THE
𝕸ERCHANT
OF 𝖁ENGEANCE

Also by Simon Hawke

THE
𝕸ERCHANT
OF 𝖁ENGEANCE

❋

Simon Hawke

FORGE®

FICTION
Hawke
JAN 0 9 2004

A TOM DOHERTY ASSOCIATES BOOK

NEW YORK

THE MERCHANT OF VENGEANCE

Copyright © 2003 by Simon Hawke

This book is printed on acid-free paper.

A Forge Book
Published by Tom Doherty Associates, LLC
175 Fifth Avenue
New York, NY 10010

www.tor.com

Forge® is a registered trademark of Tom Doherty Associates, LLC.

Library of Congress Cataloging-in-Publication Data

Hawke, Simon.
    The merchant of vengeance / Simon Hawke.—1st ed.
      p. cm.
    "A Forge book"—T.p. verso.
    ISBN 0-765-30426-0
    1. Smythe, Symington (Fictitious character)—Fiction. 2. Shakespeare, William,
1564–1616—Fiction. 3. Great Britain—History—Elizabeth, 1558–1603—Fiction. 4.
Theater—Fiction. 5. Dramatists—Fiction. 6. Actors—Fiction. I. Title.

PS3558.A8167M47 2003
813'.54—dc21

                                                                        2003049139

First Edition: December 2003

Printed in the United States of America

0 9 8 7 6 5 4 3 2 1

For

Bill Fawcett

With thanks for being there

The
Merchant
of Vengeance

1

✳

THE DAG AND DIRK was tucked away within a row of buildings on a narrow, cobbled street down by the docks, its entrance a heavy, scarred, and weathered wooden door beneath a painted hanging sign depicting a flintlock pistol and a dagger. Although it had not rained that day, the paving stones were slick and wet, partly from the river mist and partly from the waste and offal thrown out into the street. The acrid odor of the refuse mingled thickly with the briny breeze coming in off the Thames, evoking the noisome stench of rotting fish. And once inside the tavern, the smell was not much better.

"Methinks that this was ill considered, Tuck," said Shakespeare, as he looked around apprehensively at their surroundings. "Half the men in here look as if they would gladly cut our throats for the contents of our purses, whilst the other half look as if they would simply do it for a lark."

"'Tis just a tavern, Will, much like any other," Smythe replied, though he did not feel quite as certain as he sounded as he glanced around at all the patrons, most of whom were certainly a surly-looking lot. Many of the men sitting at the well-stained wooden tables over pots of ale were wherrymen, brawny and weatherbeaten, grizzled men with skin like old leather. They made their living rowing small boats on the Thames, ferrying the residents of

London up and down the river. With the streets often congested by all the carriages and carts and coaches, to say nothing of pedestrians and riders on horseback all vying for the right of way, traveling by river was often the fastest way to get around the city. Most likely the safest, as well, thought Smythe, given the steady increase in crime. And in this dockside tavern, there was a good chance that a fair number of alleymen and cutpurses were intermingled with the crowd, not to mention cutthroats.

The city constables were, for the most part, ineffective, since they were too few and far too mindful of their own self-preservation to do very much about the problem of rapidly increasing crime. The sheriff's men confined themselves largely to dealing with the riots, now almost a daily occurrence in the city with all the gangs of roaring boys roaming the streets and looking for trouble. Every now and then, some malefactor would find himself—or herself—placed under arrest and thrown into one of London's prisons, such as the Marshalsea, the Newgate, or the Clink, and there were always fresh heads to be placed upon the spikes along the bridge. For the most part, though, crime in London went unpunished, something of which Smythe and Shakespeare were all too uncomfortably aware as they gazed around at all the grim and sullen faces that stared back at them in the dim light of the tavern.

"A tavern much like any other, eh? Methinks not," Shakespeare said uneasily. "There is little of the Toad and Badger's merriment in here, Tuck. I have been to wakes that were more filled with cheer. There is a grim smell of foreboding in the very air of this place."

"'Tis because they have not changed the rushes in at least a week," said Smythe.

"Aye, well, that, too," said Shakespeare, wrinkling his nose. "Be wary where you tread. Look to your purse, as well. 'Strewth, I should be grateful if we manage to leave this infernal place in one piece."

"If it truly makes you feel so apprehensive, Will, then let us depart forthwith," said Smythe.

"Nay," said Shakespeare with a sigh, "we have come this far, we may as well go on and see it through. Although, I must admit, I cannot quite comprehend why meeting this fellow seems so terribly important to you. He wrote some decent poetry, and his plays were well received once, but he is now down on his luck, by all accounts, just another poor and dissipated poet. And 'tis not as if there is a shortage of such men in London, you know."

"Aye, I do know. I have one for a roommate," Smythe replied wryly.

"Watch it. . . ."

"In truth, Will, neither his plays nor his poems interest me so much as do his pamphlets about crime," said Smythe.

"I know, I know. You have been cluttering up our room with all his cautionary scribblings. 'Tis a most peculiar fascination."

"I have seen you reading them, as well," said Smythe, defensively.

"Out of simple curiosity and nothing more. They are somewhat edifying, I suppose, but hardly make compelling reading and certainly contribute nothing new to man's understanding of his fellow man."

"Perhaps not in the grand literary scheme of things," said Smythe, "but they do contribute a great deal to my understanding of this criminal 'underworld' in London, as he calls it. I find it all quite fascinating. Consider the way they speak, as an example, their so-called 'criminal cant.' Why, they have a language all their own. Take the way they call their victims 'coneys,' as in 'coney-catching,' likening them to rabbits they can snare. There is much practical advice to be found in these writings, Will, particularly for one who comes from the country, like myself, and knows little of the ways of criminals in the city."

Shakespeare sighed again. "Well, I shall grant you that, for I have learned a thing or two from reading him myself. Nevertheless, I cannot help but feel a little sorry for him. He is a university man, once well regarded and respected, who has had his poems published and his plays produced upon the stage. We have staged a number of them ourselves, even if they were a little dated and needed a bit of sprucing up here and there. 'Tis a pity to see him fall to such a state."

"You mean reduced to pamphleteering?"

"Oh, not at all. I never decry good, honest work. A poet has to eat, like any other man. I meant reduced to such a state as this. . . ." He indicated their surroundings with a gesture and grimaced with distaste. "If this be not the filthiest place in London, then I should not like to behold one filthier."

"Soft, Will, here comes the tavernkeeper, I believe," said Smythe.

A large and bearded man with a girth like a dray horse approached them, wiping his hands on his greasy brown leather apron. "What will ye gentlemen be wantin'?" he asked gruffly.

"We are looking for Master Robert Greene," said Smythe. "We were told he may be found here."

"He owe ye money?"

"Nay, good sir, we have not come here to collect a debt. We are but admirers of his work," said Smythe.

The tavernkeeper looked as if he could not have cared less. He simply jerked his head toward the back of the room. "That's 'im in the corner there," he said. "Stand 'im to a drink an' 'e might talk to ye. An' then again, 'e might not. Suit yerselves."

"Well, then bring him some more of whatever he is drinking," Smythe said. "And we shall have some, too."

The tavernkeeper merely grunted and moved away, the floorboards creaking ominously with every step. They turned their attention to the object of their quest, the man seated at the table in the corner, hunched over his pot of ale, which he clutched firmly with both hands.

"Master Greene?" said Smythe as they approached.

Robert Greene looked up at them slowly, as if the mere act of raising his head were a laborious task. Despite what Shakespeare had said about how Greene had fallen into dissipation, the sight of him still took Smythe aback. The man was bloated. He looked swollen, as if he were about to burst. His skin was pale and blotchy, in sharp contrast to his thick, unkempt red hair and beard. His eyes were rheumy, and it seemed to take a moment for his gaze to focus.

It took less than a moment, however, for the lean and rat-faced man who sat beside him at the table to bound to his feet and draw his dagger. "Who wants to know?" he demanded in a sneering tone.

"Sit the bloody hell down, Ball," the tavernkeeper said, coming up behind him with the ale. "These two gentlemen just bought ye both a drink. An' they say they don't want any money, mind ye."

"Eh? That so?" said Ball, gazing at them skeptically. He made no move to put away his dagger.

"They have not the look of debt collectors, Ball," said Greene, with a glance at them before his attention became fixed upon the fresh pot of ale the tavernkeeper set before him. The one he had been clutching so possessively turned out to have been empty. He wrapped his hands caressingly around the full one and slowly raised it to his lips, drinking from it deeply. He set it back down and wiped the back of his hand across his mouth.

"Please sit down, gentlemen," he said heavily. "You shall have to pardon Cutting Ball. He is my brother-in-law, in an informal sort of way, and has a tendency to be somewhat protective of me. I have of late been plagued by debt collectors, who have hounded me unmercifully and threatened me with grievous harm. Ball, here, would not wish to see his sister left without support and his little nephew left an orphan. Therefore, he looks after me when he is not otherwise engaged, for which kindness I am, indeed, profoundly grateful."

They sat down, and Cutting Ball, somewhat reluctantly it seemed, put away his knife. However, his flinty, feral gaze remained firmly fixed on both of them, even while he drank his ale. He had the look of an alleyman if Smythe ever saw one, and he made a mental note not to turn his back on him.

"So then," Greene went on, "as I perceive you are not debt collectors, what is it you wish of me? Are you from some printers? Do you wish, perhaps, to engage me to pen a pamphlet you can publish?"

"Nay, sir, we are not printers," Smythe replied, "although we do have an interest in your pamphlets. We are players with Lord Strange's Men. I am called Tuck Smythe, and this is William Shakespeare."

At the mention of Shakespeare's name, Greene stiffened and his bloodshot eyes narrowed. "Shakescene?"

"Shakespeare," Will corrected him. "William Shakespeare, at your service, sir."

"Methinks I know that name," said Greene. "You were lately with the Queen's Men, were you not?"

"Indeed, we both were," Shakespeare replied. "I am surprised that you would know that, Master Greene."

"I hear things," Greene replied, his manner very different suddenly. "So then . . . you fancy yourself a poet, do you?"

"Well, I do write some verses, as it happens. . . ." Shakespeare began, but Greene interrupted him.

"Pray tell, Master Shakescene, what university did you attend?"

"I must confess that I am not a university man, sir," Shakespeare replied, without correcting him about his name, though he gave a sidelong glance of annoyance to Smythe. "I did have some formal schooling back home in Stratford, but then—"

"Not a university man, then," Greene interrupted him again. He nodded. "Indeed, I had heard as much. I had thought, however, that I might have been misinformed, that you were in truth a master of the arts and I had not been aware of it."

"Nay, sir, I make no such claim," said Shakespeare modestly. "I never went to university."

"Indeed. An uneducated man. And yet, you seem to feel yourself somehow qualified to sit in judgment upon the writings of a master of the arts, and rearrange them to suit your fancy. You take painstakingly well-crafted literary verses and then have them jet about the stage in tragical buskins, styling yourself a poet like some upstart country crow beautifying yourself with the feathers of your betters. What do you have to say for yourself, sir?"

Shakespeare sat there stunned, completely taken aback. He looked as if the floor had suddenly dropped out from underneath him, and he could think of no reply. Smythe, too, was completely unprepared for this sudden vitriol and for a moment found himself absolutely speechless, but he recovered quickly and rose to the defense of his friend.

"Sir, I see you are offended," he said. "Please let me assure you that such was never our intent. 'Twas my idea that we come here to seek you out and meet with you, for I have read nearly all of your pamphlets and thought that—"

"My *pamphlets?*" Greene said with a snort. "For God's sake. My bloody pamphlets. A lifetime spent in pursuit of mastering the arts, Ball, and all they truly care about are my bloody cautionary pamphlets written for the common man. Tell us, Master Greene, how to avoid being cozened by some sharper, how not to have our purses lifted, how to tell if someone is cheating us at cards, or how the alleyman plies his trade, so that we may avoid being waylaid in some alley whilst out looking for some whore to bugger. And in the meantime, we shall grow fat upon your plays, rewriting them howsoever we may choose, for what are a poet's words, after all, but a lot of sound and fury, signifying nothing? Why not make a jig of them? Why must we respect an artist's original intent? Why not add a little speech in the first act and cut out one in the second, put in a jest or two, perhaps a song, take a little sample here and a little sample there, rearrange it and call it all our own. Why, 'tis brilliant, positively brilliant! What great artists we all are, eh, 'Master' Shakescene?"

Shakespeare had turned pale. He sat deathly still and speechless, a stricken look in his eyes.

"Sir," said Smythe, "meaning no disrespect, but surely a poet such as yourself must understand that plays are a collaborative medium, a crucible in which the intent of the author and the interpretation of the player comingle with the perception of the audience to yield a new alchemical concoction with every new performance."

"*Concoction?* Concoct this, you infernal jackanapes," said Greene, and dashed the remnants of his ale into Smythe's face. "You dare to lecture me? Bloody leeches! Go fatten on some other beast and leave me well enough alone!"

Smythe got to his feet, ale dripping from his chin onto his spattered tunic, and Cutting Ball was just as quick to rise pugnaciously and draw his dagger once again.

Smythe drew his own dagger. "Right, then," he said grimly. "If that is how you want it, you scurvy rogue, I shall be more than happy to oblige you." Then he felt Shakespeare take him firmly by the arm and pull him back.

"Nay, Tuck, let us be gone from this place, quickly," he said. "Please, I beg of you. Let us be gone."

Smythe kept his gaze locked on Cutting Ball, who looked somewhat undecided now, but still belligerent. For a moment, they held each other's gaze, and then Cutting Ball's eyes slid away.

"Bastards," Greene was muttering to himself. "Bloody bastards."

Slowly, Smythe backed away, keeping careful track of those around them until they had cleared the door and were once more outside in the cobbled street.

"I am truly sorry, Will," he said, "for what just happened back there."

"Why?" asked Shakespeare. "'Twas not your fault, Tuck. You have done nothing whatever for which any apology is warranted."

"I fear that I must disagree," said Smythe. "'Twas my idea that we come here to seek out Robert Greene in the first place. I should have left well enough alone. I should have listened when you told me you heard that he was dissipated and fallen on hard times. The man is deeply embittered and in a bilious humor. Yet there is simply no excuse for the foul manner in which he addressed you. And to think that I admired him."

"You admired his work," said Shakespeare. "But until now, you knew nothing of the man. And I repeat, you have done nothing for which any apology is warranted. You could not possibly have known he would have responded thus to me. 'Strewth, I never would have guessed it myself."

Smythe sighed. "Nevertheless, I feel at least in part to blame. 'Twas I who dragged you here, and more's the pity."

"And 'twas Robert Greene who took it in his head to dress me down," responded Shakespeare. "He could have greeted me in friendship as a colleague, but instead he chose to upbraid me for having the audacity to improve upon his work. Well, as it happens, his criticism was not entirely without merit. I am *not* a university man, and as such may indeed be regarded as 'an upstart crow' by the academic poets, his fellow masters of the arts. 'Beautified with the feathers of his betters.' I must say, Greene may have become a bloated old sot, but soused or not, he still knows how to turn a phrase."

" 'Twas a vile phrase, a most vile phrase, indeed!" said Smythe as they walked. "And I must disagree with you that his criticism was not without merit. I say 'twas completely without merit! Why, how can you possibly say otherwise?"

"But I *did* rewrite some of his plays."

"You rewrote some speeches here and there, and that only because the company had asked you to, for they were not working well on the stage," said Smythe. "For God's sake, Will, must I defend you to yourself? Greene's plays are full of pompous posturings and pretentious speeches that tend to ridicule the very audiences to whom he purports to play. The truth of the matter is that he fancies himself a grand literary poet superior to all but others like himself, the so-called 'masters of the arts,' if you will. Masters of conceit, if you ask me! Well, unfortunately for Master Greene, a university degree does not, apparently, elevate one above the mundane task of eating, and so for sustenance he must write plays and publish pamphlets, not for other university men such as himself, whose patronage could not support him, but for the groundlings, common people like ourselves, for whom it seems he has nothing but contempt. But then we mere mortals are not quite so ignorant as he supposes, and when he continually ridicules us in his plays, we respond accordingly and begin to look elsewhere for our entertainments. Aye, even to 'upstart crows' who may lack the advantages of a university degree, but at least do not bite the hands that feed them!"

"Upon my word, Tuck, that was as fine a speech as any Robert Greene could ever hope to write," said Shakespeare. "I can only hope that I might do as well one day."

"I have every confidence that you shall do much better."

"You are a kind soul, Tuck, if not quite an honest one. Nevertheless, I do esteem you for your kindness. But 'twould seem now that you no longer admire Greene's work, yet prior to this, I think you did. I am sorry this encounter has soured you on him."

" 'Tis the man that I have soured on, more so than the work, although in truth, after this insufferable exhibition, I doubt that I shall be purchasing any more of his pamphlets at the bookstalls. However, what I had said about his plays was what I had felt about his plays, even prior to this encounter. I was never very fond of them. 'Twas his pamphlets that I liked. They seemed much more direct and colorful, and not at all pretentious. He may write well, I do not know, for I do not presume to be a judge upon such matters, but as for how his work plays on the stage before an audience, one need not be a learned university man to be able to determine that. His plays have not done well for us. At least, not until you had doctored them somewhat. And even then, they have not drawn much of an audience, unlike Marlowe, who packs them in with his *Tamburlaine* and his *Doctor Faustus* and his *Jew of Malta*. His plays are so exciting that people cannot seem to get enough of him."

"Aye, for an Englishman, Kit is very much a Roman," Shakespeare said with a smile. "He gives them bread and circuses upon the stage. And therein, Tuck, lies the rub, you see. The audiences for plays have changed. Perhaps men such as Tom Kyd and Kit Marlowe have changed them by whetting their appetites for something new, a brew more heady than the small beer they have hitherto imbibed. Perhaps these new poets have merely responded to their jaded appetites for something more by perceiving their thirst and thus pouring stronger beverage for them. Either way, there is no question that Greene's day has come and gone. In their excesses on the stage, Kyd and Marlowe have exceeded him, so to speak. What remains to be seen now is what shall exceed them."

"It seems difficult to believe that anything could be much more excessive than Kit Marlowe," Smythe said wryly.

Shakespeare grinned, knowing it was not just Marlowe's plays Smythe was referring to. The flamboyant young poet's name had become nearly synonymous with debauchery and decadence. After a chance encounter with them in a London pub, it was Marlowe who had steered them toward their first jobs with a company of players. He had seemed like a wild man then, and in the few intervening years he had only grown even more rebellious and intemperate. Although his plays were now all the rage in London, he was treading on very dangerous ground with his outrageous behavior and public utterances.

"Marlowe has only cracked open the door," said Shakespeare. "It remains for someone else to kick it open fully. I have said before, and I believe it still, that the time for jigs and pratfalls on the stage is past. Each new production of an old standby from our traditional repertoire falls flatter than the last. The groundlings have seen such things before, and they are tired of them. They are ready now for something different, something better. Marlowe, for all his cleverness and undoubted gifts, only gives them something much more grand. He gives them spectacle, which is why Ned Alleyn so relishes playing his work. Marlowe writes speeches that a bombastic player like Ned can seize between his teeth and tear into like a rabid hound. The audiences love it. 'Strewth, I love it, as well. When he is fully in his element, Ned is a joy to watch, for all that he can often be insufferable to know. Yet mark me well, it shall not be very long before the novelty of Marlowe's grand excesses also starts to pale, and then what shall we feed these hungry groundlings?"

"What?" asked Smythe with interest.

"Meat," said Shakespeare. "We shall feed them meat."

"*Meat?*"

"Aye, once they are done with bread and circuses, my friend, they shall want meat. Something with more sustenance and substance. And I shall do my utmost to provide it for them."

"And just how do you propose to do that?"

"By being a very careful cook," said Shakespeare, "and not just tossing things haphazardly into a pot without giving due consideration to how the flavors marry. 'Tis that blend of flavors that gives a dish its fullest texture. Consider Marlowe's Tamburlaine, if you will, the very apotheosis of cruelty. Not since the ancient Greeks have we seen such terrible savagery portrayed upon the stage. And then witness Barabas, Marlowe's Jew of Malta. He slaughters more people than Caligula, each murder more gruesome than the last, until he meets his end in the last act by falling into a cauldron of hot oil and thereupon delivers his final speech, all whilst being boiled alive, mind you! Now I ask you, Tuck, as a man who has worked long hours at the forge and doubtless knows, how likely is one to declaim a bombastic, dying soliloquy whilst one's flesh is being cooked?"

Smythe chuckled. "Not very likely, I fear. When one's flesh is being burned, one is much more likely to scream with agony than deliver up a fustian speech. But then the audiences do not seem to mind that overmuch."

"Granted, 'tis because they are being given something different, something novel," Shakespeare said. "And they are hungry for such novelty at present. But in time, methinks that they shall look upon such things askance. Tamburlaine is cruelty made manifest in man, but how is man made manifest in Tamburlaine? Barabas, as we have agreed, is the very embodiment of evil, but take away that evil and what do you have left?"

"A man who has been wronged?" said Smythe.

"Aye, perhaps," said Shakespeare, "but then where is he?"

Smythe frowned. "What do you mean, where *is* he?"

"Surely, not upon the stage," said Shakespeare, with a shrug. "Aside from the fact that he is bent upon revenge, and that in this quest no evil seems to be beyond him, what else do we truly know of him?"

"Why . . . that he is a Jew, I suppose."

"But then how do we know that Barabas is a Jew?"

Smythe frowned again. "Why, we know he is a Jew because we are told he is a Jew. I am not certain what you mean, Will."

"Well, then, let us ask ourselves, what *is* a Jew?"

"One who is not a Christian, I suppose," said Smythe. "One who has rejected Jesus." He shrugged. "I cannot say much more than that for certain, for methinks that I have never met a Jew."

"And you are not alone, for neither have most Englishmen," said Shakespeare. "The Jews were expelled from England some three hundred years ago, in the time of King Edward I. What few Jews remained behind had all converted, though whether such conversion was a matter of faith or of expediency is another matter altogether. I, for one, know little more of Jews than you do. One hears the sorts of things that people say, but then in truth, these sorts of things are little different from the manner of speech they bruit about the Spaniards or the Flemish or the French, which is to say that most of it is likely arrant nonsense. We English seem to dislike foreigners, simply because they happen to be foreign. They may or may not be dislikable in and of themselves, but that is quite beside the point. The fact that they are foreign is enough for us. Hence, we dislike them."

"Whether we truly know anything of them or not, you mean."

"Just so," said Shakespeare. "Marlowe wished to present the audience with something evil on the stage, a character whom they could loathe and despise and fear all at the same time. Thus, he gave them a Jew, someone who was foreign, thus engaging the English predilection to despise the foreigner; someone who was not a Christian, thus invoking the one thing Catholic and Protestant alike could both agree to despise; someone who already has the reputation of being so undesirable and disagreeable that nearly all his kind have long since been driven out of England. Ergo, they must be evil. And, to add the crowning touch, he bestowed upon his Jew the name of Barabas, a name fraught with hatred of literally biblical proportions. And lo, there he stands before you now upon the stage," said Shakespeare, gesturing dramatically toward the street in front of them, as if he had just conjured Marlowe's character up out of his imagination. "All that is left for us to do is clothe him in a black robe and skullcap, add a nose like a promontory, and give him a wig of black tresses falling down about the ears in ringlets. *Hola!* Barabas, the dreaded, evil Jew of Malta! Boo! Hiss!"

Smythe laughed.

"But that is not a *man,* you see," said Shakespeare. "That is a masque, a Morris dancer, something all done up in bells and ribbons, nothing but a caricature. That is Marlowe's Tamburlaine, but merely in another costume. And yet, who *is* he? Who *is* this Jew?" he asked rhetorically, waving his arms in the air. "What does he *think?* What does he *feel?* Has he a wife at home, a child? Does he love them? Does he worry about them? Does he have fears of his own that keep him up at night? And if he is, indeed, as evil as Kit Marlowe paints him, then what has made him so?"

"All very good questions," Smythe replied, nodding. "But 'twould be somewhat tiresome to answer all those questions for the audience in the prologue of a play, would it not?"

"Not if they were *shown* the answers," Shakespeare replied.

"*Shown* the answers? How?"

"As a part of the unfolding of the *action* of the play," said Shakespeare. "The more I think about it, Tuck, the more I become convinced that 'tis in this direction that my true path lies! Forget

Marlowe's Jew. I will show you a Jew, by God! I will show you one who has a *reason* to be evil! A reason that any man can readily understand!"

"But Will, you have just admitted that you know no more of Jews than I do," Smythe replied. "And I, for one, know nothing of them. Why, I do not think I could tell a Jew if I chanced upon one on this very street."

"Well, that is a minor problem," Shakespeare said.

"A *minor* problem? How can you write a Jew when you have never even *met* a Jew?"

"Marlowe clearly never met a Jew, and yet he wrote one."

"Aye, and you have just finished telling me that his Jew was nothing more than a caricature. If you are determined to outdo him, then you shall have to create a character that is more man than masque, more flesh than bells and ribbons, as you put it."

"Well, a Jew is a man at heart, like any other, surely," Shakespeare said. "Like any other man, he feels sadness, he feels anger, he feels pain. . . ."

"But as you said yourself, Will, where *is* he?" Smythe replied. "What makes him who he is and what he is? After all, if you are going to outdo Marlowe's *Jew of Malta,* then do you not think that you should at least learn something of your subject?"

Shakespeare pursed his lips. "Indeed, you are quite right, Tuck. I suppose I should. The question is . . . where will we find a Jew in a country that drove them out three hundred years ago?"

Smythe grunted. "I must admit, you have me there. But you did say that some remained behind, did you not?"

"Apparently, a small number who converted."

Smythe shrugged. "Well then, can we not find one of them?"

"I would not have the faintest idea where to look," said Shakespeare with a shrug.

"Well, we know a lot of people. Surely, somebody must know."

"Surely, someone must. We shall ask around, then."

"What about your play about King Henry?" Smythe asked. "'Twas an ambitious effort, as I recall. Do you not think you should complete that first, before beginning something new?"

"I have very nearly finished it. And I have already begun work upon another."

"What, this one about the Jew, you mean?"

"Nay, that is still merely an idea, an inspiration, if you will. Still, I think it may be a worthy one. 'Twould be tempting to beat Marlowe at his own game and have everyone in London know I did it."

"Tempting, perhaps," said Smythe. "But whether it be worthy is another matter. For my part, I am not convinced that this is the best idea you have ever had."

"Great plays can spring from inferior ideas," Shakespeare said. "Look at Marlowe."

"Aye, look at him," Smythe said wryly. "Marlowe dances on the edge of the abyss. His reputation is becoming infamous, and he seems to infuriate as many patrons as he pleases. Are you quite certain that you want to emulate him?"

"Not in all things, perhaps," replied Shakespeare with a grin. "But I could do with emulating his success. And our company could certainly do with some new plays. One takes one's ideas where one finds them, eh?"

"If you say so. Either way, you humored me in my idea to go and search out Robert Greene, much to your regret now, I am quite sure, so I suppose the very least that I can do is humor you in your desire to out-Marlowe Marlowe. Let us only hope that you do not wind up suffering by comparison."

"I can assure you, Tuck, that when I am done, I will have penned a Jew that shall prove much more memorable than Marlowe's Jew of Malta."

"Famous last words?" said Smythe, cocking an eyebrow at him.

"We shall see, my friend," said Shakespeare.

"We shall, indeed," said Smythe. "Now all we need to do is find a Jew in a country where there are none."

2

✳

YOU DO NOT LOOK WELL, Elizabeth," said her friend Antonia, as they sat upon a bench, embroidering together in the garden. "Does my presence weary you?"

Elizabeth Darcie shook her head, brushing back a stray blond tress that had fallen loose from underneath her linen coif. "Nay, 'tis not so, my good, dear friend. I am neither weary nor yet unwell, thanks be to God. I am but feeling a bit sad today."

"I had hoped to cheer you with my company," Antonia said, putting down her needlework on the stone bench. "Yet I perceive that I have failed."

"Nay, I am grateful for your company, Antonia, truly," Elizabeth replied. "If my mood is pensive this day, the blame lies not with you. I was merely thinking of our friend Portia's impending marriage."

"And this makes you sad?" Antonia cocked an eyebrow at her friend. "Is it for her that you feel sad or for yourself?"

"Nay, not for her," Elizabeth replied, putting down her own embroidery with a sigh. "I am happy for Portia, truly. Thomas Locke is a most excellent young man. He has fine prospects. He is now nearly done with his apprenticeship and shall soon become a journeyman tailor. Already, his work is becoming known in fashionable circles. He shall do well. There is no doubt that he shall make something of himself."

"Despite his rather humble origins, you mean," Antonia said.

"Well, though some may hold it so, in my estimation, what his father does should be no reflection upon him," Elizabeth replied. "Thomas is making his own way in life. And 'tis not at all uncommon these days for a successful merchant or a guildsman to become a gentleman. Prosperity can do much to improve one's social standing."

"I am quite sure that Portia's father had considered that when he consented to the match," Antonia said dryly. "After all, 'tis one thing to allow one's only daughter to wed a tavernkeeper's son, and a tavern in the Liberties, no less. 'Tis quite another to let her wed a journeyman tailor who shall doubtless have his own shop before long and may one day become a gentleman."

"Aye," said Elizabeth. "Some things are more easily overlooked when the prospects of success and social betterment are in the offing."

"Unlike the prospects for a poor player who is not even a shareholder in his company?" Antonia said.

Elizabeth glanced at her with surprise, momentarily taken aback, then smiled wanly. "Am I so easily compassed, then?"

"Aye, by one who loves you well and knows your heart," Antonia replied, taking her hand. "Tuck Smythe is also an excellent young man. However, unlike Portia's young man, Thomas, he does not seem to have favorable prospects. He is also making his own way in life, as best he can, but as a poor player, I fear he can offer your father no reason to overlook his lack of social standing."

Elizabeth sighed. "Did you know that his father is a gentleman?"

Antonia's eyes grew wide. "Tuck's father? A gentleman? But you have never told me this!"

"'Tis true," Elizabeth said, nodding. "He told me so himself once. But he does not like to speak of it."

"But why?"

"It seems that his father had squandered all of his money," Elizabeth explained. "'Twas my understanding that he had barely avoided debtors' prison and was living on his younger brother's charity. 'Tis why Tuck is both poor and a player. He told me that he had always wanted to join up with a company of players, ever since he was a boy and saw a traveling troupe come through his town, but his father would not hear of it and threatened to disown him if he did. And so Tuck was sent to live and apprentice with his uncle, who was a smith and farrier. He lived with him until he learned that his father had gone bankrupt. With his inheritance gone, his father's threat was rendered moot and Tuck had nothing to prevent him from setting out to follow his heart's desire. Thus, he came to London and became a player. He does not like to speak about his father. 'Twas the only time he had ever even mentioned him, and then he never spoke of him to me again."

"Poor Tuck," Antonia said, shaking her head. "And yet . . . his father, for all that he may now be destitute, is nevertheless still a proper gentleman, is he not? That is to say, the heralds had granted him a coat of arms?"

Elizabeth clucked her tongue. "Aye, they did, but I know what you are thinking, and 'twould never do," she said.

"Why not?" Antonia asked. "Your father wants nothing more than to make a good marriage for you. He has tried again and yet again to arrange a suitable match."

"Aye, much to our mutual regret," Elizabeth replied. "I have told you of the disaster that was so narrowly prevented not so long ago, thanks to Tuck and his friend Will. I shudder to think now that I could easily have been killed by that imposter posing as a nobleman. As a result, it seems my father has learned his lesson and has at long last stopped trying to arrange a marriage for me. Besides, I told him that I would sooner die a spinster than wed a man I did not love."

"But if you were to tell him that Tuck's father is a gentleman, then surely he would be more amiably disposed toward him," Antonia said.

"Just so long as I conveniently neglected to tell him that Tuck's father is also destitute, you mean," Elizabeth replied. She shook her head. "Nay, I could never do that to him. I could not mislead my father so, nor would Tuck stand for it even if I could. He is proud and honest to a fault. And for all of his insufferable pomposity, Father tolerates Tuck now, in part because he is indebted to him and in part because he knows now that Tuck is honorable and would never do anything against his wishes. Father trusts Tuck, as he trusts me. In truth, I do believe he trusts him *more* than he trusts me. 'Tis the only reason he allows our friendship, albeit he does not entirely approve."

"But you would like it to be much *more* than just a friendship," said Antonia.

Elizabeth sighed. "I do not know. In truth, I am not certain what I want."

"Well, do you love him?"

"At times, I think I do. And yet, at other times, he vexes and exasperates me so, I think that if I were a man, I could take a club to him and beat him senseless!"

Antonia laughed. "That sounds very much like love to me."

"Oh, and you know so much about it!"

"You might be surprised at what I know," Antonia said slyly. "You may be older, Elizabeth, but do not forget, I am the one who is married."

"Everyone is married," Elizabeth replied dismissively. "Marriage merely teaches a woman what it means to be a wife. I have not observed that marriage has much to teach a woman about love."

"Once married, a woman can learn to love her husband, even if she does not love him from the start," Antonia said with a shrug.

"I suppose that one can also learn to love a tonic of tart vinegar and scurvy-grass if one must drink it daily," Elizabeth replied dryly. "However, that still does not make it a pleasant-tasting brew."

"You shall make a fine spinster, methinks," Antonia replied.

"You already have the tongue for it. Here I am trying to help you with my best advice, and you abuse me for it."

"Forgive me, Antonia," Elizabeth said. " 'Twas unkind of me, I know. I am simply in a dreadful humor. Perhaps 'tis my lot in life to be a spinster."

"Oh, what arrant nonsense," said Antonia. "You have had more than your share of suitors. And if you had not frightened all of them off with your shrewish tongue and willful manner, then you would have an army of them still. Why, you could have a husband at any time you chose, if only you would behave more amiably toward those who came to court you. The trouble with you is not a lack of suitors. What you seem to want, Elizabeth, is what you cannot have."

"And what is that, do you suppose?"

"You want a man, but you want him only on your terms. What you want is a husband who is not a husband, one who is strong enough to tame you, but at the same time does not attempt to rein you in. You want a man with whom you can discourse as an equal, and to whom you do not owe obedience, unless it be your choice. You want someone who can provide for you, but at the same time with whom you can feel passion." Antonia shook her head. "Elizabeth, my dear, you do not want a husband. What you want is a lover."

"Antonia! That is a scandalous thing to say!"

Antonia merely shrugged. "Nevertheless, 'tis true. 'Tis what you truly seem to want. And 'twould seem that Tuck Smythe could be all of those things for you, save one. He could not provide for you. But then, you have your father to do that, at least for the present. Then, when he finally tires of supporting you and puts his foot down once and for all and insists upon your taking a husband, why then, take one who can provide for you and does not make too many demands. And then keep Tuck as your secret lover."

"Antonia!" Elizabeth was shocked. "You cannot possibly be serious!"

"And why not, pray tell?"

"You mean that you would wish me to be unfaithful to my husband?" Elizabeth asked, astonished at the very suggestion.

"What I would wish is for you to be happy," Antonia replied calmly. "If you could find your happiness in being faithful to a husband, then I would wish no more for you. But if not, then I would wish for you to find some means whereby you might find the happiness you seek. I was merely suggesting one path that you could take. The choice is yours."

"Could. . . ." Elizabeth hesitated and glanced at her friend askance. "Could *you* ever be unfaithful to Harry?"

Antonia laughed. "Oh, Elizabeth! Harry is my father's age, and I am but eighteen! What do *you* think?"

Elizabeth stared at her friend as if seeing her for the first time. "You mean to say that . . . that you have. . . ."

"Had a lover?" Antonia said, raising her eyebrows. "Aye, several."

"Several!"

"Well, two, to be exact," Antonia said. "Does that amaze you? Do you think less of me now that you know? Does it make you think I am a strumpet?"

"Nay, Antonia, I would never think that of you!" Elizabeth replied. "But in truth, I . . . I do not know what to think!"

"For all that you are older, Elizabeth, you know so little of the world," Antonia said. "Do you truly believe that men are faithful to their wives? Who do you suppose patronizes all the brothels in the Liberties?"

"Why . . . I have never even thought about it," Elizabeth confessed. "I would have thought that . . . well . . . men who had no wives, I suppose."

"You mean men like Tuck?" Antonia asked mischievously.

"I cannot believe that Tuck would ever set foot within a brothel," said Elizabeth with firm conviction.

"Yet he is employed within a playhouse," Antonia replied. "And 'tis well known that whores ply their trade in playhouses. Why, the men who own the playhouses often own the brothels that can be found close by."

"I cannot believe that Tuck would ever even venture into such a place," Elizabeth said.

"Well, perhaps Tuck is one of the rare men who would not," Antonia replied. "Indeed, he is as upright as a maypole. And any fool can plainly see he is in love with you. Nevertheless, he is still a man, and sooner or later, a man will have his passion wane should it remain unrequited."

Elizabeth glanced sharply at Antonia. "Are you suggesting that I should requite his passion?"

Antonia chuckled. "I was thinking more that you should indulge your own, my dear."

"And if I were to do that," Elizabeth replied, "which is not to say I would, mind you, then what if one day I should marry another, a man who could provide for me, as you suggest? What then would I say to my proud husband on his wedding night?"

Antonia raised her eyebrows innocently. "Why, you would lower your eyes demurely and inform him that you were afraid and meekly ask him to be gentle with you."

Elizabeth rolled her eyes. "Indeed! And do you suppose that he would fail to perceive that I was not a virgin?"

"Men are not very perceptive, as a rule," Antonia replied dryly. "And there are ways to make a man perceive that which you would wish him to perceive."

Elizabeth looked skeptical. "I should think that 'twould take a very foolish man, indeed, to be so gulled."

"Men are often quick to call us women foolish," Antonia replied, "and yet 'tis men who are often made to play the fools. On the morning of your wedding, all you need do is pay a visit to a cunning woman and procure from her a bladder cut from a small sheep and filled with blood. Then, as you prepare to receive your new husband in your wedding bed, conceal your counterfeit virginity within, and as your husband consummates the marriage, the resulting flow shall surely satisfy him of your purity."

Elizabeth stared at her friend with open-mouthed astonishment. "God's mercy, Antonia! You take my breath away and nearly leave me speechless! However do you *learn* such things?"

Antonia shrugged. "The same way that you have learned them now. One woman passes on wisdom to another. 'Tis the ancient way."

"And the woman who passed this wisdom on to you," Elizabeth replied, "would not be a woman by the name of Granny Meg, by any chance?"

It was Antonia's turn to look surprised. "And how would *you* know of Granny Meg?"

"Mayhap I do not know so little of the world as you may think," Elizabeth said with a touch of defensive smugness. "As it happens, I have had occasion to consult with Granny Meg myself."

"*You?* Gone to see a witch?"

"Do you find that so surprising?" asked Elizabeth, a bit annoyed that she should be thought so innocent, especially by someone younger than herself.

"What did you go to see her for?" Antonia asked. "Was it to obtain a love potion?"

"I hardly think I should require a love potion," said Elizabeth. "From what I can see, love brings naught but trouble to its victims."

"What then? What did she give you?" asked Antonia eagerly. "Was it a charm of warding? A binding spell to hold off your father's wishes for you? Or did she, perhaps, work a spell of divination to foretell your future?"

"Never you mind what Granny Meg did," Elizabeth replied. "'Twas between the two of us, and let that be an end to it. I would not have said as much save that you were so smug in thinking you knew more than I did about everything. In any event, some things are best left unspoken, and so I shall say no more."

Antonia's eyes grew wide. "Oooh, 'twas something nasty, was it not? 'Twas some black magic that she worked for you?"

Elizabeth said nothing. She merely looked away.

Antonia's hand went to her mouth. "Oh! I knew it! 'Twas something dark and terrible!"

It was, of course, nothing of the kind, but Elizabeth was not about to tell Antonia that. She merely gave her a sidelong glance and said, "I shall not speak of it."

Antonia gasped and shrank away from her. "Elizabeth! What have you *done*? You have involved yourself with witchcraft! Oh, how could you?"

"Why, I have done no more than you," Elizabeth replied.

"Nay, I never!"

"You never what?"

"I never went to Granny Meg!" Antonia said.

"You said you did!"

"I never did!" Antonia protested. "I merely asked you how you knew of her!"

"Antonia! You *told* me that you had been to see a cunning woman, that 'twas she who told you of the trick to counterfeit virginity!"

"I never told you that I had been to see a cunning woman," Antonia replied. "I said that you should go to *see* a cunning woman if you wished to fool a husband into believing that you were a virgin when you were truly not; I never said that *I* had gone to see a cunning woman myself."

Elizabeth folded her arms and scowled at her friend. "Antonia, you purposely led me to believe that was *just* what you had done!"

"Well . . . perhaps I did," Antonia replied, "but I did not lie! And I did not mean to deceive you."

"I think that was precisely what you meant to do," Elizabeth said. "And I can see that I shall have to be more careful what I tell you in the future."

"Oh, that was unkind!" Antonia said. "Elizabeth, I would never betray your trust! Surely, you must know that!"

"I am not certain that I do," Elizabeth replied. "But I suppose that we shall see. Time shall tell how well you keep a confidence."

"I shall never tell a soul, I swear it!"

"If you do, Antonia, then I may go see Granny Meg about another sort of charm," Elizabeth replied.

Antonia brought both hands up to her mouth. "Elizabeth! You wouldn't!"

"See if I would not!"

Antonia swallowed hard, her eyes very wide. "I shall be as silent as the grave, I swear!" She crossed her heart.

"Well, then we shall speak no more of it," Elizabeth said, once more picking up her embroidery.

Antonia swallowed hard again and nodded, resuming her own needlework. A moment later, she gave Elizabeth a sidelong glance and softly said, "Was she very frightening?"

"Who?" Elizabeth asked, without looking up.

"You know . . ."

"I thought that we agreed to speak no more of it."

Antonia threw down her needlework. "Oh, Elizabeth, be *reasonable,* for mercy's sake! You simply cannot tell me that you have been to see a fearsome witch and then not tell me what it was like! 'Tis hardly fair!"

Elizabeth suppressed a smile. "Well, for one thing, she was not fearsome."

Antonia leaned forward eagerly. "You mean to say that you were truly not afraid?"

"Oh, I was afraid . . . at least a little," Elizabeth replied, "but when I met her, I did not find her fearsome."

"Was she very ugly?"

"Nay, she was beautiful."

"Beautiful?" Antonia asked with surprise. "But I had heard that she was old!"

"Well, beautiful in the way an old woman can be beautiful," Elizabeth said. "Her hair was white and very long, and her face was aged, and yet nearly unlined by age. Her eyes were blue as periwinkles, clear and bright, and you could still see what a beauty she must have been when she was young."

"I had thought that all witches were ugly old crones," Antonia said. "Do you suppose 'twas a spell? That she had made a pact with the devil?"

Elizabeth shrugged. "I could not say. But she did not seem evil in the slightest. Quite the contrary, she was very kind."

Antonia pursed her lips and nodded knowingly. "'Tis how they get you," she said in a low voice.

"I do not think she *got* me," Elizabeth replied. "After all, I am here, am I not?"

"I meant . . . your soul," Antonia said, her voice barely above a whisper.

"I do not recall pledging my soul or signing anything in blood," Elizabeth said. "There was no talk of the devil, nor did she demand any tokens of me. 'Twas nothing at all like what I had expected. 'Twas more like going to visit a kindly old maiden aunt or grandmother."

"That must be how they fool you," Antonia said, nodding.

"I did not have the sense of being fooled," Elizabeth replied.

"Well, of course not! For if you knew that you were being fooled, then you would not be fooled, for to be fooled, you must not know it, whereas if you knew that you were fooled, then you were never truly fooled, were you?"

Elizabeth glanced at her with an irritated expression. "I have absolutely no idea what you have just said. And in all likelihood, methinks, neither have you."

"Well, at least it has taken your mind away from contemplating Portia's wedding."

Elizabeth grimaced. "Indeed, it had, until you just mentioned it once more."

"Oh. Drat. Well then, let us speak of something else."

"Aye, let us do so, by all means."

"Have you heard what they say about her intended's father?"

"I am glad to see that we are not speaking of Portia's wedding any longer," Elizabeth said wryly.

"I was speaking of Thomas Locke's father, *not* Portia's wedding."

Elizabeth sighed. "Very well, then. What do they say? That aside from owning a tavern, he is also a brothelkeeper? That is hardly news, Antonia, we all knew that already. 'Tis certainly no secret."

"Nay, this is something different." Antonia leaned closer and added in a conspirational tone, "They say he is a *ruffler!*"

"What, you mean a criminal? A thief?"

"Not *just* a thief," Antonia said, pleased to see she had once more surprised her friend. "They say . . ." She leaned still closer, looking around cautiously as if they could be overheard. "They say that he is a master of a thieves' guild!"

"A thieves' guild!" Elizabeth frowned. "Antonia, that is absurd! How could thieves possibly have a guild? 'Twould be against the law!"

"Nevertheless, they do," Antonia insisted. "They meet in secret. And they say that Charles Locke is their master. Or one of them, at the very least. It seems that there are several masters in the guild, one for the alleymen, one for the pickpockets and the foists, one for the sturdy beggars, one for the sharpers, and so on. But they say that Charles Locke is one of the main leaders of them all."

"Where in Heaven's name do you hear all of these things, Antonia?" asked Elizabeth. "Who has been filling your ears with all this arrant nonsense? And pray do not tell me you got it from some cunning woman, for we know *that* is not true, either!"

"'Tis the truth, Elizabeth!"

"That you got it from a cunning woman? Nonsense. Granny Meg would never have aught to do with the spreading of such rumors. And I know of no other cunning woman in the city."

"Nay, I know 'tis true because I read it," said Antonia.

"You *read* it?"

"Aye, here in this pamphlet, see?"

Antonia reached inside her embroidery basket and pulled out a slim pamphlet that was sharply creased from being folded. It had a crude black-and-white illustration on the cover, a woodcut depicting what appeared to be a room inside a tavern, with men seated at wooden trestle tables, smoking pipes and drinking from large tankards. There were a few bawdy-looking women in the crowd, some sitting on the men's laps, others standing around in postures that did not seem very ladylike. And holding forth from what appeared to be a sort of pulpit on one side of the room was a bearded man with long hair and dark clothing, one hand raised dramatically overhead, forefinger extended, the other also raised, but slightly lower and clenched into a fist. The title of the pamphlet was *The Guild of Thieves,* and the subtitle read, *Bringing to Light the Notorious and Secret Practices of Divers Thieves and Scoundrels and their Underworld Guild of Cozeners and Coney-Catchers, Written by Robert Greene.*

"Wherever did you come by this?" Elizabeth asked, examining it.

"I bought it at a bookstall in Paul's Walk last Sunday," Antonia replied. "It makes for most fascinating reading. And it mentions Thomas's father by name."

"By name, do you say?"

"Aye, right here, do you see?" Antonia indicated the passage. "And Master Greene would never write it if 'twere not true."

"Well, perhaps not," Elizabeth replied skeptically, "but I see by the title here that this is all about the 'notorious and secret practices' of this supposed thieves' guild, and I should like to know just how secret these practices could be if they were notorious. And I should also like to know how Robert Greene should happen to know all about them, unless he were a thief himself and a member of this guild. And one would think that if he were, why then, his fellow thieves and scoundrels in the guild would not take very kindly to his 'bringing to light' all of their secret practices."

"But Master Greene is *not* a thief," Antonia said. "He is a respected master of the arts! I should have thought that you would surely know of him, Elizabeth, for he has written numerous plays, many of which were staged at the very playhouse where your Tuck once worked, and in which your father has an interest."

"Well, my father does not speak much of playhouses of late," Elizabeth replied dryly. "Ever since the Lord Admiral's Men began to play together with Lord Strange's company at the Rose, the attendance at the Burbage Theatre has been greatly in decline. My father has witnessed the value of his investment dwindling steadily. That Tuck has left the Queen's Men, together with his friend Will Shakespeare, has only served to strain relations further with my father. Not that Tuck's departure from the company made much difference one way or another, for he was never an important player, but Will had become their resident poet and was beginning to make a reputation for himself. Now, Philip Henslowe has both him *and* Christopher Marlowe, which greatly increases his ability to stage new productions at the Rose, whilst the Burbages are in danger of losing their lease, in which event Father would likely lose all the money that he had invested with them. So even though Tuck and Will have done my father good service in the past, we do not speak of them these days, nor do we speak of playhouses or companies of players in this house."

"Oh. I see. Well then, I can tell you that Master Greene is a university man and a respected, well-known poet who has written a considerable number of these pamphlets with an aim to keeping the honest citizen informed of the ways in which the criminals of the underworld conduct their shadowy practices, so that good people may avoid being robbed and cozened."

"The underworld, is it?" said Elizabeth. "It all sounds quite dramatic. What makes you think that he is not simply making it all up?"

"Well, he did not make up Charles Locke, did he?" Antonia countered. "He is real enough. As is Moll Cutpurse, whom he also mentions in this pamphlet."

"And what would you know about Moll Cutpurse?"

"I know that she is real, because Tuck has met her. He has told me so."

Elizabeth raised her eyebrows. "Did he, indeed? And just where and when, pray tell, did you two have this conversation?"

"Why, at the bookstall, when I purchased this," Antonia replied. "He was buying one, as well. It turns out that he is a great admirer of Master Greene and has read nearly all of his pamphlets about cozeners and coney-catchers." She hesitated. "He asked about you, of course."

"Ah. How good of him."

"As it happens, 'twas he who recommended that I purchase this," Antonia continued blithely.

"Indeed! And why did he do that, do you suppose?" Elizabeth asked, trying to mask her irritation. She felt irritated that Antonia had met Tuck at St. Paul's, and at the same time it irritated her that she felt irritated.

"Why? Oh, I suppose because I told him that I was looking for something new to read and then asked him what he was going to purchase," Antonia replied, as yet unaware of Elizabeth's reaction.

"So now it seems you both have an interest in common," Elizabeth said dryly, wondering even as she said it why her irritation with Antonia was growing. She had always enjoyed Antonia's company before, but now it seemed she was only getting on her nerves. Elizabeth told herself that it was not as if she had any sort of claim on Tuck Smythe, after all. Their relationship, such as it was, was ill defined, if indeed it could be said to be defined at all. Was it possible that she was feeling jealous of her friend? Though she was young and very pretty, Antonia was a married woman. But then Elizabeth reminded herself that Antonia had also just confessed to having taken lovers. And if she could so easily be unfaithful to her husband, could she not just as easily be unfaithful to a friend? *Or had she been already?* It was a disquieting thought, and Elizabeth found herself looking at Antonia in a new and not very favorable light.

"Elizabeth, I do believe that you are jealous," said Antonia, as if suddenly reading her mind.

"Nonsense. Why should I be jealous?" asked Elizabeth, trying to keep her tone neutral and hoping that her face was not turning red. "Tuck is free to meet with anyone he chooses, and at any time he pleases. As are you, I suppose." She flinched inwardly, wishing that she had not added that last comment. It had sounded tart even as she said it.

Antonia glanced at her and raised her eyebrows. "You *are* jealous!" she said. "And I do believe you disapprove of me."

"Not so much of you as of your behavior," admitted Elizabeth, somewhat reluctantly.

"My behavior," Antonia repeated. "Do you mean my behavior as it regards my husband or my behavior as it regards Tuck Smythe?"

"I do not know that there was anything in your behavior as it regards Tuck Smythe that anyone could fault," Elizabeth replied. "Or was there?" She kicked herself mentally for that. It had sounded less like a question than an accusation. She felt exasperated. Why did she keep doing that? What on earth was the matter with her?

"I do not think that there was anything wrong in my behavior toward him," Antonia replied. "But 'twould seem *you* are afraid there might have been. Or may yet be, more to the point. Is it because you suspect that I may have designs upon him?"

"Oh, Antonia, do not be ridiculous!" Elizabeth replied, sensing the telltale flush in her face even as she spoke. She wanted nothing more than to end this conversation. It was absolutely maddening.

"Ridiculous, am I?" Antonia replied. "Well, do you want to know what I think?" And she proceeded to tell her without waiting for a response. "I think that you like Tuck a great deal more than you truly care to admit. And though 'twould be the height of folly, I daresay you may even love him. Nay, hear me out," she quickly added, raising her hand when she saw that Elizabeth was about to interrupt. "There is much about Tuck to commend him to any woman, as you well know. He is strong and handsome, honest to a fault, amiable and agreeable and possessed of a good heart. But regrettably, he is also a player and poor as a churchmouse, which means that he would never be considered suitable, not by your father certainly and, if you have any sense at all, not by you, either. So then where does that leave you? As far as I can see, it leaves you with but three choices. The first would be to realize that you could not have a future together, for your father would never agree to the match, which would mean that the only sensible thing for you to do would be to forget all about Tuck and wait for the right sort of man to come along, one that could be acceptable to both you *and* your father. However, I have never known you to be particularly sensible, so I rather doubt that you would choose the sensible course."

"I see," Elizabeth replied dryly. "And what would be the second choice?"

"The second choice," Antonia continued, "would be the romantic one, in which you would throw all caution to the winds and defy your father, absconding with Tuck to some far-off place where the two of you could begin a new life together, with both of you as poor as churchmice and struggling to survive as best you could, hoping that you could somehow live on love. And while I do think that you have a romantic side, Elizabeth, I do not think it overshadows your practical nature, though it does tend to interfere with it somewhat. Aside from that, methinks that Tuck would never agree to such a plan, for 'twould place you at a decided disadvantage and take you away from the sort of life to which you have grown accustomed, not to mention that 'twould also take him away from the life of a player, which is what he has always wanted. You would both wind up unhappy, and you would only make one another miserable in the end."

"I suppose we would," Elizabeth agreed with a grimace. "And so what is the third choice?"

"The third choice is the practical alternative," Antonia replied. "And that is to take Tuck as a lover, indulge your passion, allow it to run its course, and then, when it is spent, get on with your own life and let him get on with his. And 'tis that choice which seems to me to be the best for you. If you think it over, and then discuss it plainly and honestly with Tuck, I suspect that in the end you will both see that I am right."

Elizabeth was not quite sure how to respond to that, but before she could gather her wits to respond in any way at all, the sound of running footsteps accompanied by an anguished, sobbing cry made them both look up to see Portia come running in through the stone, ivy-covered arbor entrance to the garden. They both jumped to their feet as Portia came running up to them, holding up her skirts so that she would not trip, her hair in disarray, her face wet with the tears that were streaming down her cheeks. She came rushing up to Elizabeth and threw her arms around her, sobbing into her shoulder.

"*Portia!*" Elizabeth exclaimed with concern, as she tried to comfort her. "Dear Heaven, Portia, what has happened? What is wrong?"

"Oh, woe is me, for I am the most miserable girl who ever lived!" Portia wailed. "My life is over! My one chance for happiness has flown! Father has called the wedding off!"

"He called it off?" Antonia said. "But 'twas to take place within a fortnight! I thought that he approved of Thomas and gave all his blessings to the match! Whatever could have happened to make him change his mind and call it off?"

"A disaster has happened!" wailed Portia. "A most untimely, untoward, and unfair disaster! Father has discovered that Thomas's mother was a Jewess, and so that means that Thomas is himself a Jew! He has called off the wedding and has forbidden me to see or ever speak with Thomas again! Oh, fie! Oh, unbid spite! I think that I shall die!" And with that she buried her head in Elizabeth's shoulder and started sobbing once again.

Antonia met Elizabeth's gaze and shook her head. "And you thought *you* had problems," she said wryly.

3

✳

THE SHOP OF BEN DICKENS, the armorer, was one of the busiest in Cheapside. It was always full of hammering and clanging noises as the journeymen and apprentices worked at the forge and at the anvils on the heavy wooden trestle tables in the smoky room, bending and shaping metal into cuirasses and bucklers, leg harnesses and gauntlets, helms, visors and gorgets, elbow cops, and other pieces that made up heavy suits of armor, most of which, in all likelihood, would never see a real battle.

The advent of firearms had made the armored, mounted knight all but obsolete, save for ceremonial tournaments largely staged for entertainment. And if a nobleman did not require a full suit of polished and elaborately engraved armor for competing in a tournament—although such tournaments were truly not so much competitions as exhibitions and parades—then he would most likely order one, or several perhaps, to stand in a conspicuous location in his home. There it would often become a part of an elaborate display of arms, including swords and shields, pikes and halberds, and maces and axes, all bejeweled or otherwise embellished and mounted on the walls, often over coats of arms, so that they might give ostentatious testimony to the noble aristocracy of their owner, who probably did not have the faintest idea how to employ any of them in combat.

Ben Dickens accepted all this philosophically. Unlike the vast majority of his customers, he had actually been to war and knew from firsthand experience just what terrible damage such weapons could inflict. Consequently, he had no trouble with the fact that most of the weapons that he made were put primarily to passive, peaceful uses. Nevertheless, unlike some other armorers who did a brisk business in weapons that looked better than they functioned, Dickens prided himself on crafting weapons that could, if need be, serve their owners every bit as well upon the field of battle as they did upon the wall. In some cases, they did, for while most of his clients were members of the aristocracy, more than a few were mercenaries or privateers. Though their weapons were generally plain and unembellished, they were no less well made for lacking ostentation.

As Tuck and Smythe came in, Dickens looked up, saw them, and waved. To one who did not know him, it would have been difficult to tell who the owner of the shop was, for Dickens looked as young as any of his journeymen. Tall, fit, and well formed, with chestnut hair and dark eyes, he was dressed simply in well-worn brown leather breeches and a matching doublet, over which he wore a leather apron. He spoke for a moment to several of his craftsmen, and then approached them with a smile, a very large and ornate war sword in his grasp.

"What do you think?" Dickens asked, holding up the two-handed great sword for Will and Tuck's examination.

"Well . . . 'tis very large," Shakespeare ventured uncertainly.

Dickens sighed and shook his head. "What do *you* think, Tuck?"

"'Tis a very handsome sword, indeed," replied Smythe. "Too bad about the flaw."

"*Hah!* There, what did I tell you?" Dickens said triumphantly, turning back to several of his journeymen who were looking on. "Did I not say that he would see it straightaway?"

Shakespeare frowned. "What flaw?" he asked.

"There, in the blade, see?" Dickens pointed it out to him. "'Tis a flaw in the metal."

Shakespeare looked more closely. "Now that you point it out, I can see it," he said, "but 'tis barely noticeable."

"Nevertheless, 'twould make the blade fail in combat," Dickens said, tossing it aside contemptuously. It fell to the floor with a clatter.

"Fail how?" asked Shakespeare.

"'Twould break," said Smythe, bending down and picking up the sword. "This cannot be one of yours, Ben."

"It very nearly was," Dickens replied. "One of my own journeymen tried to pass this off as being acceptable, since 'twould only be employed for decoration. I gave him the boot. Some of the others thought that I was being too harsh. When you came in, Tuck, I told them that you would spot the flaw in an instant. They disagreed and wagered you would not." He laughed. "Gentlemen," he cried out, thumping the table, "pay up!"

With sour expressions, several of the journeymen placed their coins upon the tabletop.

"Consider it a lesson cheaply bought!" Dickens told them. "Mark me well, for I shall not tolerate inferior craftsmanship!"

"Where shall I put this?" asked Smythe, holding the sword.

"I care not," said Dickens. "What good is it? Throw it out."

"Why not hang it upon the wall back here, as a symbol of what shall not pass out of this shop?" asked Smythe.

"Now that is an excellent idea," Dickens said. "I shall do just that. You should come and work for me, Tuck. You know your steel. You would make a splendid armorer."

Tuck smiled. "You have asked me before, Ben, and I fear my answer has still not changed."

"But *why?*" asked Dickens. "You do work for that cantankerous old smith Liam Bailey. What can he offer you that I cannot?"

"The freedom to come and go as I please, for one thing,"

Smythe replied. "And I enjoy working in a small smithy, for another. It reminds me of my boyhood, working with my Uncle Thomas. Besides, my first loyalty shall always be to our company, Ben, you know that."

"Aye, I know," said Dickens with a smile. "And I understand, too. I was a player once myself, remember. But 'tis indeed a pity. You would be a wonderful addition to my shop."

"You are too hard a taskmaster, Ben," Smythe replied with a grin. "I fear that you would grow impatient with me."

"Nonsense. But have it your way. My offer stands. There shall be a place for you here anytime you choose."

"Thank you, Ben," said Smythe. "Your kind offer means more to me than I can say. Perhaps I may even take you up on it one day. But if I may, I should like to discuss the purpose of our visit."

"By all means. I am all attention."

"Well," said Smythe, "we have considered that of all the people that we know, you are doubtless the most widely traveled and have thus seen much more of the world than anyone else of our acquaintance."

"Perhaps," said Dickens with a shrug. "I have traveled widely, that is true, and I have seen much. I would not pretend that this has given me great stores of wisdom, but I may have learned a thing or two along the way. If my experience can be of any benefit to you, then please say how I may be of service."

"Do you happen to know any Jews?" asked Shakespeare.

Dickens raised his eyebrows. "Now, there is a curious question! Of all the things you could have asked of me, I must say, I would never have expected that. Why do you ask?"

"Will is intent upon writing a play about a Jew, so as to outdo Kit Marlowe's *Jew of Malta*," Tuck replied.

"Well now, you need not have put it quite *that* way," Shakespeare said, somewhat petulantly.

"How else should I have put it?" Smythe asked.

"You could have simply said that I was considering writing a play about a Jew and left it at that. You need not have added that I was trying to outdo Kit Marlowe. That makes it seem as if I am trying to compete with him."

"But you *are* trying to compete with him. You told me so yourself."

"Well, never in so many words."

"As I recall, it took you a great multitude of words to say so. I merely said it much more sparingly."

"Perhaps you should be the one to write the play, then!"

"I do not pretend to be a poet . . . unlike some people of my acquaintance."

"*Aghh! Aghh!*" Shakespeare clutched his chest theatrically. "Stabbed to the quick! Oh, traitorous blade! *Et tu, Tuckus! Et tu!*"

"Oh, for Heaven's sake!" said Smythe, rolling his eyes.

"I have known a number of Jews, as it happens," Dickens said, watching them with a bemused expression. "Or was that merely a rhetorical question?"

"What are they like?" asked Shakespeare. "Are they at all like Englishmen, or are they very foreign in their nature? And what do you suppose it means to be a Jew?"

"Well, that is a rather difficult thing to say," Dickens replied with a contemplative frown. "Although I have met some Jews during my travels, I make no claim to any true knowledge of their religion, so as to all the ways in which 'tis different from ours, I could not even begin to tell you. As to your question about their seeming foreign, I suppose that they might seem rather foreign to most Englishmen. Their customs are very different from ours in many ways, and yet in others they are very much the same. I cannot say what it means to be a Jew, for in truth only a Jew could tell you that. I can venture to say, however, that to be a Jew must require great strength of faith, for I can think of no faith that has been so sorely tested."

"You mean because they are so reviled by Christians?" Smythe asked.

"In part," Dickens replied. "But at the same time, 'tis not so simple as all that. Here in England, they were driven out many years ago, save for a small number who remained and were confined to certain areas, tolerated in large part only because there was a need for them. But in other lands, if they have not likewise been driven out, they have often been very harshly used. And yet despite that, they still cling to their faith. All I can say is that a faith that can claim such strong adherents under such duress must surely offer much to its believers."

"Ben, you said that those who had remained in England after most of them were driven out were tolerated only because there was a need for them," said Smythe. "What did you mean by that? What need?"

"One of the oldest and most common needs in all the world, Tuck," replied Dickens with a shrug. "The need for money."

"Ah. I have heard it said that Jews are greedy in their love of money," Shakespeare said.

"Have you, indeed?" said Dickens with a wry smile.

"Why do you smile so?" Shakespeare asked.

"Because I have heard it said, also," Dickens replied. "And yet, have you ever considered *why* people would say so, and then, for that matter, if it were even true?"

Shakespeare shrugged. "I must confess to you that I had not. At least, not until this very moment."

"And so what does your present consideration tell you?" Dickens asked, raising his eyebrows.

"Having never had any dealings with a Jew, nor even met one, I cannot in truth say yea or nay to that," said Shakespeare.

"Indeed, and neither can most Englishmen," said Dickens. "Nevertheless, I have heard it oft repeated as if 'twere gospel. I think 'tis because the Jews are oft engaged in the trade of moneylending. But why, do you suppose? Why that particular trade more than any other?"

"Truly, I have no idea. Because they have some special aptitude for it, perhaps?" said Smythe.

"Well, some may, and some may not," Dickens replied, "as would be the case with any man, in any trade, whether he be Jew or Christian. However, if he were a Christian, and thought himself truly devout in his belief, then he could not choose to be a money-lender, for the Holy Scripture forbids usury."

"It does?" asked Smythe. "I must confess, I have little knowledge of such things, save for *The Poor Man's Pater Noster*, from which my uncle read to me when I was a boy."

"Well, I am no great scholar in such things myself," said Dickens. "As it happens, 'twas a Jew who explained it to me, as I shall now explain to you. In the Bible, there is a verse in which God says, 'If thou lend money to any of my people that is poor by thee, thou shalt not be to him as an usurer, neither shalt thou lay upon him usury.' Therefore, if a Christian wishes to remain devout, he must perforce refrain from the trade of moneylending, for to profit from it would be usury. To a Jew, however, the words 'my people' could be considered to apply only to other Jews."

"I see," said Shakespeare, nodding. "Thus it would follow that if one were a Jew, then nothing would forbid the lending of money at a profit to those who were *not* your people."

"Just so," Dickens replied. "And therein lies the rub. For in almost every nation where their wandering tribes have spread, the Jews have been forbidden to engage in one trade after another, until only one was left to them, the trade of moneylending, which was, conveniently, the only one forbidden to devout Christians. Thus, forced by Christians into the only trade that was left open to them, the Jews then became reviled by Christians for engaging in it."

"But there are more than a few Christian moneylenders here in London, are there not?" asked Shakespeare.

"Oh, indeed, there are," Dickens replied. "Not all Christians are so devout in their adherence to the Holy Scripture as they are in their pursuit of profit, which is why there came a time when Italian and French bankers started to arrive in England and the Jews could safely be expelled, for once there was enough Christian money to be borrowed, one did not require money borrowed from the Jews."

"I cannot imagine what it must be like to be thrown out of my own country," Smythe said, shaking his head.

"Can you imagine what it must be like to know you do not even *have* a country?" Dickens replied. "We were born here in this land and can thus count ourselves Englishmen and Christians, but a Jew who has been born here can only count himself a Jew. And even then, he must do so circumspectly."

"The Jews have your sympathy, it seems," said Shakespeare.

"No more so than anyone who is unjustly used, Will," Dickens replied. "Perhaps that is what having been a 'soldier of misfortune' has taught me. I have seen men unjustly used too many times to unjustly use a man myself. Now, I shall give a man his just desserts, mind you, as I threw out that laggard who forged yon miserable blade, but to judge a man because of what his faith is or who his people are? That is not justice in my view."

"Nor mine," said Smythe. "I, for one, should not like to be judged for who my father is, much less judged for his forebears. I would much prefer to be judged for my own self."

"As would I, Tuck, as would I," said Dickens. "But then, there are many who do not feel as we do. 'Twas not all that long ago, remember, when Protestants were persecuted under the rule of 'Bloody Mary' right here in our own land. Now the tables have been turned and the Catholics must hide their priests in cubbyholes. And I recall only too well those villainous roaring boys Jack Darnley and Bruce McEnery, along with their murderous crew, the Steady Boys, who wanted nothing better than to break the head of every foreigner in London, for no better reason than that they were foreign. It shames me now to think that I once counted them my friends. Their hatred of all foreigners brought about the murder of my good friend Leonardo, and then doomed them, as well."

"A fate they richly deserved," said Shakespeare emphatically.

"For the murder, aye," said Dickens. "But what of the hate that drove them to it?"

"Well, were they not punished for that also?" Smythe asked.

"Of course," said Dickens. "But what I meant was that they had to learn that hate from somewhere. No child is born with hate. It must be taught. And children learn best from the examples that they see around them. 'Tis a pity that they do not learn more love than hate."

"A most ironic sentiment coming from an armorer," said Shakespeare.

"Perhaps," Dickens replied. "If this were a better world, or, more to the point, if we who peopled it were better, then there would have been no need for me to have apprenticed in this trade and I would instead have learned another. But a weapon does not kill by itself. It takes a man to wield it. And he may choose to wield it to oppress another or else to defend himself. The choice is his, not mine. For my part, I would be just as pleased to see every weapon that I made hung upon a wall and never taken down save to be polished and hung up once again."

"In that event, what would it matter if a blade were made well or poorly, so long as its appearance was pleasing to the eye?" Shakespeare asked.

"I shall reply to your question with another question, Will," said Dickens. "If you wish to write a play about a Jew, then why not simply write one in which you imagine your Jew howsoever you might please? Why ask what a Jew is like? And how Jews may be different from ourselves? And whether or not 'tis true that they are greedy? Why not simply make your Jew out of whole cloth, repeating all the things that you have heard said about them, whether they be true or not? What difference would it make, one way or the other, so long as the play itself was pleasing to the audience?"

Shakespeare smiled and nodded. "I can see why you are an excellent armorer, Ben. When you drive home your point, you make your thrust sharp and to the quick. You are quite right, of course. 'Tis not enough simply to satisfy the audience. A good poet must first satisfy himself. And even though the audience might not be aware of the play's faults, I would be aware of them, and that is what would matter most."

"You see?" said Dickens, clapping him upon the shoulder. "We are not so very different, after all. One good craftsman can always understand another, even if their crafts are not the same, because at the heart of it being true to your craft means crafting truly. Do you not agree, Tuck?"

"Oh, I agree completely," Smythe replied. "My Uncle Thomas oft expressed a similar sentiment. He used to say, 'To thine own self be true.' He meant do what you *know* is right, regardless of what others may think or counsel."

"To thine own self be true. I like that," Shakespeare said. "I wish I had thought of it."

"Never fear," Smythe said, "you shall."

"Go suck an egg."

The front door of the shop suddenly swung open with a slam, and a very agitated-looking young man came rushing in. "*Ben! Ben!*"

Dickens turned toward him with consternation. "Thomas! What is it? What is wrong?"

"Oh, Ben, a dreadful thing has happened! I am lost! I am undone!" the young man cried.

To Smythe, the young man looked familiar. Tall, slim, and dark, he was perhaps eighteen or nineteen, clean shaven, with well-formed, handsome features. His shoulder-length black hair was in a state of disarray, no doubt from running through the streets while clutching his bonnet in his hand. It was a soft cap of dove gray velvet, matching his short cloak, and he kept fumbling with it, crushing it up in his hands and turning it nervously, apparently without being aware of what he was doing.

"What has happened, Thomas?" Dickens asked with concern. "Good now, sit, you look all out of breath." He pulled out a stool.

Thomas shook his head. "Nay, I cannot," he replied. "I must stand, I cannot sit. I am in such a turmoil, I cannot think what to do. I feel as if my heart shall burst!"

"What are you all gaping at?" Dickens shouted at his workers, who had stopped everything to stare at the new arrival. "Get back to work! You, Robert! Go fetch some wine! Be quick about it!" One of the apprentices immediately jumped to obey, and Dickens turned back to the upset young man.

"Forgive me, Ben," said Thomas. "I see now that you have customers."

"Will and Tuck are good friends of mine who came to visit," Dickens replied.

"Perhaps we should depart, Ben," Smythe said.

"Pray do not leave on my account, although I would not wish to burden you with my woeful tale of misfortune," said Thomas. He stared at Smythe a moment. "Say, I know you, do I not?"

"Methinks you do," said Smythe, finally placing him. "You ride a bay mare with a white blaze across her nose and white upon her forelegs."

"The Rose!" said Thomas. "I remember now, you work at the Rose Theatre! That is how I know you, you are an ostler there."

"Among other things," said Smythe.

"And I have seen you there, as well," Thomas said, looking at Shakespeare. "You are a player, are you not?"

"I am," Shakespeare replied. "Will Shakespeare is my name. And this is my good friend and fellow thespian Tuck Smythe."

"Well met, my friends," said Thomas. "Or mayhap poorly met, for I am in a sad state, indeed."

"This is my good friend Thomas Locke," said Dickens, introducing him. "I know him of old, when we both were young apprentices, before I went off to the wars. He is a tailor, and a right good credit to his craft."

"Forgive me, good sirs," Thomas said. "I am bereft of courtesy today. My manners have all left me. I can scarcely think what my own name is, much less give it to others. Besides, I know now 'tis not worth giving, for it becomes a plague upon the ears of those who hear it."

"What speech is this?" asked Dickens with a frown. "What terrible misfortune has befallen you that you should so defame yourself?"

"Only this morning I awoke the happiest and most fortunate man in all of London," Thomas said. "Now I am the most miserable and unfortunate man in all the world! Oh, call back yesterday! Bid time return! I was to wed a sweet and gentle lady whose every glance and smile had bestowed a lightness on my heart, but now Portia's father has forbidden her to marry me and I am not allowed to see or speak with her again!"

"Why, what had you done?" asked Shakespeare.

"I was born!" said Thomas miserably, as he kept pacing back and forth. "Such is my guilty crime! My father is a Christian and my mother is a Jewess, which in the eyes of Jews and Christians all alike thus makes me born a Jew. And for naught but that accident of birth, Portia's father has withdrawn consent for us to marry, saying that he will not have his family defiled by a Jew!"

"Here is a sad coincidence," said Shakespeare softly in an aside to Smythe, who nodded.

"I am sorry, Thomas," Dickens said. "Here, sit down and have a drink." He poured a goblet from the bottle the apprentice brought, then poured goblets for Tuck and Smythe as well and handed them around.

As Thomas tossed back half the goblet in one gulp, Smythe asked, "Who is the girl's father?"

"Henry Mayhew," Dickens replied, "a prosperous haberdasher, and an insufferable stuffed shirt. He is a widower with a beautiful young daughter possessed of grace and a most amiable disposition. Until now, he had found in Thomas nothing lacking, and had deemed him eminently suitable to take his daughter's hand in marriage. His consent had already been given, and the marriage was to take place within a fortnight."

"Now he has called it off and withdrawn his consent," said Thomas bitterly. "And Portia is forbidden ever to see or speak with me again."

"But you have not lived as a Jew, Thomas," Dickens said. "I have often seen you in church, and always known you to live life as a Christian."

"Indeed, 'tis so," Thomas replied. "I was not raised in my mother's faith, but in my father's, not that he is the most Christian of all men, by any means, but he does go to church each Sunday. So I have always done, as well."

"And what of your mother?" Shakespeare asked. "Had she become a Christian?"

Thomas shook his head. "She always went with my father to the church, but she was never truly converted to the faith. She was raised a Jew, and at heart she had always remained a Jew. Nor did my father ever try to force her to be otherwise. She was always circumspect in her belief, for she always knew that there were many who would condemn her for her faith. And who am I to judge her? She is my mother. But woe that I was ever born her son!"

"Oh, but that is a bitter thing to say about a parent," Smythe replied.

"Aye, truly, and ashamed am I to speak thus," Thomas said, hanging his head. Then he looked up again, with anguish in his eyes. "But what am I to do? I love Portia with all my heart! She is my world, my life, my breath! I cannot bear the thought of losing her, of never being allowed to see or speak with her again! If you had ever been in love, then you would understand my desperate plight!"

"I understand, perhaps better than you know," Smythe replied, thinking of Elizabeth. "But what does your Portia say to this?"

"I do not know," said Thomas, hanging his head and running his fingers through his hair, clutching at his thick locks in exasperation. "I have not spoken with her since her father banished me from his house and from his sight."

"Well," said Smythe, "'twould seem, then, that you must contrive a way to see her, and discover where her heart stands, with her duty to her father or her love for you."

"I am certain that her heart shall be with me," said Thomas, "but her obedience must perforce be to her father."

"Must it?" Smythe asked.

Shakespeare glanced at him, raising his eyebrows with surprise, but saying nothing.

"What do you mean?" asked Thomas. "How could it be otherwise?"

"If you truly cannot bear to lose her, and if she is, indeed, your world, your life, your breath, then methinks that you must take the measure of her love," said Smythe.

"Speak then, and tell me how," said Thomas, looking up at him intently.

"You must find a way to see her so that you can ask her how she truly feels," said Smythe. "If she truly loves you as you believe she does, as you say you love her, and if your love for one another is truly as great and all-encompassing as you believe, why then, you could elope and make your way to some place where you could live your lives together, as you wish, without hindrance from her father."

"You are right!" said Thomas, banging his fist upon the table. "You give sound counsel, friend! That is just what I shall do!"

"Well now, wait, Thomas," Dickens said, glancing at Smythe and taking Thomas by the arm as he got quickly to his feet. "Stay a moment and do not act too rashly. Before your passion drives you to take a course you may regret, consider that you have now nearly completed your apprenticeship. And what is more, your work has begun to attract favorable notice here in London. One year more and you shall become a journeyman, and you shall be well on your way to making a good life for yourself."

"But what good would any of that be without the woman that I love?" asked Thomas.

"What good would having the woman that you love be without having the means to properly provide for her?" Dickens countered. "And that is something that Portia should consider, also. 'Tis always best to think with your head and not your heart."

"That is a simple enough thing for you to say, Ben," said Thomas, "for you have married the woman that you loved. Your happiness is now assured, and you may think of other things. But I can think of nothing else but Portia and how I cannot bear to go another day without her!" He turned to Smythe. "Thank you, my friend, for your good counsel and your understanding. I shall do as you advise. And if her love for me is true, as I believe her love to be, then we together shall determine what our course must be!"

He clapped Smythe on the shoulders and hurried out the door.

Shakespeare sighed. "The course of true love never did run smooth," he muttered, "for love is blind and lovers cannot see."

"What?" said Smythe. "Why do you look upon me so, Ben, with such a February face, so full of frost and storm and cloudiness?"

"I shall wager that he thinks what I am thinking, Tuck," said Shakespeare, with a disapproving grimace, "that you have just done poor Thomas a profound disservice. If that wench is as besotted with him as he is with her, then they shall doubtless follow your advice and run away together, and thus they will ruin both their lives."

"But why?" asked Smythe. "Why should their lives be ruined if they are both together and in love? I should think they would be happy!"

"They would, indeed, be together and in love and happy at the very first," said Shakespeare wryly, "but at the same time, they would be together and in love and poor. For a time, a short time, they could live on love, but ere long, there would doubtless be children from that love, and then they would be together and in love and poor and hungry and with children, and not long after that, they would be together and poor and hungry and with children and unhappy. And soon thereafter, they would be together and poor and hungry and with children and miserable with one another, a state commonly known to one and all as a settled marriage."

"I am well familiar with your thoughts on marriage, Will," said Smythe defensively, "but they are not shared by one and all. There are people who find happiness in being together, even if they are poor and hungry and struggling to survive, for being together in such circumstances is a far better thing than being alone."

"And what of all the years that he has spent in laboring at his apprenticeship?" asked Dickens. "If he runs off with Portia, he shall be throwing all of that away. Why, within a year, his term as an apprentice will have been completed and he would then be free to open his own shop. Already, his work has gained favor with a number of wealthy customers who would have helped his business grow and prosper. In a few years, he would have been successful on his own, perhaps even a wealthy man. And if this Portia was not deemed good enough for him right now, why, in a few years' time, there would have been a plentiful supply of eager, marriageable young wenches all vying for his favor, without regard to questions of his lineage."

"And if his heart were broken from losing the one woman that he loved?" Smythe asked. "Then what good would all those eager wenches be?"

"Forgive the lad," said Shakespeare, "he knows not whereof he speaks."

"If you believe that I was wrong in what I said to Thomas," Smythe said, "then why do you not go after him and tell him so?"

"Because I know Thomas well enough to know that once he sets his mind on something, he cannot be dissuaded," Dickens replied. "And because, Tuck, I know all too well how foolish a young man in love can be. 'Twas only a few years ago that I was that young man, and I had set my mind upon a course that took me off to foreign wars in the mistaken notion that I would return wealthy from the spoils. As it happened, I was fortunate to have returned at all, and in one piece. Yet back then, I turned deaf ears to all the prudent counsel I received, as now Thomas turns deaf ears to mine."

"Then why does my counsel bear more weight with him than yours, a man who knows him better?" Smythe replied.

"Because you have shown him a way that he may achieve his heart's desire," Dickens said.

"Mayhap not so much his heart, methinks, as some vital organ lower down," said Shakespeare wryly.

"Oh, that was base," said Smythe. "Anyone can see that Thomas is very much in love."

"Is it Thomas that you are truly thinking of or is it not yourself?" asked Shakespeare, raising his eyebrows.

"What? What do you mean?" asked Smythe.

"Methinks that Thomas finds himself in a situation not all that much unlike your own," Shakespeare replied. "You are hopelessly moonstruck over Elizabeth Darcie, whose father, while he does not forbid your friendship, would never grant consent to proper courtship. She is much too valuable a piece of goods to waste upon the likes of you, when she might still attract and wed a wealthy gentleman or, better still, a nobleman. And because he knows that you are an honorable young man, and also because he is indebted to you, Henry Darcie permits you to see his pretty daughter, whom he trusts not to do anything foolish. Thus, you two have a friendship made piquant by the pain of exquisite frustration, where you both yearn for what you both know you cannot have. Now here comes young Thomas, plagued with another Henry, less tolerant than yours, and for that, perhaps, less cruel. You hear his story, and you are moved to counsel him to do that which you wish that you could do yourself, but know that you cannot. You counseled Thomas not for his sake, but for yours. He heard your counsel, and not Ben's, because when one is in love, one hears only that which one wishes to hear. Now he has gone to do that which he wishes to do."

"For that you lay the blame with me?" asked Smythe, glancing from Will to Ben and back again.

"Thomas is old enough to make up his own mind," said Dickens with a shrug. "Still, 'tis a young and reckless mind, and you need not have set spurs to it."

"Mayhap some wise counsel from his parents could serve to give him pause and rein in unwise ambition," Shakespeare said thoughtfully.

"And at the same time allow you the opportunity to meet a Jew?" asked Smythe.

"Is there any wrong in that?" asked Shakespeare.

"Perhaps not," said Smythe. "For if I am wrong in what I said and you and Ben are right, then I must try to check young Thomas in his headstrong flight."

Dickens shook his head. "Why is it that you two seem to find trouble no matter where you go?"

"Methinks that trouble has a way of finding us," said Shakespeare. "But then we are not the first who, with the best meaning, have incurred the worst. Come, Tuck, let us away, and see what other mischief we can accomplish on this day."

4

✳

HE WHERRY RIDE ACROSS the choppy, windswept river took them to the area known as the Liberties, outside the city proper on the south bank of the Thames. They disembarked not very far from the Rose Theatre and the Paris Gardens, where the residents of London, or at least those with a taste for bloodier drama than they could see portrayed upon the stage, could watch the sport of bear-baiting in the ring or, on occasion, see a chained ape tormented by a pack of hounds. In this same area, close by the theatre, a number of thriving brothels could be found, as well as several taverns and gaming houses. A short walk in a southeasterly direction took them to the residence of Thomas Locke's parents, Charles and Rachel Locke, on a tree-lined dirt street near the outskirts of Southwark.

"For a mere tavernkeeper, Charles Locke lives in a rather large and handsome home," said Shakespeare, observing the three-story, oak-framed house with its white plaster walls and steeply pitched thatched roof.

The timbers of the house had been tarred, blackening them so that they stood out dramatically against the white plaster of the walls. In between the upright timbers were shorter boards arranged in opposing diagonal directions, resulting in a dramatic herring-bone effect that made the house stand out from all those around it.

"Strange that we never should have heard of him before," said Shakespeare. "I would have thought by now that we knew all of the taverns hereabouts."

"Methinks that he is rather more than a mere tavernkeeper," Smythe replied. "When Ben told us his name, it seemed somehow familiar to me, although I could not then call to mind just why. Yet now it comes to me at last. If this is the same Charles Locke that I am thinking of, and not just a coincidence of names, then he also owns a brothel and is a master of the Thieves Guild."

Shakespeare glanced at him with surprise. "Now, how in the world would you know something like that?" he asked.

"Of late, I read it in a pamphlet that I bought in a bookstall in Paul's Walk," Smythe replied.

"Oh, no," said Shakespeare, stopping in his tracks. "Do not tell me 'twas one of Robert Greene's works about the so-called 'dark and murky underworld' of London!"

"Well . . ."

"Good Lord, Tuck! You *saw* the man! He was living in his cups, for God's sake, if you could even call that living. I had heard that he was fallen on hard times and dissipated, but the sight of him alone more than confirmed it, to say nothing of his bilious and caustic disposition. How could you possibly take anything he wrote seriously, considering the source?"

"If we were to dismiss the work of every writer ever known to take a drink," said Smythe, "then there would be no literature left in all the world. And I might add, whilst we are on the subject, that you yourself have been known for your supine presence 'neath the tables in many of the lesser alehouses of the city."

"You infernal bounder!" Shakespeare sputtered. "Do you mention me in the same breath as that hopeless, rheumy-eyed, and bloated souse?"

"Not yet rheumy-eyed and not yet bloated, at the least," said Smythe, "but if there be not a flask of brandy somewhere about your person even as we speak, then I shall herewith eat your bonnet!" He swiped the floppy velvet cap off Shakespeare's head and held it underneath his nose. "Well? What say you now, Master Shakescene?"

Shakespeare stared at him squinty-eyed for a moment, then flatly said, "There is no flask."

"Why, you saucy, timorous, and motley-minded liar!" Smythe said. "What will you wager that if I picked you up and shook you, one should not fall out from somewhere within your doublet?"

"You would never dare!"

"Oh, would I not!"

Smythe reached out quickly and spun him around, then seized him about the waist from behind and easily lifted him up into the air.

"*Gadzooks!* Put me *down,* you great baboon! Have you lost your senses?"

Then Shakespeare yelped as Smythe turned him upside down and shifted his grip so that one hand grasped each of his ankles. "Now," Smythe said, "what shall I do, I wonder? Shake you or make a wish?"

"*Tuck! Damn you for a venomous, double-dealing rogue, let me down at once, I say!*"

"Hmmm, now what was it you said just now?" asked Smythe, holding him aloft. "There is no flask, eh? Was that what you said?" He started shaking the helpless poet up and down.

"*Tuuuuuuuuuuuck!*"

Something fell out of Shakespeare's doublet and struck the damp ground with a soft thud.

"Well, now!" said Smythe, "what have we here?" He turned slightly so that Shakespeare, still held upside down, could see what was lying on the ground. "Is that a flask, or do mine eyes deceive me?"

"Ohhhhh, I am going to beat you with a stick!" said Shakespeare through gritted teeth as he vainly tried to strike out behind him. Smythe merely held him out farther away, at arm's length.

"Aye, I do believe that is a flask I see down there at my feet. I do not suppose 'twould happen to be yours, by any chance?"

"God's body! You are as strong as a bloody ox!" said Shakespeare. "Let me down, I pray you, the blood is rushing to my head."

Smythe released him. "Very well, then. Down you go."

It was not very far to fall, no more than a foot or so, but from the way Shakespeare cried out, it might have been a precipice that he was dropped from. He fell to the ground in a heap, groaning.

"Now then," Smythe said, looking down at him with his hands upon his hips, "what was it you were saying about not taking seriously anyone who drank?"

"You know very well what I meant, you great, infernal oaf," grumbled Shakespeare, getting up and dusting himself off. "There is a deal of difference between a man who drinks in moderation and a man who drinks to excess."

"*Moderation?*" Smythe replied. "Compared to you, half the drunks in London drink in moderation, and the other half are bloody well abstemious!"

"Gentlemen," a deep voice said from behind them, "if the two of you are intent upon a brawl, might I suggest a tavern, or perhaps some wooded place where you could maul each other to your hearts' content?"

They turned to see a tall, gray-bearded, and barrel-chested man with sharp, angular features and thick, shoulder-length gray hair standing between them and the front entrance to the Locke house. In his right hand, he held a stout quarterstaff with one end resting lightly on the ground. "Either way," he continued, "I would much prefer that you conduct your mischief elsewhere, and not at my front door, if you please."

"Master Charles Locke, I presume?" Smythe said. He started

toward him, but immediately stopped when he saw Locke raise the quarterstaff and hold it across his body in the defensive posture of a man who was prepared to fight.

"Who are you?" Locke demanded, gazing at him suspiciously. "What do you want?"

Smythe held out his hands, palms forward. "Your pardon, good sir, we mean you no harm. My friend and I were merely having a bit of sport, is all. As it happens, 'tis you we came to see. My name is Tuck Smythe, and this is my friend Will Shakespeare."

Locke frowned and maintained his staff held at the ready. "I know you not. What is it you want of me?"

"'Tis a matter concerning your son," said Shakespeare.

"Thomas?" Locke said, narrowing his eyes. "What have you to do with him?"

"In truth, not a very great deal," Smythe replied. "We have met him for the first time but this afternoon, at the shop of our good friend Ben Dickens, the armorer."

"I know of him," said Locke curtly. "And yet I still know naught of you."

"We are players, good sir," said Shakespeare, "at present with the august company of Lord Strange's Men."

"And so what is that to me?"

"Indeed, sir, it may be naught to you," Shakespeare replied, a touch defensively, "but the news we bring you of your son may not be naught at all."

"*Bah!* Do not plague me with your riddles, you mountebank! What news have you of my son? Speak plainly and try not my patience!"

"We believe that your son is planning to elope," said Smythe.

"Elope!" Locke gave out a barking laugh. "What nonsense! What earthly reason would he have to do such a damned fool thing?"

"Because the father of the prospective bride has now withdrawn his consent to the marriage and forbidden Thomas ever to see or speak with her again," Smythe replied.

"And we have heard this from your son's own lips this day," added Shakespeare.

Locke frowned and lowered his staff. "Indeed? And did he tell you why Mayhew has done this?"

Smythe hesitated slightly, then replied, "He said 'twas because his mother is a Jew."

For a moment, Locke simply stood there, saying nothing. His already stormy countenance betrayed little more response. Then he finally replied. "If you are lying about this because you are bent upon some sort of mischief, then so help me Almighty God, I shall have your hearts cut out."

Shakespeare swallowed nervously and turned a shade paler. Smythe merely returned Locke's steely, level gaze. "Sir, I know full well just who you are, and that you are fully capable of making good upon your threat. Given that knowledge, then, consider how foolish we would have to be to play at making mischief for a man such as yourself."

Locke's gaze never wavered. He merely nodded once, then curtly said, "Why do you come to me with this? What concern is it of yours? Did you hope to gain some favor or ask for something in return for imparting this most unfortunate news?"

"Indeed, sir," Shakespeare began, "the truth of the matter is that we had thought the doing of a favor for a man in your particular position could be of some considerable benefit to struggling players such as ourselves, and—"

Smythe interrupted him before he could continue. "Nay, the truth, sir, is that 'twas all my fault and, as such, my conscience did bid me try to make amends."

"Oh, Good Lord. . . ." muttered Shakespeare, rolling his eyes.

"Explain yourself," said Locke curtly.

In as few words as possible, because he could clearly see that

Locke would not have any patience for long-winded explanations, Smythe described how it happened that he advised Thomas to elope with Portia if he truly believed that he could not bear to live without her. Locke listened impassively. When Smythe was finished, he took a deep breath and exhaled heavily. He looked down at the ground for a moment, as if digesting everything that he had heard and considering it carefully, then he looked up once again, fixing Smythe with a very direct, unsettling gaze. The wind from the river had picked up, and as it blew the old man's hair back, away from his face, and plucked at his dark, coarse woolen cloak, Smythe thought he looked for all the world like some biblical prophet, an angry Moses about to cast his staff down before the pharaoh.

"Methinks you are a man who does not shy from the consequences of his actions," he said to Smythe. "I respect that. But there is one thing that you have not yet told me, and that is *why* you saw fit to offer your opinion on this matter to my son, who was essentially a stranger to you."

"I suppose 'twas meddlesome of me," said Smythe, with a self-conscious grimace. "But in truth, at the time we spoke, I did not truly realize why I had done so. My friend here helped me to comprehend my motives, which I myself had not considered. Like your son, I also am in love, but sadly, with one who is much above my station. And whilst my own situation is not quite the same as that of your son, in that this woman's father, owing me a debt of gratitude, does not forbid our friendship, yet that friendship is the only sort of bond he can permit. In hearing your son's anguish over being forbidden to wed or even see the girl he loved so deeply, I took it much to my own heart and counseled him to do that which, perhaps under different circumstances, I wished that I could do myself."

Locke nodded. "I see," he said. "Well . . . I can understand that, perhaps better than you know." He looked off into the distance for a moment, in reflection, and then continued. "I must ask your pardon, gentlemen. I would invite you both to come inside, but I do not wish to distress my dear wife with this most untimely and unfortunate news."

"We understand completely, sir," said Smythe. "Would there be anything more that we . . . or that I could do to be of service to you in this matter?"

"I am tempted to say that you have already done more than enough," said Locke dryly, "and yet, young Master Smythe, I shall not hold you entirely to blame, for I know my own son. He is possessed of a passionate temper, much like his mother, and what he feels, he feels most deeply. I believe that had you not mentioned elopement as a possible course for him to take, then he would doubtless have come to it on his own. And knowing what my reaction would have been, to say naught of how his mother would respond, he never would have told us. Nor would Mayhew have sent any word to us concerning his decision, so I would have continued on in ignorance of how things stood until 'twas much too late." He nodded to himself. "There is one thing you can do for me, and I would be indebted to you for that favor."

"You have but to name it, sir, and if 'tis within my power, then it shall be done," said Smythe.

"Find my son," said Locke. "I do not wish to see him throw away everything that he has worked for all these years. In time, I believe, he would regret doing so himself, although now, impassioned as he is, doubtless he cannot think so clearly. There are certain things that I can do to prevent him from making such a costly error if he should choose to continue on this course regardless of my wishes, but I shall need some time to make arrangements. In the meantime, find him for me, and communicate to him my feelings on this matter. Remind him also of my love for him, and in particular that of his mother, and bid him consider the effect that this would have upon her."

"I should be glad to do so," Smythe replied.

"I shall tell you of some places where he may be found," said Locke. "He is most regular in his habits, and with luck you shall not take long in finding him. The first place you must seek him is the tailor shop of Master Leffingwell. . . ."

"Well, here is another fine mess you have got us into," Shakespeare grumbled, folding his arms across his chest and huddling in his cloak as the small boat bobbed up and down in the choppy current of the Thames. "Pray tell, why is it that you always have to go sticking your nose into other people's business?"

Smythe sighed. "I am sorry, Will. You are quite right, of course. The entire matter was really none of my concern. Thomas is Ben's friend, not ours, and I should, indeed, have kept my foolish mouth shut. I apologize. I truly do."

"Well . . . we still have some time before our next performance," Shakespeare said, although he sounded a bit dubious. "With any luck, we shall find Thomas at his master's shop, pass on his father's message, and then make it back across the river to the theatre by the first trumpet call."

"I hope so, but I am not so certain," Smythe replied. "We may be cutting it a bit too close. For certain, we shall miss rehearsal."

"Never fear," said the grizzled wherryman, in a gruff and raspy voice, without missing a stroke as he rowed them across. "'Twill rain cats 'n' dogs within the hour. Ye won't be havin' any show this night, ye can be sure o' that."

Smythe glanced up at the sky. "'Tis a bit gray, indeed," he said, "but how can you be so certain?"

The wherryman spat over the side. "I can feel it in me bones, lad. I been scullin' this 'ere river since afore yer birth. If'n I say 'tis gonna rain, 'strewth 'n' ye count on rain. Wager on it, if ye like."

He pulled hard and steady on the short oars of the sharp-prowed wherry as they cut through the choppy water. About twenty feet in length and narrow in the beam, the wherry could carry up to five passengers. On this short cross-river journey, though, only Will and Tuck were being rowed by the sole wherryman, whose powerful arms pulled on the sculls with strong and purposeful strokes.

The Company of Watermen consisted of several thousand wherrymen much like him, a rough-and-tumble lot who plied the waters of the Thames in boats of various sizes, rowing the citizens of London across and up and down the river. With all the traffic on the narrow, crowded, and muddy city streets, many of which still remained unpaved, it was often easier to get around London by traveling the river. Thus, the Company of Watermen was one of the largest companies in the city.

The weather-beaten boatmen, known as watermen or wherrymen or scullers, made their living ferrying the citizens of London on the Thames for the very reasonable fare of about one pence per person. On any given day, their boats dotted the surface of the river like waterflies upon a country pond. There were even Royal Watermen, who rowed solely in service to the queen and her court. A veteran such as the old wherryman who rowed them had very likely also spent some time serving in the Royal Navy, which often turned to the Company of Watermen for impressment. Consequently, there was little point in questioning his knowledge of the river and the weather. If he said he knew that it would rain, then it would surely rain.

"Well, 'tis a pity that we shall not be able to perform tonight," said Shakespeare, "but all the same, it serves us just as well. I should not have liked hastening back for our performance before we could have done Locke's bidding properly. He is not a man to be trifled with, methinks."

"Ye mean Shy Locke?" the wherryman asked. "You two on a job for 'im, are ye?"

"Shy Locke?" said Shakespeare. "Nay, one Charles Locke, a Southwark tavernkeeper, was the man I meant."

"Aye, 'tis 'im," the wherryman replied. "Shy Locke, they call 'im." He grinned. "Ye want t' know why?"

"Somehow I have the distinct impression that you are going to tell us," Shakespeare said wryly, drawing his cloak about him against the chill.

"'E's an important man in 'is own way, 'e is," the wherryman replied from somewhere behind his thick and bushy beard as he bent to the oars. "But ye would never know it to see 'im in 'is tavern, mind. 'E 'ides 'is light under a bushel, ye might say, like a shy sort. Never acts important. Never puts on airs. An' yet, not a thief or alleyman in the city plies 'is trade without ole Shy Locke's permission, if ye please."

"There, you see?" Smythe said. "What did I tell you? Greene was right."

"Robby Greene, what writes them pamphlets?" asked the wherryman.

"*Robby?*" Shakespeare said, raising his eyebrows. Somehow, the familiarity did not seem to fit the bitterly resentful ruin of a man that they had met.

"Aye, 'e knows whereof 'e speaks, ole Robby does," the wherryman continued as he rowed. "A regular chronicler of the underworld, 'e is."

"One might think people like that would resent his writing all about them and telling all the world their business," Shakespeare said.

"Aye, one might think that, indeed," the wherryman replied. "And yet, strange as it might be, they seem to like it. I often 'ear 'em talk about it in the taverns or when I 'ave 'em in me boat. Robby Greene makes 'em famous, see? Get yer name in one o' those pamphlets 'e writes an' then yer cock o' the walk in that lot."

"How curious," said Shakespeare. "Much as noblemen often

have their pet poets who write sonnets to extol their virtues, so 'twould seem that criminals in London have their own poet in Robert Greene. And, as such, I could see how 'twould be a measure of their status to be mentioned in his writings."

"'Twould help explain why he has a cutthroat like that Cutting Ball at his beck and call," said Smythe.

"Oh, aye, 'e's a bad one, all right," the wherryman replied with a knowing nod. "I would be givin' 'im a right wide berth if I was you. One time, one o' Robby Greene's creditors sent a bill collector after 'im. The man found 'im, all right, but Cutting Ball was with 'im, and 'e gave the poor sod a choice to eat the bill or 'ave his throat cut."

"I imagine that he ate it rather promptly," Shakespeare said dryly.

"Washed it down with ale, then took to 'is heels like the devil 'imself were chasin' 'im," the wherryman replied with a chuckle.

"That sounds like just the sort of thing that ruffian would do," said Smythe with a grimace. "I must admit, the more I learn about Master Robert Greene, the less and less I like the man."

"Oh, 'e's an 'orrible man!" the wherryman exclaimed. "Vile tempered and mean-spirited as they come!"

"And a university man, at that," said Shakespeare. "A master of the arts, no less." He shook his head. "He was a good poet in his time. 'Tis a pity what has become of him. A sad thing. A very sad thing, indeed."

"A harbinger of things to come, perhaps?" asked Smythe with a smile.

"Perish the thought!" Shakespeare replied with a shudder. "I should sooner go back to Stratford than see myself reduced to such a state! Nay, I shall not be fortune's fool, Tuck. Thus far, I have achieved some small measure of success, and I am most grateful for it. I shall endeavor to make the most of it, you may be sure of that, but if I see that my run of luck has ended, then I shall know well enough to quit. I promise you. A wise guest knows not to overstay his welcome at Dame Fortune's table."

" 'Ere we be, good sirs," the wherryman said, as he shipped the oars and let the boat drift up to the flight of stone steps coming straight down the bank to the river. There were many such "pairs of stairs" along the riverside, built expressly for the purpose of small boats pulling up to them. "Watch yer step, now!"

The warning was as traditional as it was unnecessary. Everyone knew how slick the steps could be, especially on a damp day. The rough-cut stones had been smoothed by both the elements and foot traffic over time and were often slippery. Smythe and Shakespeare stepped out gingerly, one at a time, while the wherryman held the boat steady, close to the steps.

"Look sharp, good wherryman," Smythe said, flipping him an extra coin. "For a swift passage and the benefit of your wisdom."

"Thank ye, lad," the old wherryman replied, catching the coin. "Mind now, ye go muckin' about with the likes o' Shy Locke and 'tis fortune's darlings ye will need to be to come out with your heads all in one piece. Do what ye please, but just remember old Puck the Wherryman and what 'e told ye."

"We shall do that, Puck, and thank you," Smythe replied, as the wherryman pulled away in search of another fare. "A right good fellow, that," he said to Shakespeare.

"Aye. A good fellow, indeed. But did you happen to pay any mind to what he said?"

"He said 'twould rain soon."

"*And* that we would do well to avoid any dealings with the likes of this Shy Locke if we wanted to keep our heads from being broken," Shakespeare said.

"We have already had some dealings with him," Smythe replied, as they ascended the steps to the street, "and thus far, we seem to have survived with our heads unscathed."

"Thus far," Shakespeare replied with a grimace.

"Oh, stop worrying so much, Will," said Smythe with a grin. "'Tis a simple enough matter. All we need do is deliver his message to Thomas Locke and there will be an end to it. 'Tis not as if we were embarking upon a precarious journey to some den of thieves!"

"It seems to me that when all of this started, 'twas merely a simple matter of going to a tavern so that you could meet your favorite pamphleteer," Shakespeare replied dryly. "Your 'simple matters' have a disconcerting tendency to become byzantine in their complexity."

"And this from a man who cannot seem to get a single play finished before he begins a new one," Smythe replied. "How many are you working on at present? Three? Or is it four?"

"A poet must follow his inspiration," Shakespeare replied.

"He might do better to generate some perspiration by applying himself to only one task at a time," Smythe said.

"Oh, indeed? And where, pray tell, did you learn your mastery in the craft of poetry? Whilst apprenticing with your Uncle Thomas at his forge? Doubtless, you declaimed the classics to one another between hammerblows upon the anvil. Beat the verses into submission, I suppose. Iambic bent-ameter, if you will."

"I am a *what?*"

"Oh, never mind," said Shakespeare, rolling his eyes. "To you, a heroic couplet probably suggests Greek ardor."

"What the devil are you talking about?"

"Your education, sirrah, or, more to the point, the lack of it. 'Tis showing as brightly as a pinked sleeve. I shall take your lead when it comes to smithing or weaponry or knowledge of the criminal underworld, about which you have read so exhaustively and exhaustingly, but when it comes to poetry, my friend, I shall thank you to speak little, or, better yet, speak not at all."

"Do you know, if you expended as much effort in your writing as you do in tongue lashing, then your productions would be hailed throughout the world," said Smythe.

"And if you spent half as much time learning your lines as you do in finding fault with me, then London would forget Ned Alleyn and hail you as the greatest actor of all time!"

"Hark, methinks I hear a kite screeching," Smythe said sourly.

"Whilst I hear a tiresome and rustic drone," Shakespeare replied.

"Rustic? *Rustic,* did you say? And this from a bog-trotting, leather-jerkined Stratford glovemaker! See how yon pot calls the kettle black!"

"*Bog-trotting, leather-jerkined glovemaker?* Oh, that was vile!"

"Well, if the muddy gauntlet fits. . . ."

"Why, you base and timorous scondrel! You call *me* a leather-jerkined bog-trotter whilst *you* lumber about London in country galligaskins and hempen homespun like some hedge-hopping haggard? You raucous crow!"

"Unmannered dog!"

"Rooting hog!"

"Yelping cur!"

"Honking goose!"

"Balding miscreant!"

"*Balding? Balding?* Why, you vaporous churl. . . ."

"*Hey, you, down there! Shaddap!*" A stream of odoriferous slop came pouring down from a second-story window above them as somebody threw out the contents of a chamberpot, just barely missing them.

"Why, that miserable, misbegotten—"

"Never mind, never mind," interrupted Shakespeare, pulling on Smythe's arm to hurry him along. "We really do not have time for this. I should very much like to complete our errand and return in enough time to attend at least part of today's rehearsal. Henslowe has said that he would be fining us from now on if we did not attend."

"Well, I suppose you are right," Smythe grumbled, allowing

himself to be led away. He shot a venomous glance back toward the building from whence the excrementory assault had come. "We should be nearing Leffingwell's shop, in any event."

"I believe 'tis right around the corner," Shakespeare said, as they came around a bend in the curving street and entered a small, cobblestoned cul-de-sac containing a number of shops with painted wooden signs hanging out over their doors.

Several of these shops had display windows in the front with one large wooden shutter that was hinged at the bottom, so that it swung down to open and swung up to close, then was latched from the inside. When swung down in the open position, this shutter, supported by chains or ropes, functioned as a display table upon which the craftsmen could show their wares to passersby in the street. Of course, it was often necessary to fasten the goods down or have someone there to watch them; otherwise a thief could make off with something without even entering the shop. Here, however, such a snatch-and-grab would be rendered more difficult, since these shopkeepers had all joined forces to hire a couple of burly, rough-looking men armed with clubs and daggers to act as guards. They sat upon wooden kegs at the entrance to the cul-de-sac, leaning back against the building walls with their thick arms folded across their massive chests, giving everybody who came past them a close scrutiny.

Smythe and Shakespeare entered the tailor shop where Thomas Locke had served his apprenticeship and now worked as a journey-man. The owner of the shop, a lean and severe-looking master tai-lor, approached them, looked them over quickly, and did not quite manage to mask his purse-lipped disapproval of their attire, which was neither very fashionable nor very expensive. Still, there was always the possibility that they might be looking to upgrade their appearance, and so he put on a polite smile and asked them if he could be of any assistance.

"In truth, sir, we came in search of Thomas Locke, who we

were told is employed here as a journeyman," said Smythe. "We have a message for him from his father."

The tailor sighed and rolled his eyes. "Indeed, everyone seems to be looking for Thomas today," he replied with irritation. "I, too, would very much like to know what has become of him. He should have been here hours ago. 'Tis most unlike him to be so late."

"What do you mean, everyone seems to be looking for him?" Shakespeare asked. "Has someone else been here asking for him, as well?"

"Aye, three women came by in a carriage a little while ago," the tailor replied. "They were asking about him, too. One of them was his betrothed, or so she claimed."

"Did she give her name as Portia?" Smythe asked.

"Aye, she was the one," the tailor replied. "A pretty young thing, if you like that sort. A bit on the coltish side, if you ask me, but with the right style of clothing, in a fuller cut, she could present a decent figure, I suppose. I know not who her tailor is, and did not presume to ask, but she could certainly do better. The other one was not all that much different. Antonia, I think she said her name was, a bit more brassy looking, but well dressed in silks and damasks in dark hues that set off her coloring to good advantage. However, the flaxen-haired one, Mistress Elizabeth, now, there was a woman who knew how to wear clothes. The moment I saw that exquisite green velvet cloak, I told myself this was a woman of excellent taste and sensibility."

"*Elizabeth?*" said Smythe, interrupting him abruptly. "Do you mean Elizabeth Darcie?"

"Aye, Darcie was her name, indeed. Master Henry Darcie's daughter. Now there is a gentleman I would be proud to count among my customers. Mistress Darcie admired some of my bolts of cloth and said she might return and order a dress or two. Aye, she had excellent taste. Excellent taste, indeed. My most expensive silks and velvets were what caught her eye. In my humble opinion, Thomas would have done himself a deal of good had he set his cap at her rather than that other one."

"Oh, good Heavens!" Shakespeare said, throwing his arms up in exasperation. "How has Elizabeth managed to become mixed up in this business? Is there nothing the two of you do not stick your noses into?"

"Mixed up in what business?" the tailor asked, frowning. "Thomas has not done anything wrong, has he?"

"Nay, I am certain he has not," replied Smythe. "'Tis only that his father was most anxious to speak with him concerning some family matter and, as we have just come from him, he asked us to convey the message to him."

"Well, if you see him, you may convey another one to him from me," the tailor said. "You may tell him that Master Leffing-well is not in the habit of employing journeymen who do not show up for work. He never behaved this way when he was my appren-tice, and if he thinks that becoming a journeyman means that he may now come to work only when it pleases him, then he is very much mistaken. And you may tell him that I shall expect him here tomorrow, promptly, and I shall want a full accounting from him concerning where he was today, indeed I shall!"

"We shall be sure to tell him, Master Leffingwell," said Smythe. "But we are not certain where he may be found. Perhaps you could assist us. Did he not reside somewhere nearby?"

"I can only tell you what I told the three young ladies," the tai-lor replied. "Thomas has a room he rents above the mercer's shop across the street. However, as I had already sent one of my appren-tices there earlier today, to see if perhaps Thomas had fallen ill, I can of a certainty tell you that he is not there. As to where he may be found, I fear I cannot say. 'Tis not my habit to keep track of everyone who works for me. I merely expect them to be here on time and to do their jobs properly."

"Well, thank you just the same, Master Leffingwell," said Smythe. "We shall endeavor to find him on our own."

"Well, that would seem to be that," said Shakespeare, as they left the tailor's shop. "We have done our best to deliver Locke's message to his son, but his son was simply nowhere to be found. Certainly, no one can hold us to account for that."

Smythe frowned. "I am rather more concerned about Elizabeth," he said. "I cannot think what she and Antonia were doing here with Portia, unless 'twas their intention to help the two of them elope."

"Well, of course, that is their intention," Shakespeare replied irately. "That should seem obvious. Elizabeth is simply incapable of resisting the urge to meddle, especially when it comes to matters of the heart. She is a decent and good-hearted soul, but she has not the sense God gave a goose. I tell you . . . wait, where are you going?"

"Across the street," said Smythe.

"But Leffingwell has already told us that Thomas is not there," Shakespeare replied.

"He has told us that he sent an apprentice there earlier today, to see if perhaps Thomas had fallen ill," said Smythe, recalling the tailor's words exactly.

"Well then?" said Shakespeare. "Did you not believe him?"

"Oh, I believed him. But what do you suppose that apprentice must have done when he went over there?" asked Smythe. "He knocked on the door and waited for an answer, and then when there was none, he returned. But suppose that Thomas was there and did not answer to the knock?"

"'Tis possible," said Shakespeare. "But why would he fail to answer?"

"What if he were packing his things as he prepared to run away with Portia? Or perhaps he was not there at the time the apprentice was sent, but has returned since. In any event, I should like to go and see for myself."

Shakespeare sighed. "Oh, very well, if you insist. But I should not like to spend the remainder of the day questing for Thomas all over the city. This has already taken up too much of our time to no good purpose."

They crossed the courtyard at the end of the cul-de-sac and went into the mercer's shop, where they learned that Thomas Locke's room was on the third floor. With people from all over the countryside flocking to London in search of work, accommodations were often difficult to come by, and people with rooms to rent could make a handsome profit. It was not unusual for one room to be shared by a number of unrelated people splitting the rent among them, and with such crowded conditions, rooms were often used only for sleeping. That Thomas Locke was able to afford a room all to himself, albeit a small one, already said something about his success as a new journeyman tailor.

Perhaps he had made some arrangement with the mercer in which he bartered his tailoring skills in exchange for part of the rent. Either way, thought Smythe, he certainly had a comfortable arrangement: his own room in a reasonably decent section of the city, where he only needed to walk across the street to get to work in a job where he was doing well. A great many people in London had to make do with a great deal less, Smythe thought, himself included. And yet, Thomas Locke was apparently willing to leave it all behind for an uncertain future in some unknown place. He would gain the woman that he loved, but he would lose everything else. And, Smythe thought with some self-recrimination, he was the one who had given him the idea in the first place.

He could not help wondering if he would do the same if Elizabeth were willing to run off with him. He did not delude himself that she would ever agree to do such an incredibly foolish thing, but nevertheless, he had to wonder. Would he have the courage to do the same in Thomas Locke's place? He discovered, with somewhat mixed feelings, that the answer was not immediately forthcoming.

Perhaps it was not entirely a question of courage. He loved Elizabeth, of that he had no doubt, but then he also loved being a player, something he had dreamed of all his life. When he had left home and set off for London to pursue his dream at last, he had nothing but the clothes upon his back and a few personal possessions. On the way, he had met Will Shakespeare at a roadside inn, a chance encounter of two strangers who, by coincidence, were both in pursuit of the same goal. They had achieved that goal, when so many others who came to London following their dreams were doomed to bitter disappointment. Smythe knew that he had been very fortunate, indeed. Would it not be wrong to turn his back on his good fortune when others had been so much less fortunate than he?

Aside from that, he had good friends now. Shakespeare and the other players in the company were all like brothers to him, even Kemp, cantankerous and quarrelsome as he was; they all seemed like family. He had never had such friends as these. And then there was the old smith Liam Bailey, who in many ways had taken the place of his beloved Uncle Thomas, not to mention the illustrious and adventuresome Sir William Worley, the knight who had befriended him and trusted him with secret knowledge. He had a life here now, a life that meant something to him. He did not think that he could simply walk away and leave it all behind, even if Elizabeth were somehow willing to run off with him.

For that matter, even if she was—not that he could ever ask her—what sort of life would he be able to offer her? Her father was a gentleman. She could never be a player's wife, and the only other trade he knew was that of a smith and farrier. Elizabeth Darcie was simply not the sort of woman who could leave everything she had and live the life of a humble country blacksmith's wife. Such a step down would be a disgrace to both her and her family. But it was all nothing more than pointless conjecture.

Thomas Locke's situation was completely different. He and

Portia Mayhew were in love and were going to be married until her father had suddenly withdrawn his consent, while he and Elizabeth had never declared their feelings to each other. It was an unspoken thing between them, never openly acknowledged.

Shakespeare had been right. He had no business meddling in this affair in the first place. It did not concern him and was nothing more than wishful thinking on his part, in which he had suggested a course to Thomas Locke that he wished that he could take himself, but in all likelihood would not, even if such a possibility were open to him. Still, he thought, it was interesting that Elizabeth had coincidentally become involved in this affair, as well, from Portia's side.

"You are being strangely silent," Shakespeare said as they reached the top of the stairs to the third floor. "Are you thinking about Elizabeth again?"

Smythe smiled and shook his head. "You know me much too well," he said. "I do not think that I could ever keep a secret from you, Will."

"'Tis your face that is to blame," said Shakespeare. "Whenever Elizabeth is in your thoughts, it assumes a woeful, maudlin aspect and you look for all the world like a small boy who has dropped his favorite sweet into a drainage ditch."

Smythe grimaced. "I shall have to cultivate a new expression, then, for that one sounds altogether insufferable."

"You should see it from my angle," Shakespeare said. "Perhaps we can work on some new ones in the tavern later, when we have finished with this nonsense. Then we can sit in comfort over some bread pudding and tankards full of ale and make faces at each other."

They came to the door, and Smythe knocked upon it several times. There was no answer. He knocked again, a bit harder.

"Well, so much for that," said Shakespeare, turning to go back down the stairs.

"Wait," said Smythe. He had tried the door and it had opened.

"Look," he said. A sudden and ominous clap of thunder outside announced the arrival of a storm.

Shakespeare turned and sighed with resignation. "I suppose you simply *must* go in?"

"Well, 'tis open," Smythe said with a shrug. He opened the door wider and went inside.

"Oh, I just know that nothing good can come of this," said Shakespeare, following him in. "Perhaps he has already packed up all this things and left."

"Nay, he is still here," Smythe replied heavily.

The body of Thomas Locke lay upon the floor in a puddle of blood, a dagger sticking up out of his back.

5

✻

TRUE TO THE WHERRYMAN'S WORD, it had started to rain within moments after they had found the body. The gray sky had darkened, and the clouds had opened up to disgorge a hard and pelting rain that had forced the cancellation of that day's performance. All the other players in the company had gathered at the Toad and Badger by late afternoon, but Smythe and Shakespeare did not return till after nightfall, because it had been necessary to report the murder and bring the sheriff's men to the scene, and then remain to answer all of their questions. At the tavern, the rest of the company were waiting for their fellows anxiously, demanding to know why they had missed rehearsal.

They explained about discovering the murder, and how they had narrowly avoided being arrested themselves, which would have made a very convenient solution for the sheriff's men.

"Bloody laggards," Shakespeare exclaimed with disgust as he described the incident to his fascinated audience in the tavern. "They cared not who had actually done the foul deed so much as they were anxious to have it disposed of neatly and with a minimum of effort. Had we not told them that we could produce witnesses who could account for where we had been all day, then 'tis certain that Tuck and I would both have been thrown into the Clink upon the spot."

Smythe felt his stomach knotting at the thought. The Clink was notorious for being one of the worst prisons in London, and from all that he had heard and read, none of London's prisons could boast conditions that were anything less than nightmarish.

"Who do you suppose killed the poor fellow?" asked John Hemings, as he cut off a thick slice of the hearty Banbury cheese they were all enjoying, tore off a large chunk of barley bread, took a big bite out of each, and then washed it all down with beer, a relatively new beverage that had recently become available in London. It was not quite as rich tasting or as hearty as ale, but it had the virtue of being considerably cheaper. Between the wheel of cheese upon the table, loaves of rye and barley bread baked with beans and oats mixed in, and several large clay pitchers full of beer, the players were having themselves a filling and satisfying supper, spiced now by news of the murder.

"I have not the foggiest notion who murdered the poor lad," Shakespeare replied after taking a long drink. "I am just grateful that we were able to convince the sheriff's men not to blame the devilish deed on us!"

"Do you suppose the girl's father may have had it done?" asked Augustine Phillips. "To prevent the elopement, I mean."

"'Twould not have been much of an elopement had the girl's father known about it in advance, now, would it, Gus?" Will Kemp observed sarcastically.

"Well . . . he could have found out about it, somehow," Phillips replied defensively.

"Oh, really? How?" asked Kemp. "As Shakespeare tells the tale, there was not even any *plan* of an elopement until sometime late this morning, when Smythe here put the foolish notion into the unfortunate boy's head."

"Thank you so much for the thoughtful reminder, Kemp," said Smythe with a sour grimace. "It makes me feel ever so much better about how everything turned out."

"Well, it serves you right for poking your nose into other people's business," Kemp replied testily. "Instead of coming to rehearsal, as you were supposed to have done, you chose to spend the day in profitless and pointless gallivanting about town, dragging our book holder to some low-class alehouse only to have him be insulted by some drunken lout of a poet, and then convincing some poor lad you did not even know that he should run off with some wench you also did not know, only to have this boy turn out to be the son of a man who could easily have both of you sewn up into sacks weighted down with stones and then thrown into the river . . . which he might very well do when he discovers his beloved son was murdered. Does that about sum it up, you think?"

Smythe pressed his lips together and nodded glumly. "Aye, 'twould about sum it up, indeed."

"Well done, Kemp," Shakespeare said dryly. "Now if you could only manage to remember your lines as well as you recalled every last detail of our story, then we would all be infinitely better off."

"Perhaps if you wrote lines that were more memorable, I might find that I remembered them more easily," riposted Kemp.

"'Strewth, I do not know if I would be capable of writing anything that you would find easy to remember," Shakespeare said. "Perhaps if I were to rhyme it with some sound that is cherished by thine ear. Speed, old fellow, pray tell, what rhymes with fart?"

"Art," Bobby Speed replied at once, and belched profoundly.

"Hark, methinks we have here the makings of some truly memorable poetry for Kemp," said Shakespeare. "Indeed, 'tis a veritable epic. Now then, what rhymes with belch?"

"Smelch," said Thomas Pope, with his mouth full.

"Smelch? *Smelch?*" Shakespeare frowned. "Preposterous! There is no such word."

"Is so."

"Is *not!*" said Shakespeare. "You are being quite ridiculous, Pope. Go on and use it in a sentence, then, you knave."

"Kemp farted and the smelch was terrible," said Pope.

"Odd's blood! You know, I do believe I rather like the sound of that," said Shakespeare. "Pity there is no such word. Perhaps there ought to be."

"Go on and use it, then," said Pope. "Put it into one of your plays."

"Indeed! The very thought of it! And by what right would you have me take such license with our language?"

"The right of every bard and poet to coin whatever words or phrases please him," Pope replied.

Shakespeare raised his eyebrows. "The devil you say! And what do you call this marvelous right of linguistic libertinage?"

"Um . . . I call it . . . poetic license," Pope mumbled around a mouthful of bread and cheese.

Shakespeare simply stared at him.

"What, no clever rejoinder?" Kemp asked archly.

Shakespeare shook his head. "Nay, Kemp, I have none. He leaves me quite speechless."

"Good," said Pope, his mouth still full. "Now pass the beer."

"About this poor lad's murder," Gus Phillips said once more, getting back to the subject at hand, "you do not suppose that this Shy Locke will hold the two of you to blame? I mean, with what Kemp said and all . . . you do not suppose he will?"

"I most certainly hope that he shall not," Shakespeare said uneasily. "Truly, I do not see how he can. After all, we did not have anything at all to do with poor Thomas's murder!"

"That may not be how he shall see it," Kemp replied.

"Well, I doubt very much that he shall even remember our names," said Shakespeare.

"Only you did tell him that we were players with Lord Strange's Men," said Smythe.

Shakespeare frowned. "I did?"

"You did."

"Bollocks. Well, perhaps he shall not remember it. In any event, we were able to convince the sheriff's men that we had nothing to do with it, so I am sure we shall be able to convince him likewise, if need be."

"You had best hope so," Kemp replied. "Else we may be in need of a new book holder, as well as a new . . ." he waved his hand dismissively, "whatever 'tis you are, Smythe."

"'Hired man,' I believe, is the proper term for my position with the company," replied Smythe tartly.

"'Strewth! Do you mean to say that we actually *pay* you?" Kemp replied with mock astonishment.

"Why not?" asked Pope, masticating furiously as he shoved a wedge of cheese into his mouth, immediately followed by a large chunk of barley bread. "He remembers his lines at least as well as you do."

"Methinks he has you there, Kemp," said Shakespeare.

"You are both impertinent," Kemp said with a disdainful sniff.

"Oh, good Lord," said Smythe, staring toward the tavern entrance with dismay. "As if this day has not brought ill tidings enough."

Shakespeare followed his gaze, looking at the man who had just walked in and now stood just inside the doorway, glancing around the tavern. "I say, Tuck, 'tis your father, is it not?" he said.

"Tuck's father?" Hemings said with surprise. He turned around on the bench, looking over his shoulder. "Truly?"

At once, everyone else turned toward the door. Smythe sighed wearily and brought his hand up to his forehead, which had suddenly begun to ache fiercely. "Oh, this can bode no good," he said. "No good at all."

Symington Smythe II swept the tavern with an aristocratic gaze, then spotted his son, tossed his dark brown cloak back, and started toward them with a regal air.

"Tuck, you never mentioned having any family in London,"

Hemings said, turning back toward him. "Did you not tell us that you came from a small village in the country?"

"Aye, I did," Smythe replied. "Unfortunately, my father chose to follow me to London."

"Ah, Symington, my boy, there you are!" his father said in a tone that sounded so jovial, Tuck knew that it was forced.

"'Allo, Father," Smythe said, rising to his feet politely. "Allow me to introduce my father, everyone . . . Symington Smythe II, Esquire. Father, permit me to present the company of Lord Strange's Men." They rose and he quickly introduced them all, noting as he did so that his bluff and hearty, hail-and-well-met manner notwithstanding, his father did not really have the slightest interest in meeting any of them. "And, of course, Father," he added at the end, "you remember my good friend Will Shakespeare."

"A pleasure, sir," said Shakespeare with a slight bow.

"Indeed," replied the senior Smythe, barely even glancing at him. "Son, I wonder if I might have a word with you in private for a moment?"

"Of course," said Tuck, somewhat awkwardly. He excused himself and allowed his father to lead him away to an empty table in the corner. He sighed as they took their seats. "'Twas rather rude of you to treat them so curtly, Father, if I may say so. These are my friends. The very least you could have done was to exchange a pleasantry or two, instead of treating them all as if they were nothing but dirt underneath your feet."

"They *are* nothing but dirt underneath my feet," his father replied with a disdainful grimace. "Bounders, louts, and scalawags, every last man jack of them. Gypsies, moon-men, vagabonds." He snorted. "A fine lot you have taken up with, I can see that."

"They are my friends, Father."

"Indeed. You know that one may judge a man by the company he keeps."

"Well then, if I be judged now, I must surely stand condemned," said Tuck dryly.

"Do not be insolent with me, young man."

"Or else what?" said Smythe wearily. "You shall disown me? That old and tired hound simply shall not hunt, Father. You have naught left of which you can disown me, not that it would make the slightest bit of difference to me if you did, one way or the other. Do as you please."

"Oh, how very bravely said, now that you know I have suffered some reverses," his father said wryly.

"Reverses, is it?" Smythe replied. "'Strewth, sir, you have lost everything you had, including that saucy young tart who had the presumption to call herself my stepmother when she was scarcely older than myself. You shamefully cheated Uncle Thomas out of his share of the inheritance, foolishly squandered it all, and then fastened on to him like a leech until even he could no longer tolerate your abuses and gave you the boot. Now, at long last, you come to me, your unloved and long-neglected son who had disgraced you by joining a company of players. So, then . . . what is it you wish of me? More money to spend on clothes and carriages? How much this time?"

"My word, how very high and mighty we seem to have become," his father said scornfully. "Such a lofty, noble, moral tone for a mountebank in motley! I see now what comes of having sent you to be raised by my good brother. You have become as insufferable a prig as Thomas ever was. On you, however, the mantle of morality does not sit quite as well, considering the company you keep."

"Did you come here merely to trade barbs with me, or was there something that you wanted?" Tuck said curtly.

His father glared at him for a moment, looked as if he were about to launch into a sharp rejoinder, and then abruptly changed his tack. He smiled and said, "I was going to ask if you would consider acting as the best man at my wedding."

Tuck simply stared at him, speechless with astonishment.

"Of course, if 'twould be asking too much, then I suppose that I could find someone else to stand beside me when the time comes, although I have no idea who in London I would know well enough to ask," his father said.

Tuck finally found his voice. "You are getting married? But . . . how? When?" He shook his head in confusion.

"As to when, I am not yet quite certain. There are yet some small details that need to be worked out. As to how, well, 'tis quite a simple matter, really. One stands before a minister in church and speaks some nonsense and 'tis done."

"But . . . but you are *already* married!"

His father shrugged. "The ungrateful wench ran off."

"God's wounds! You think that makes a difference?" Smythe replied, astonished at his father's arrogant presumption. "You cannot simply marry once again! 'Strewth, not that I have any fondness for that miserable, smug, and grasping woman you had the poor judgment to marry after Mother died, but 'tis not as if she were a horse that bolted and ran off and you simply went and bought yourself another! For God's sake, 'twould be bigamy if you married someone else! 'Twould be a sin!"

"A minor matter," said his father dryly, with a dismissive wave. "'Tis of no consequence. However, if 'twould make you feel any better, I suppose I could arrange to have the first marriage annulled."

"*Annulled?* Upon what grounds?" asked Smythe with disbelief.

His father shrugged. "What difference does it make? Doubtless, a suitable justification can be found. She never bore me any children. I suppose I could claim that the marriage was never consummated. And 'tis not as if precedent did not exist. After all, King Henry had it done, you know."

Smythe was absolutely speechless. His mouth worked, but no words would come out. However, his father continued speaking blithely, as if completely unaware of how casually and lightly he had placed himself on the same level as the monarch who had placed himself above the Church of Rome and presided over the Dissolution.

"In any event, 'twould be seemly for someone of my family to be present at the wedding; after all, one must consider appearances, and since my good, dear, sanctimonious brother Thomas has seen fit to wash his hands of me, well, I suppose that leaves only you."

"How kind of you to think of me," said Tuck dryly.

And, apparently unaware of how he had just slighted his own son, the senior Smythe continued by adding insult to injury. "Of course, 'twould never do for anyone to know you were a lowly player, so I have said you are a journeyman armorer. After all, between hammering shoes onto plowhorses and what all, Thomas *did* teach you to make knives and such, so 'tis not entirely a falsehood, is it? Come to think on it, perhaps you could see your way clear to forging up some trinket as a gift for the father of the bride. You could do it at the shop of that blacksmith friend of yours, what was his name? Well, no matter. 'Twould be a nice gesture, I should think. An ornamental sword or some such thing. How soon do you suppose you could have it ready?"

Smythe stared at the man sitting across from him, the man who he knew beyond a doubt was his father and yet, in almost every other respect save that accident of birth, was nearly a complete stranger to him. He had often felt that in his childhood, but never more so than at that very moment. They shared the same name, but otherwise he could not imagine what the two of them could possibly have in common. He did not even wish to speculate upon the matter. How in God's name, he thought, could I possibly be related to this man?

"Father," he began, somehow managing to find the words, "I fear that I could not possibly comply with your request."

"Well, 'twould not have to be something as fancy as an ornamental sword," his father said. "If that would be too difficult, then I suppose a dagger would do nicely, mayhap with some engraving on the blade—"

Smythe felt the throbbing in his temples building to a point that seemed unbearable. "Father, I do not think you understand," he interjected. "I cannot, and shall not, be a party to *any* of this duplicitous coney-catching."

"Coney-catching!" said his father. "Now, see here—"

"Nay, sir, *you* see here," Smythe interrupted him with a fierce intensity. It was only through great force of will that he was able to refrain from shouting. "I shall *not* do it. Can you understand that, sir? 'Tis important to me that I make my meaning very clear to you. I shall not have *anything* to do with this at *all*. What you plan to do is *wrong*, sir. 'Tis immoral and outrageous, unlawful in the eyes of God and man, and I cannot believe that you would think, even for one moment, that I could ever go along with it. 'Tis a vile scheme that you propose, and knowing what I know of you, I can only think that there is but one purpose to it. You seek to enrich yourself through this marriage so that you might regain all the money you have squandered, and, in the process of so doing, you shall ruin and bring shame upon some poor and blameless woman and her family who have never done aught to you save given you their trust. I am appalled, sir, that you would even consider such a shameful course, much less come to me with this request."

"Do you mean to say that you would refuse your own father?"

Smythe stood up so quickly and so forcefully that the bench he sat upon went crashing to the floor. "My God, sir, have you heard *nothing* that I said?"

An irritated and rather put-upon expression came over his father's face. He gave one of his characteristic disdainful sniffs, a gesture that he presumed made him appear aristocratic. "Well, I see that you are determined to be quite unreasonable about this," he replied, as if what he was asking were a perfectly reasonable thing. "I would have thought that a son would see it as his duty to support his father in seeking some solace and companionship in his old age and embarking upon a new course in life, but 'twould seem that you do not care about such things. So be it, then. I shall trouble you no longer."

"Would that I could have that surety in writing," Smythe replied.

His father stood and drew himself up stiffly, throwing one side of his cloak back over his shoulder in a cavalier manner. "I will have you know that this marriage should set me up quite well, quite well, indeed. You might do well to consider that, Symington. You might do well to consider that, indeed. I am still a gentleman, whatever you may think of me, and despite having suffered some misfortune of late, a knighthood is not yet beyond my grasp."

"Oh, Father, you are dreaming," Smythe replied, shaking his head. "You could have been satisfied with what you had. Methinks most men would have gladly traded places with you. You had a small yet very comfortable estate, a goodly amount of money, a young and pretty wife—who married you for that money, although you did not seem to mind that very much—and you had finally managed to obtain your precious escutcheon and become a proper gentleman."

He paused for a moment, thinking he could also have added that he had a son who had once wanted very much to love him, but whose love was never deemed important. However, he decided not to say that, because he knew that it would serve no purpose.

Instead, he said, "One would think that all these things would have been enough to satisfy most any man. But not you. And in truth, Father, I have never understood why not. Uncle Thomas had ever so much less than you, and yet he always thought he had a great deal more. In time, I came to understand that he did have a great deal more, indeed, because he knew how to be grateful for all the things he had, rather than lust for all the things he lacked." He shook his head. "Nay, I will not help you in this, Father. You were wise . . . or perhaps 'crafty' would be more appropriate, methinks . . . to be careful not to tell me the name of this unfortunate woman upon whose estate you have designs, for if I knew her name, then rest assured that I would seek her out and warn her about you. And I would entreat her family most urgently to bar their doors against you, for you are a scoundrel, sir, and I am ashamed to call myself your son."

His father gazed at him with scorn, his lips compressed into a tight and angry grimace. For a moment, they simply stared at one another, and then Smythe had to look away, for he could not bear to face that smug, superior, and unrepentant gaze. It was too painful. Finally, his father spoke.

"I see how matters stand between us, then," he said in a tone of affronted dignity. "Apparently, it does not shame you to associate with scalawags and strumpets, but it shames you to be my son. Very well, then, I shall free you of that noisome burden." He lifted his chin and uttered his next words as a pronouncement of the utmost gravity. "You may consider yourself disowned."

Smythe sighed wearily. "You have already disowned me once before, Father, when I left home for London. Yet you conveniently managed to forget that when you came to me last time to ask for money and I gave you all I had. And I suppose, when all is said and done, that compasses it all between us. I gave you all I had, and I have naught else left."

"I shall remember that," his father said stiffly, "on the day you come to me with hat in hand, as I know one day you shall."

"If you knew me at all, Father, then you would know that I do not wear hats," said Smythe.

With a contemptuous sniff, his father turned on his heel and stalked out of the tavern without another word or backward glance. As Smythe turned to watch him go, he saw the other players all looking at him, their expressions ranging from curious to puzzled to, on at least one face, concern. The furrow was still present on Shakespeare's brow as Tuck returned to their table.

"It did not go well?" he asked.

"Aye, Will, it did not go well," said Smythe as he sat back down. "Thomas, pass that pitcher, will you? I have a mind to get good and drunk this night."

"Suits me," said Pope, passing him the pitcher.

"And me," echoed Bobby Speed. "Stackpole, you old reprobate, more beer!"

And for a time, as other spirits flowed, Smythe's sunken spirits were somewhat uplifted. For a time.

Henry Mayhew was very much displeased with his daughter. He had done her—and himself, he felt—a very great service by saving her from a marriage that would have brought disgrace upon her—and himself, of course—and in return, she was not only ungrateful, she was angry. It simply passed all understanding. Instead of thanking him profusely for preventing what would have been a truly horrible mistake, she had cried and sobbed and carried on and blamed him for ruining her happiness and then had fled the house, against his wishes. Now here it was, growing quite late, and Portia still had not come home. He was torn between feeling angry and concerned.

"I tell you, Winifred, I simply do not know what has become of young people these days," he complained to his intended, the widow of a prosperous ironmonger who had left her quite well off when he had obligingly dropped dead the previous year. "Apprentices roaming the streets in unruly gangs and rioting, young women gallivanting about town unescorted and having assignations in Paul's Walk . . . I tell you, Winifred, that sort of thing simply did not happen in my day!"

"I am certain it did not," Winifred Fitzwalter replied, glancing up at him calmly from her embroidery, "as I am equally certain that grieving widows did not go unescorted to the homes of widowers at night and sleep under the same roof with them."

For a moment Mayhew looked shocked, perhaps not so much at what she said as at the fact that she had said it. However, he recovered quickly. "'Tis hardly the same thing, Winifred," he said, somewhat huffily. "'Tis nigh on a year now since your husband died, and there has been quite sufficient allowance for the customary period of mourning." He grunted and nodded and patted his ample stomach with both hands, as if to reassure himself. "Aye, more than sufficient time to satisfy propriety. And as for your presence in my home, dear Winifred, 'tis perfectly proper, perfectly proper, indeed! We are betrothed, and our betrothal has been formally announced. What is more, on the occasions when you visit here and spend the night, you are duly attended in your own room by a maidservant, so there can be no question of propriety at all, nay, none at all."

"Nevertheless, that does not mean that people will not talk, you know," said Winifred with a slight smile.

"Well, people can say what they will," said Mayhew with a grimace. "The fact remains that propriety has been observed in all respects, in all respects, indeed. What is more, you are a mature woman, Winifred, not a young girl like Portia."

"Why, thank you, Henry. 'Tis always a comfort for a woman to be reminded of her advancing age," she replied.

"Oh, for Heaven's sake! You know what I mean! Odd's blood! Where the devil *is* that girl?"

"I would venture to say that she has gone to the home of one of her friends," Winifred replied calmly, "where she will doubtless remain for as long as she can, the better to cause you concern. Rest assured, Henry, that she is not out wandering the streets, and even if she were, the watch would surely stop her, question her to find out why she was abroad alone at this time of night, and then escort her home."

"And supposing they thought she was a whore out plying her trade?" asked Mayhew.

"Oh, Henry, I should hardly think so," Winifred replied. "No one in his right mind would mistake Portia for a strumpet. She is much too innocent a girl."

"Well, perhaps you are right, but there are still evil men abroad who would not hesitate to despoil an innocent young girl," said Mayhew.

"All the more reason she would not be out wandering the streets," Winifred replied. "She has been protected, yet not quite sheltered, and Portia knows full well the dangers of the city streets at night and what parts of the city to stay out of in the daytime and what sort of people to avoid. She may be headstrong, Henry, but Portia is not foolish."

"Well, 'tis true, I suppose," he said, somewhat mollified. "She is my daughter, after all. The apple does not fall very far from the tree."

"Indeed," replied Winifred, nodding over her needlework and thinking that, all things considered, Portia must have fallen much closer to her mother's tree than to her father's. "I am quite certain that there is no cause for concern. She will return in due time, when she is ready, when she has had some time to have her cry and think things over."

Mayhew grunted. "Bloody lot of nonsense, if you ask me. I do not know what she has to cry over. The very idea! All I did was save her from marrying a heathen Jew."

"Now, Henry. . . ."

"One would think the world were coming to an end from the way she carried on!"

"To her, perhaps, it was," Winifred replied. "To Portia, Thomas Locke is not a 'heathen Jew,' as you say, but the young man with whom she fell in love and whom she had planned to marry. She was so looking forward to it. 'Tis an important event in a young woman's life, the most important event of all. She stood upon the threshold of becoming a woman, Henry, a wife and soon, no doubt, a mother. Now all that has changed, and changed quite suddenly. She has had no time to prepare for it. Her feelings are surely in a turmoil. Oh, Henry, can you not remember being young yourself?"

"Hmpfh! When *I* was young, Winifred, I had no time for such nonsense. I was much too busy working. My family was poor. We had no time for 'feelings.' We could not afford them."

"Well, I should think you could afford them now, Henry," Winifred replied, her voice as steady and methodical as her needlework. "And if you find that you cannot, then perhaps I should go out and buy a plentiful supply for you, so that you could afford to spare some for your daughter."

"Most amusing, Winifred," Mayhew replied with a grimace. "Most amusing, indeed. I suppose you think that I am being much too hard on the girl."

"I think, Henry, that you did what you thought was right," she replied. "You have prevented her from marrying someone that you found unsuitable. Now give her some time. Once she has given the matter due consideration, no doubt she will come to understand."

"I should certainly hope so," Mayhew replied. "Can you imagine? My daughter married to a Jew? God shield us! What would people say? 'Twould be the ruin of us, the absolute ruin, I tell you!"

"Well, you have stopped it, Henry."

"Aye, indeed, I have! Indeed, I have! There shall be no chance of that now, I can tell you that! No chance at all!"

"Calm yourself, Henry," Winifred said quietly. "You are

becoming all red in the face. And when Portia returns home, pray do not go on about it. Leave her be. She will be like a willful steed now; let her have her head and she shall come around, you will see."

"Hmpfh. What makes you so certain?"

"A woman knows these things," she replied reassuringly.

"Indeed? Well, a man knows a thing or two, as well. And I have taken steps to ensure that this does *not* happen again!"

Winifred looked up at him and frowned. "What do you mean? What sort of steps?"

"I have already begun making arrangements to ensure that she shall marry someone much more suitable. Much more suitable, indeed," he replied.

Winifred looked startled. "Have you? So soon?"

"Aye, I have, indeed. And what is more, I intend to waste no time about the matter. I shall have Portia married off well and properly before she can get herself into any more trouble, you may rest assured of that!"

"To be quite fair, Henry, you cannot blame Portia for something she could not have known," Winifred replied. "Nor did you know it, for that matter. Do not forget that you gave your approval to the match, at first."

"Well, 'twas because I was misled," Mayhew replied testily. "The young man seemed entirely suitable and presented himself as such. A journeyman tailor, well spoken and well settled and employed in a good shop, with excellent prospects all around. . . ." He grunted and scowled. "Zounds, what is this country coming to when such people are permitted to mingle with their betters? Why, to think of that . . . that . . . spawn of that detestable tribe of usurers with his hands upon my daughter. . . ."

"*Henry!* You are growing all red in the face again! I fear that you shall become sanguine in your humor, and then we shall have to summon a physician to bleed you!"

"Never you mind my humors, madame," Mayhew replied irritably. "There is no distemper in my disposition, I assure you. As I have told you, I have taken steps to set things right. In due time, this entire matter will be settled, and there shall be an end to it."

"What are these steps that you have taken, Henry?" Winifred asked with a slight frown. "I must confess that I am much surprised at how quickly you have acted. What, exactly, is the nature of these arrangements you have made?"

"Ah, well, there, madame, you may see the mettle of the man that you shall marry," Mayhew said with a self-satisfied air. "As it happens, fortuitous circumstance led to my making the acquaintance earlier today of a certain gentleman lately arrived in London from his country estate. A proper gentleman, mind you, to the manner born, one who dresses in the height of fashion, with his escutcheon embroidered on his handkerchiefs in gold and silver thread! He carries himself most excellently, most excellently, indeed. And, as we engaged in conversation, I discovered, by pure chance, that he was looking for a wife!"

"Happy chance," said Winifred.

"Oh, I should say so, Winifred! I should say so, indeed! He was most interested when I mentioned that I had a marriageable young daughter—a very comely marriageable young daughter— for whose hand, of course, there had been more than a few suitors, although none quite suitable had as yet been found."

"And I presume you did not tell him that she had but lately been betrothed to Thomas Locke," said Winifred.

"For Heaven's sake, Winifred!" Mayhew replied. "This is a gentleman of quality! Do you suppose that he would even for one moment consider a match with a girl who has already been betrothed, much less to one who. . . ." He shook his head, as if he could not bear even to complete the thought.

"Nay, I suppose not," Winifred said quietly. "Not if he were a *proper* gentleman. You did not tell him, then."

"Perish the thought! If word of that were to get around, then I should be saddled with a spinster for a daughter! Or else be forced to have her married to some lowly ostler who stank of horse manure or, worse yet, a player! Nay, Winifred, we have our own lives and our reputations to consider."

"And if Portia were married to a gentleman, a proper gentleman, of course, that would considerably enhance our lives and reputations," she replied.

"Just so, Winifred, just so! Why, it may be possible for me to become a gentleman myself! I should think that after a lifetime of hard work, now that I have the means at last, obtaining an escutcheon would be a fitting reward, indeed. Can you not see yourself married to a gentleman, Winifred, a proper gentleman with his own coat of arms emblazoned on his mantelpiece and painted on his coach?"

"And embroidered on his handkerchiefs, no doubt, with gold and silver thread," she murmured softly.

"Eh? What was that you said?" he asked.

"Eh? 'twas nothing, Henry," she replied. "I was merely counting my stitches to myself."

"Ah. I see," he said. "Well, count away, then. Do not let me distract you. 'Tis only our future I am speaking of."

"I have finished, Henry. And I am all attention. So tell me, who is this gentleman of whom you speak?"

"His name is Symington Smythe II, Esquire," Mayhew replied, as if savoring the sound. "And what is more, Winifred, 'tis my understanding, although he most humbly and modestly requested that I refrain from speaking of it, that he is presently a candidate for knighthood! Think of it, Winifred, my daughter, Portia, married to a knight! Can you imagine what that could mean for us? 'Tis most fortuitous, most fortuitous, indeed! One disaster narrowly averted, and now this great good fortune falls into our laps!

Just wait until Portia hears of this! I imagine that then you shall see gratitude, indeed!"

"I can imagine just how grateful she will be," Winifred replied with a slight furrow in her brow.

"Aye, Winifred, things are looking up!" said Mayhew. "Things are looking up, indeed!"

6

✳

THE DISCOVERY OF THOMAS LOCKE'S body briefly displaced Smythe's concern about Elizabeth's involvement with Portia Mayhew, but it had been simmering away at the back of his mind ever since they had left Master Leffingwell's tailor shop. Then he began to think about it once again as soon as his father left the tavern.

Just the thought of his father getting married while still being married to his errant second wife was disconcerting enough all by itself, but it only served to remind him once more of Thomas Locke's plan to elope with Portia Mayhew, a plan that Thomas might never even have considered had he not suggested it to him in the first place. And now it seemed to have resulted in his death. Ben Dickens had been right, Smythe thought; he should have kept his mouth shut and his mind on his own business.

He wondered how Elizabeth was involved with Portia Mayhew, whom he knew only by name. Presumably, they had known each other all along. Perhaps that should not have been surprising. After all, Elizabeth's father and Portia's father were both successful and wealthy merchants who most likely traveled in the same social circles and probably did business with one another. And it was not as if Elizabeth were in the habit of introducing him to all her friends. He understood that. He was under no illusions that he was a suitable companion for someone of her class. He could hardly expect her to acknowledge their relationship to everyone she knew.

He had never met or even known about Antonia, for example, until she had happened upon them together by chance in Paul's Walk one day. As he recalled, Elizabeth had clearly felt a little awkward introducing them. It had been the most cursory sort of introduction. Elizabeth had introduced her merely as "my friend Antonia." He did not even know her last name. Later, when they had once again chanced upon each other at the bookstalls in Paul's Walk, this time without Elizabeth being present, Antonia had greeted him in a warm and friendly manner, doubtless only being polite, of course, and it had seemed, under the circumstances, a bit presumptuous to ask her full name. Not that he had given it much thought at the time. Their conversation had quickly turned to their tastes in reading matter, for they were both there to browse the bookstalls. But at the same time, he had felt that Antonia had been very curious about him and the nature of his relationship with Elizabeth. She was, however, much too well bred to question him about it, and they had soon gone their separate ways.

Then he found out that both she and Elizabeth had been at Leffingwell's tailor shop with Portia, looking for Thomas only a short while before he had arrived there with Will on the same errand. He had known better than to tell the sheriff's men about that, and fortunately Will had refrained from mentioning it, as well. However, the sheriff's men would almost surely question Master Leffingwell and probably find out about it then. And that, in turn, meant that they would doubtless pay a call on Henry Darcie soon thereafter. His relationship with Elizabeth's father was already somewhat strained. This would certainly not serve to improve matters between them.

The entire matter had somehow turned into a hopeless, tangled, tragic muddle, with him in the center of it all. The headache that began with his father's arrival at the tavern had continued to build in intensity until he had started drinking with his friends, and then for a time it went away. Now, with the advent of the morning, it had returned full force, much worse than it had been the previous night.

"Here," said Shakespeare, bending over to help him sit up, "have some of this." He held a tankard up to his lips.

Smythe wrinkled his nose at the smell. "Good Lord, not more beer!" he said, groaning at the sound of his own voice. "Odd's blood, Will, I should think that I have had enough," he added miserably.

Shakespeare chuckled. "More than enough, I would say. Yet drink this just the same. 'Tis the hair of the dog that bit you. 'Twill make you feel somewhat better."

Smythe sipped and groaned again. "'Strewth!" he said. "If this is what comes of getting drunk, then I swear that I shall never drink again!"

"I have heard that a time or two, methinks," said Shakespeare. "In your case, however, I may well be inclined to believe it. You never did much care for spirits, and I have never seen you drink but sparingly afore last night. I had cautioned you to have a care, but you seemed disinclined to listen."

"I do not remember," Smythe replied.

"Well, that does not surprise me," Shakespeare said with a smile. "Here, have a little more."

Smythe took another sip and moaned. "I feel sick to my stomach," he said. "God! Does this happen every time one has too much to drink?"

"To varying degrees," Shakespeare replied, nodding. "Men who are not used to drink should not drink more than they are used to."

Smythe had seen Shakespeare in similar straits a number of times before, but until now he had never fully appreciated how it felt. "How in Heaven's name can people stand it? Lord, the way Speed drinks, I should think 'twould be an utter agony!"

"Well, if Speed ever sobers up, no doubt his head shall burst," Shakespeare replied. "But he seems to maintain an even strain upon his constitution, having apparently learned the fine art of balancing his inebriation through long experience. If he were an alchemist with such precision, then he would have long since turned lead into gold, though doubtless he would have drunk up all the profits from it. Are you feeling any better yet?"

"Not really," Smythe replied.

"Here, have a little more. If you feel the need to spew or pluck a rose, then I shall bring the chamberpot."

"Nay, there is no need," said Smythe, shaking his head, and then instantly realizing his mistake as the room began to move. He shut his eyes and brought his hands up to his head. "Oh, Lord. 'Tis a right worthy penance I receive now for a night of folly."

"'Twill get a little worse, I fear," said Shakespeare, handing him a note. "This came for you by messenger a little while ago. 'Tis from Elizabeth."

"Have you read it?"

"I did take that liberty, considering your indisposition, since I thought that it might have some bearing upon recent events."

"And?" said Smythe, still holding the message with its broken seal of red wax. He almost didn't want to read it.

"And it did, indeed," said Shakespeare. "'Twould seem the sheriff's men came by her house early this morning."

Smythe groaned and put his hand over his eyes. "Oh, I am fortune's fool. What said her father?"

"She did not say," Shakespeare replied. "You may read it for yourself, but she writes little more than that. She wishes to meet you at Paul's Walk this morning."

"This *morning*?" Smythe quickly opened the note and read it. "What is't o'clock?" he asked.

"Nearly ten o' the clock," said Shakespeare.

"Zounds! I shall be late!"

"Not if you run," said Shakespeare.

"You villain. I believe you are enjoying this," Smythe accused him.

"Rather a great deal," Shakespeare said with a smile. "For a change, the shoe is on the other foot. Next time, perhaps you may have more sympathy for a man in this condition."

"A man who allows himself to fall into this condition deserves no sympathy," said Smythe, hopping about as he got dressed. "And nor do I deserve it. But just the same, I shall endeavor to be more tolerant in the future."

"Good luck," said Shakespeare. "And do not forget rehearsal!"

It had felt hellish to run at first, but the brisk pace he forced himself to maintain and the cool air rushing over his face had improved the way he felt. Although the headache had not completely gone away by the time he reached St. Paul's, the intensity of it was greatly diminished, much to his relief.

The churchyard was a bustle of activity, as usual. Still an impressive edifice, even after its tall spire had been destroyed by lightning, the cathedral of St. Paul had nevertheless seen better days. Since the Dissolution, no incense was permitted, organ music was prohibited, and candles could not be used at all except at Christmas. What statuary had not been removed was broken. Overall, the majestic cathedral was in a sad state of disrepair.

Morning prayer service was usually held between seven and eight o'clock, with evening prayer held from two to three. Following the separation from the Church of Rome during King Henry's time, the Act of Uniformity had decreed that the *Book of Common Prayer* was to be used for services, and all recusants were severely punished. The harboring of priests had been declared high trea- ·

son, punishable by death. It was unlawful for shops to be open during the time of common prayer, on Sundays, or on holy days, though the enforcement of these laws was entirely another matter. Wednesdays had been set aside for abstaining from meat, although it was said that this was less for spiritual reasons than to help the fishing industry. And in a similar manner, there was a great admixture of the sacred with the profane in the cathedral of St. Paul.

There was much demand among the citizens of London for "good books," such as the *Geneva Bible* and the *Bishop's Bible,* of course, as well as collections of prayers, sermons, aphorisms, and religious stories, such as *Foxe's Book of Martyrs,* or translations from the French of Calvin's commentaries, or the popular devotional works of Thomas Bacon. All of these and more were for sale in the bookstalls, along with more prosaic and sensational matter, not only outside in the churchyard, but inside the cathedral itself, as well.

St. Paul's School had been established on the grounds to give a grammar school education to young boys, but if they happened to venture out of the school and down the main aisle of the cathedral, known commonly to one and all in London as Paul's Walk, then they could quickly receive a different sort of education altogether. Since the Dissolution, Paul's Walk was less a quiet and somber aisle in a church than it was a busy thoroughfare, where the citizens of London came to hear the latest news, as well as meet with lawyers, many of whom kept more or less permanent stations at certain pillars in the cathedral where they could conduct business with their clients. Men in search of work often loitered in the Walk, hoping to find someone who would hire them for endeavors either legal or illegal. Merchants set up their stalls at the tombs and at the font, where they sold such commodities as ale and beer, bread and fruit, and even fish.

For a time, there were even horses ridden through the cathedral, as well as carts drawn along the Walk by either mules or oxen, though a law was finally passed prohibiting such traffic. Nevertheless, from time to time, some young bravo on a prancer would still take a trot along the Walk, enjoying the sound his horse's hoofbeats made as they echoed above the general din. Paul's Walk was also known as a place of assignations, and London's lovers, either married or unmarried, often met there. And related activities, although of a considerably less romantic nature, were also conducted at the pillars and in shadowed corners. Many religious houses had been taken over following the Dissolution and converted to other uses, but perhaps none served quite as many or as varied uses as St. Paul's.

For Smythe, once he overcame his initial shock at the spectacle of what St. Paul's had become, Paul's Walk served two primary purposes. It was a place he often came to purchase books and pamphlets, and it was also where he came to meet Elizabeth Darcie now and then.

His friendship with Elizabeth—for it was truly little more than that—was a source of both joy and misery to him. He was hopelessly in love with her, and had been ever since the day he met her at the Burbage Theatre, where he and Will had gained employment as ostlers upon first coming to London. From the very beginning, there had seemed to be a spark between them, but she had arrived in a fine black coach to meet a gentleman to whom she was betrothed. And, he had thought at the time, even if she were not already spoken for, she was still too far above him for him to entertain any serious thoughts of courtship.

She was the beautiful daughter of a wealthy merchant who was also a partner in the Burbage Theatre, while he was a lowly working-class ostler whose greatest hope in life was to become a player. With such a daughter, a wealthy man like Henry Darcie could easily arrange a marriage that would advance his family both socially and financially. Shakespeare, who had quickly realized his friend was smitten, had vainly pointed out to him that someone like himself had about as much chance of courting Elizabeth Darcie as a player had of being knighted. And it might have ended there had fate not brought Elizabeth to seek his help in freeing herself from a betrothal to a man who turned out in the end to have been an imposter, a murderer, and a spy.

The situation had served to bring them closer, and a grateful Henry Darcie, as a way of acknowledging his debt, had allowed their friendship to continue. He could still not countenance any sort of formal relationship or courtship, but because he owed a debt to Smythe and trusted both him and his daughter to behave honorably, he could at least, somewhat grudgingly, look the other way. And in that Smythe found both relief and frustration.

He enjoyed his meetings with Elizabeth immensely and looked forward to them, but at the same time he often found them agonizing. He could not simply come out and tell her how he felt about her. He had no right to do so, nor did she encourage him—at least, not in any direct way—either because she could not or would not. He was never really certain which. Maybe it was both.

They had long conversations every time they met, but there was often another sort of conversation that took place between them, one that went unspoken. He was convinced, despite Shakespeare's repeated assertions that he was only deluding himself, that Elizabeth cared for him more than merely as a friend. And a number of times, she had come close to saying it outright.

She was at an age when many young women of her class would have already been married. Yet she had obstinately resisted every attempt by her father to arrange a suitable match for her, insisting that she would not marry for any reason save for love, an attitude her father found maddeningly unreasonable. To his way of thinking, she had at most another five years of opportunity to find a suitable husband, one that would advance Henry Darcie's own position as well as hers. Much past the age of twenty-five or-six and she would be considered a spinster.

Given her beauty, there had certainly been no shortage of suitors. However, her fiery and assertive nature had given her the reputation of a shrew, a term that she wryly defined as "a woman who does not do all that a man wishes." At times, that same strong sense of independence led to arguments between them, but no argument, however passionate, was ever enough to break the bond they had. Quite the opposite, in fact.

They met most frequently in Paul's Walk, a crowded place where people of all classes mingled, where, if necessary, the convenient fiction of a chance encounter could explain their being together. Yet, in Antonia's case, that had not been quite enough. She had seemed suspicious of them from the start, although Smythe had the feeling that she suspected a great deal more than she had reason to suspect. It was in the way that she had looked at him, with a sort of smug and knowing glance. It had irritated him and at the same time, curiously, made him feel guilty, like a small boy caught doing something wrong.

He soon spotted Elizabeth's familiar long, dark green velvet cloak and hastened toward her. As usual, she was at the bookstalls, perusing the titles. It was not merely for the sake of appearances, however. She was a great reader, although their tastes were not the same. He liked to read pamphlets about London's criminal underworld and about the adventures of sailors and soldiers and such, while Elizabeth was much more interested in poetry. Nevertheless, their love of reading was something that they had in common.

"Elizabeth, I received your message and came as soon as I could," he said.

She turned toward him and, once again, as every time, he was so struck by her beauty that he was rendered speechless for a moment. Like most unmarried women, she did not wear a coif, and her blond hair fell out in a thick braid from beneath the hood of her cloak and hung down the side of her chest to her waist, which was naturally narrow even without the aid of a boned, stiff-pointed bodice and stomacher. Much to her mother's chagrin, since turning twenty, she had obstinately refused to wear the latest fashions, claiming that they were too confining and would not let her breathe. She preferred much simpler clothing, such as gowns cut in the kirtle style, similar to those worn by working-class women. However, so as not to utterly scandalize her parents, she had hers made from silks and three-piled velvets, the better, very costly kind that was cut into three heights and imported from Italy or France. And, unlike most women of the upper and middle classes, she did not dye her hair or paint her face, because she claimed that it was too much trouble and made her face feel as if it were caked with grease.

This was her rebellion against having been dressed in fashionable, adult clothing from an early age and dragged around her father's ever widening social circles, "paraded before the gentry and the aristocracy like a Judas goat staked out for bait," as she described it. For, having realized early on that he had a daughter of surpassing beauty, with soft, flaxen hair, deep blue eyes, high cheekbones, and creamy, nearly translucent skin, Henry Darcie had seen an opportunity that might otherwise have been denied him, regardless of how hard he worked and how successful he became.

He knew that an alliance through marriage to a family of rank and long-standing position might allow him to overcome the handicap of his common birth and become a gentleman. Unfortunately for Henry Darcie, his own pride and overreaching ambition had ultimately kept him from achieving his goal. He could easily have married off Elizabeth a dozen times over when she was younger and more tractable, but none of her suitors had ever seemed quite good enough. He had always believed he could do better. Why settle for a gentleman when he might net himself a knight? And then why settle for a knight when his daughter's charms might snare a nobleman?

Yet as Elizabeth grew older and her intelligent, willful personality became more and more assertive, she became more and more difficult to handle. Potential suitors whom her father now found quite suitable enough were often quickly discouraged by her independent disposition and by her refusal to subordinate her will or her intelligence to theirs.

Quite impractically, she had announced that she would marry only if she were in love, an idea her father blamed upon a tutor who had instructed her in poetry and who had been summarily dismissed for putting such foolish notions into her head. Sadly for Henry Darcie, once that notion had taken root, it was not so easily dislodged. He believed the day would come when Elizabeth would finally come to her senses and realize that her own future, as well as that of her family, depended upon making a good marriage. However, since his last attempt at arranging a marriage for her had nearly ended in disaster, he had, at least for the present, given up trying to make a match for her. Perhaps, he thought, having tried everything else, if he left Elizabeth alone for a time and allowed her at least some of the freedom that she seemed to crave so much, she might eventually become more settled in her disposition and more amenable to practical decisions.

Meanwhile, so long as her attention seemed to be occupied by books, her women friends, and a rather loutish but honorable and good-hearted young player, she would probably keep out of trouble. She had enough sense that she could not possibly consider anything more than friendship with him, and he, in turn, had proven himself trustworthy, even if he was insufferably working class. Remove the reasons for her rebellion, Henry Darcie thought, and her rebellious spirit might dissipate in time. At least, this was his fondest hope.

Smythe both knew and understood this. What Elizabeth had not explained to him, he could easily surmise from his acquaintance with her father, who was, for all his pomposity and ambition, basically a good and decent man. He trusted them both to behave properly, something Smythe found flattering and frustrating at the same time. There were men, he knew, who would not hesitate to take advantage of such a situation, but he could not. And he did not think Elizabeth could . . . or would. Therein lay the exquisite agony of their relationship.

"You look as if you have been running, Tuck," Elizabeth said to him. "You are all flushed and out of breath. Are you unwell?"

"Nay . . . well, perhaps only a little. I fear I drank too much last night and overslept, and when I awoke, my head was fit to burst."

She raised her eyebrows. "You were *drunk?* 'Tis not very like you, Tuck. Is your friend Shakespeare becoming a bad influence upon you? Or is it that something causes you distress?"

"The latter, I confess, although 'tis still a poor excuse for such behavior, and I have learned my lesson painfully," Smythe replied, rubbing his still-aching head. "My father came to visit me last night at the Toad and Badger. Our conversation was exceedingly unpleasant, but 'tis a matter of no consequence at present. I am more concerned to learn that the sheriff's men came to your house this morning. What happened?"

"Methinks that you already know," she replied. "They wanted to know about poor Thomas."

"Leffingwell told them that you were at the shop, no doubt," said Smythe with a grimace. "I was afraid he would. I had hoped to keep you out of it."

"How are *you* involved in this?" she asked with a frown.

He sighed. "'Twas all my fault, I fear."

Her eyes went wide. "*What?*"

"Oh, I do not mean his murder," Smythe quickly replied. "I had naught to do with that, but I fear 'twas I who had set events in motion that must have led to the foul deed. And now I feel myself responsible for the tragedy that came to pass."

"But how?" Elizabeth asked, as they proceeded together slowly down the crowded Walk. "I did not know you even knew him."

"Until yesterday morning, I did not," said Smythe, and he quickly told her what had happened since the time that he and Will went to see Ben Dickens at his shop. He did not tell her the full scope of his conversation with Thomas Locke, for that was a bolt that struck a bit too close to home, but he did convey the essential substance of it. "So, you see," he concluded, "'twas all my fault that Thomas had decided to elope with Portia Mayhew, for had I never mentioned it, the idea might never even have occurred to him."

"I see," Elizabeth replied. She took a deep breath and exhaled heavily before continuing. "Well, in that event, perhaps you might feel somewhat relieved of your guilt in this sad matter if you knew that the idea would surely have occurred to him whether you had suggested it or not, for I had also suggested it to Portia."

"*What?*" said Smythe, staring at her with astonishment. "You mean to say that you told Portia that she should elope with him? But . . . when did this occur?"

"From what you have just told me, I would surmise it must have been at nearly the same time that you spoke with Thomas at Ben's shop," Elizabeth replied. "So 'twould seem not to be possible, in truth, to determine for a certainty which of us was first to offer our counsel."

"Odd's blood!" said Smythe, thinking Shakespeare had been right. "So that was why you went to Leffingwell's tailor shop? You were looking for Thomas so that Portia could tell him that she was willing to run off with him?"

"Quite so," Elizabeth replied. "But she never had the chance to speak with him, poor girl. And now she has been driven nearly insensible with grief over what has happened."

"When did she learn of it?" asked Smythe.

"When I did, this morning," Elizabeth replied. "She was staying at my father's house with me."

"But why was she at your house?"

"Because she was angry at her father for refusing to let her marry Thomas," she replied. "And now she refuses to go home, because she is convinced that her father had poor Thomas killed."

"He may well have done so," Smythe said. "He would seem a likely suspect, especially if he knew the two of them planned to elope. But then, I do not see how he *could* have known. There would not seem to have been enough time or opportunity for him to have made such a discovery."

"Unless he met with Thomas and Thomas told him outright what he planned," Elizabeth replied.

"But why would he do that?" asked Smythe. "'Twould seem very foolish to forewarn him."

"Mayhap Thomas did it out of spite, to defy Portia's father and flaunt in his face that there was nothing he could do to stop them," Elizabeth replied.

"Would he have done such a thing?" asked Smythe with a frown. "Was Thomas that much of a hotspur?"

Elizabeth shook her head. "In truth, I do not know," she said. "I did not know him. We had never even met."

"What, never?"

She shook her head. "Not even once. I never did lay eyes upon him."

"But I thought Portia was your friend?"

"She was, and is, my friend," Elizabeth replied. "But there was never an occasion for me to meet Thomas. They had only but lately become formally betrothed, and I had not seen very much of her of late. I had heard her speak of him before, but you would know him much better than I, for all the brief time that you spent with him. Did he strike you as a man who was possessed of a bold and fiery disposition?"

Smythe considered for a moment. "Nay, I would say that he did not. He seemed quite driven to distraction by what had happened, but I would say his disposition was more one of desolation and dismay than of scorn or anger. He did not strike me as some roaring boy. Quite the contrary, he seemed more . . . well, if you had met him, I do not think that you would have taken him for anything but what he was, a tailor."

"And you do not think that he could have gone to Mayhew's home and stood up to him? Cannot even a tailor be driven to a fury born of anger and frustration?"

"I suppose 'tis possible," said Smythe. "But I should think that he would have wished to speak with Portia first. After all, how else would he have known she would be willing to elope with him? And you just told me that Portia was with you and had not seen him. At least, not since Will and I had met him at Ben's shop."

Elizabeth shook her head. "Nay, she had not. We had been together all that time. And Antonia was with us and may vouch for that."

Smythe frowned and gave her a sharp glance. "Why would she need to?"

Elizabeth grimaced. "You would not ask that had you seen the way the sheriff's men behaved," she said. "They were very boorish and suspicious."

"They merely want someone to deliver up to the hangman for the crime," said Smythe contemptuously. "I believe they would have arrested me and Will for it if they thought they could have pinned the blame upon us without too much trouble."

"Well, Portia could never have done such a terrible thing," Elizabeth replied. "In any event, she was with me and Antonia when it must have happened."

"How did she respond to their questioning?" Smythe asked.

"She could not speak with them," Elizabeth replied. "She ran from the room, sobbing with grief. I was left to answer all of their questions, and then I gave those ruffians a good talking-to for the way they treated her!"

"I should imagine that you did," Smythe said with a smile, easily able to picture it. "Where was your father during all this?"

"He was away on business," she replied. "Else he would have had a thing or two to say about it, too!"

"I have no doubt," said Smythe, feeling at least momentarily relieved. "And your mother?"

"In the country, visiting her sister," said Elizabeth. "And just as well, I should say. I see no reason to trouble my parents with any of this."

"Nor do I," said Smythe, nodding. "At least, not unless anything should happen that might involve you further. Well then, given what they had heard from Will and me, and what they learned from you this morning, I would gather that they next went to Henry Mayhew's house. I take it that Antonia was there with you, as well, when the sheriff's men came?"

"Nay, she had gone home to her husband yesternight," Elizabeth replied, "after we had failed to find Thomas."

"So then you never went to his room across the street from Leffingwell's?"

She shook her head. "There was no reason, as Master Leffingwell had said he was not there." She shuddered. "Thank God we had not gone there. Then we should have found him slain."

"A sad business, indeed," said Smythe. "I wonder if they have arrested Henry Mayhew?"

"Do you suppose he did it?" Elizabeth asked.

Smythe shook his head. "I do not know. What sort of man is he?"

"Well . . . I should not think he was the sort who would be capable of murder," Elizabeth replied, "but then one never truly knows, does one?"

"Nay, one does not," Smythe agreed. "If there is one thing I have learned, Elizabeth, 'tis that most any man could be capable of murder, given the right circumstances and the provocation."

"Even you?" she asked, cocking an eyebrow at him.

"Aye, even me," he said. "In truth, I can imagine certain circumstances that could drive me to it, such as if some villain were to harm . . . someone that I cared about."

She gave him a sidelong glance. "You mean Will?" she asked, in a slightly mocking tone.

"Well, Will is my closest friend," he said, a little awkwardly. "But I can think of others on whose behalf I might be moved to some act of violence, if the occasion warranted."

"If the occasion warranted," she repeated. "Aye, there's the rub, indeed. Who is to say what sort of occasion may warrant such a deed? You? Or I? Or Portia's father? If he believed that his daughter had been disgraced or, worse yet, defiled, might he not consider that an occasion which warranted an act of violence? Or even murder?"

"I suppose that would depend upon what he believed may have occurred and how strongly he detested Jews," he replied. "Strangely enough, come to think of it, 'twas the desire to learn more about the Jews that started all of this."

"Indeed?" Elizabeth asked with a slight frown. "How so?"

Briefly, Smythe explained to her how he and Will had met with Robert Greene and how that, in turn, had led to the discussion of Marlowe's *Jew of Malta,* which Shakespeare had determined to surpass.

"So that was why you went to see Ben Dickens?" asked Elizabeth. "So that Will could find out if he knew any Jews?"

"Aye," said Smythe. "Ben is the most well-traveled person that we know, and we supposed perhaps he might have met some in his soldiering days. Little did we suspect that we were about to meet one in the flesh." He frowned. "Although I must admit, the thought of Thomas being a Jew did not impress itself upon my mind especially, save that he had mentioned it as being the reason for his troubles. Otherwise, he seemed much like any other man."

"Why would he not?" she asked.

"Well, in truth, I do not know," Smythe said. "But he was nothing at all like Marlowe's evil villain. He seemed a decent enough fellow, and struck me as no different from any other Englishman."

"Did you expect him to be different somehow?"

Smythe shook his head. "I do not know that I expected anything, in truth, having never met a Jew. Perhaps I had expected that a Jew would look different somehow, more like Marlowe's Barabas, I do not rightly know. But then, Thomas Locke's father is an Englishman."

"And so is he," Elizabeth replied. "Or, I should say, *was* he," she added sadly. "Did he not go to church? I seem to recall Portia telling me that they had gone together."

Smythe nodded. "Aye, since you mention it, I recall he did say so. Thomas told us that he had been raised in his father's faith, and not his mother's. Was that not the only way a Jew could have remained in England?"

Elizabeth shook her head. "I truly know nothing of such

things. But from what I understood from Portia, 'twould make no difference to her father yea or nay. Once he had discovered that Thomas's mother was a Jewess, then that made Thomas a Jew, as well, even by the standards of his own people."

"Curious. I wonder how Mayhew would have known that," Smythe said. "And how did he happen to discover that Thomas's mother was a Jewess?"

"Portia made no mention of it," Elizabeth replied. "But 'tis an interesting question, I must say. Unless he had found out from Thomas."

"Why would Thomas even mention it, especially to Mayhew?" asked Smythe. "Knowing that Jews had been barred from England since King Edward's time, one would think 'twould be the last thing he would do."

Elizabeth glanced at him. "You have become all caught up in this, I see."

"And you have not?"

"To the extent that Portia is my friend, I have," she replied. "But for me, it ends with my concern for her. Not so with you, however."

"Well, as I told you, I feel at least in part responsible for what has happened," he replied.

"And as *I* have told *you,* even had you not spoken with Thomas at all, he still would have at least considered an elopement, if not purely on his own, then certainly after Portia told him that she was willing to run off with him."

"Except by that time, he would already have been dead," said Smythe. "'Tis the timing of it all that troubles me. Like a hungry dog that worries at a bone, I cannot seem to let it go. Did Portia happen to mention if Thomas had any other enemies? Perhaps someone with whom he may have quarreled of late?"

Elizabeth frowned, thinking for a moment, then shook her head. "Nay, I do not think she mentioned Thomas having any enemies. Of course, that does not mean he did not have them. Are you thinking that Henry Mayhew may *not* have been the one who did it?"

"Well, 'twould seem unlikely he would have done it by himself," said Smythe. "He could have hired someone and had it done, which would not have been very difficult at all." He glanced around. "We could probably find men willing to perform such work right here. And yet, the more I dwell upon it, the more it troubles me, Elizabeth. I do not think Mayhew could have acted so quickly to have had it done within so brief a span of time."

"Unless he had already planned to do it earlier," Elizabeth replied.

"'Tis possible," said Smythe, nodding as he considered it. "And yet, methinks 'twould seem unlikely."

"Why so?" she asked.

"Consider this," he said. "Mayhew discovered somehow that Thomas was a Jew, and let us not trouble for the moment about how he happened to come by this knowledge, although that is a point which puzzles me considerably. We shall assume, for the moment, that he was outraged and infuriated by this knowledge to the point where he was willing to commit murder, or else hire someone else to do it. Well then, why not simply go ahead and have it done? Why bother formally withdrawing his permission for the marriage? Why bother saying anything at all, to Portia or to Thomas or to anyone, for that matter? Would it not have been simpler by far for him to have poor Thomas killed, and then feign ignorance and commiserate with his daughter over the terrible tragedy that had occurred? In that event, would anyone have seen any reason at all to tie him in with it? Assuming that he was not an utter fool, which he could not have been, else he would not have made such a success in business, then would he not have found such a course much more expedient?"

"Indeed, 'twould seem so," Elizabeth replied, after considering it a moment. "So then, why did he not do so?"

"Perhaps," said Smythe, "because he was not the one who did it."

"But . . . if that is true. . . ." Elizabeth began with a worried frown.

"Then the sheriff's men may very likely be arresting an innocent man even as we speak," said Smythe.

7

✳

BUILT TO HOUSE THE COMPANY of players known as the Lord Admiral's Men, the Rose Theatre was the crown jewel of Philip Henslowe's various enterprises, among which were also a pawnshop and a number of thriving Southwark brothels situated conveniently nearby. Originally hexagonal in shape, the playhouse was three stories high and timber framed, with thatch-roofed galleries and an open yard. At considerable expense, the Rose had recently been renovated and enlarged by pushing back the walls behind the stage, along with the stage itself and the tiring room behind it, then lengthening the sides of the building. This expansion increased the available area for the groundlings, those members of the audience who paid the cheapest admission price of one penny and stood in the open yard, the surface of which had been mortared and sloped upward, so that those who stood toward the rear could enjoy an unobstructed view. This sloping of the yard also facilitated drainage, so that rainwater and other natural fluids could run down to the wooden box drain that ran from just behind the stage to a ditch beyond the playhouse walls. This made cleanup after the performances easier and, with the regular changing of the rushes, helped keep down the smell. Now shaped like an assymetrical polygon, the playhouse was currently home to both the Lord

Admiral's Men and Lord Strange's Men, the company to which Smythe and Shakespeare now belonged.

They had left their first company, the Queen's Men, though not without some regret, for they had thought of the Theatre as their home ever since they came to London. Dick Burbage, the son of the owner, James Burbage, was a fellow player and had become a good friend to them both. However, despite the Theatre's legacy of lending its name to other stages—all playhouses in London were now increasingly being called "theatres"—the Queen's Men had fallen upon hard times. The company had been in decline ever since the death of Dick Tarleton, their celebrated comic player, followed by the defection of their star, the celebrated Edward Alleyn, who had joined the Lord Admiral's Men. Ned had subsequently married Henslowe's daughter, thereby cementing his relationship to the entrepreneur and assuring his own future. To make matters worse, the Queen's Men had then lost both of their juvenile apprentice players when one had died of the plague and the other, perhaps fearing the same fate, ran off.

After that, the company's bad luck only continued to grow worse.

Will Kemp, for all his efforts, had never quite been able to fill Dick Tarleton's shoes, and before long he, too, had left the company, following Alleyn to the Lord Admiral's Men. The lengthy forced closure of the playhouses due to plague and a dismal touring season for the company had already strained the finances of the Queen's Men to the limit. Most of the players were broke, and a number of the hired men had quit and gone in search of other work. And in a time when work in London was becoming increasingly difficult to come by, this bespoke a degree of desperation that was telling. When the playhouses had at last reopened, the powerful combination of Ned Alleyn's bombastic acting and Kit Marlowe's luridly dramatic writing drew most of the Queen's Men's audience to the Rose. The wind was whistling through the empty galleries of the Theatre, and even the ever optimistic Dick Burbage had seen the ominous writing on the wall.

"Go," he had told them, when Will received an invitation to join Lord Strange's Men. "Go on and join them. Never fear for me. 'Tis true that things do not look very promising at present. The company is but a shadow of what it once had been; our audiences have deserted us, and our greedy landlord keeps threatening not to renew our lease upon the property in the hope that he may seize the playhouse for himself. But though the carrion kites may circle overhead, my friends, my father and I are far from finished. For a time, Henslowe and the Lord Admiral's Men have us at a decided disadvantage, to be sure, but remember that fortunes ever change. We are already planning a *new* Theatre, much improved over the present one, and although the time is not yet ripe, our plan will soon come to fruition. But in the meantime, you must eat, my friends, and you must pay your rent, and though your loyalty is the very nectar of sweet nourishment to me, I fear 'tis but poor provender for you. So please, I beg you, go with my blessings, both of you. There shall yet be another time for us to play together."

And so, with a bittersweet mixture of sadness and anticipation, they had joined Lord Strange's Men, who in turn had combined forces with the Lord Admiral's Men shortly thereafter due to a poor season and hard times for all the companies in London. Over the next few months, players came and went; companies formed, disbanded, and re-formed. And sadly, the Queen's Men, once the nation's most illustrious company of players, did not survive the various upheavals.

Bobby Speed came with them to Lord Strange's Men, as did John Hemings soon thereafter. The departure of a second shareholder in the company signaled the end to all the others. Hemings was in due course followed by Tom Pope, George Bryan, and Gus Phillips. Will Kemp had joined their new company, as well. He had not gotten on well in the Lord Admiral's Men, having managed to quickly raise the ire of both Ned Alleyn, their star player, and their resident poet, the young and irrepressible Kit Marlowe. Unfortunately for Kemp, when the two companies joined forces, he was once more thrown in with both of them.

Alleyn had little patience with Kemp's ever increasing reluctance, or perhaps growing inability, to learn his lines, something he had previously covered with improvised songs and caperings. However, the conventions of the stage were changing, and Marlowe's sensational and gory dramas had no place for such buffoonish antics. Thus, when Kemp forgot his lines and resorted to his usual comic bag of tricks, Marlowe flew into hysterical rages, screaming and throwing things at him, at one point actually drawing steel and chasing him around the playhouse with his sword, threatening at the top of his lungs to disembowel him. Had it been anyone else but Marlowe, Kemp might well have taken it for nothing more than a grandiose display of temper and dramatics, something not at all uncommon in the world of players and poets. However, this was not just any player or poet, but Kit Marlowe, whose flamboyant excesses and mad, Dionysian behavior were legendary throughout all of London. Kemp took fright and ran to his old friends for protection.

So the old crowd, for the most part, was back together once again. But although the Rose was home now to both companies, and they often played together, sharing members back and forth depending on the needs of their productions, there was still a feeling of competitiveness and rivalry between them—and, in a few cases, even animosity. It was not the most harmonious of marriages.

Ned Alleyn's ego was as expansive as his gestures on the stage and, having been the star of two companies in succession, he had a natural tendency to lord it over everyone. Being widely acclaimed throughout the country as the greatest actor of the age had certainly done nothing to restrain him. Where he had once tolerated

Kemp when they had played together in the Queen's Men, he now openly detested him and, knowing that Marlowe absolutely loathed Kemp, often tried to pit the one against the other. And Will Kemp was an all-too-easy victim. He simply could not restrain his wicked sarcasm, which was his natural defense, and Marlowe did not know the meaning of restraint to begin with, all of which meant that their rehearsals often became boisterous and tumultuous affairs that nearly degenerated into riots. On a number of occasions, Smythe had to separate the two of them, able to do so only because his size and strength made him an effective barrier between them and because Marlowe, having once fought alongside him in a barroom brawl, was well disposed toward him.

Fortunately, for all his passionate and violent nature, Marlowe was, at heart, neither evil nor mean-spirited, and his rages would usually dissipate as quickly as they would erupt. Nevertheless, Kemp had become so terrified of him that he had developed a nervous twitch that manifested itself whenever Marlowe was around, and this only served to irritate the flamboyant poet further.

"And so I rose," boomed Alleyn from the stage, sweeping out his right arm in a grandiose gesture of encompassment, "and looking from a turret, did behold young infants swimming in their parents' blood. . . ."

Now Alleyn paused dramatically and posed, sweeping both arms out wide, right arm to the side and bent slightly at the elbow, left arm to the other side and raised, with elbow sharply bent, fingers splayed, eyes wide and staring, as if at a lurid vision of unimaginable horror. His voice rose and fell dramatically as he continued with the speech.

". . . scores of headless carcasses piled up in heaps, and half-dead virgins, dragg'd by their golden hair and flung upon a ring of pikes. . . ."

"'And *with main force* flung *on* a ring of pikes'!" shouted Marlowe from the second-tier gallery, springing to his feet and pounding his fist on the railing. "And the line is 'headless carcasses piled up in heaps,' not '*scores* of headless carcasses'! God blind me, Ned, must you always change the lines?"

"Methinks that '*scores* of headless carcasses' sounds ever so much more dramatic, Kit," Alleyn replied in his stentorian tones, gazing up him.

"Well, if they are piled up in bloody fucking heaps, methinks 'tis likely that we may assume that there are bloody fucking *scores* of them!" shouted Marlowe, throwing up his hands in exasperation. "Why can you not read the lines the way I *wrote* them? *And why is that man shaking?*" he added, his voice rising to a screech as he leaned over the gallery rail and pointed an accusatory finger toward the stage, straight at Kemp.

"Must be all those infants swimming in their parents' blood," Shakespeare murmured quietly to Smythe as they stood together near the back of the stage, holding spears up by their sides.

Smythe snorted as he barely repressed a guffaw.

"*Kemp?* Is that *you* again?" shouted Marlowe.

In vain, the trembling Kemp tried to conceal himself behind John Hemings, who was far too thin to help conceal much of anything.

"I can still *see* you, Kemp, you horrible man!" shouted Marlowe. "Why the devil are you twitching about so?"

"Doubtless he is attempting to upstage me," Alleyn said petulantly. "Kemp is forever attempting to upstage me."

"*Liar*! I . . . I was *not!*" protested Kemp, clutching at Hemings for protection. "John, tell them I was not!"

"He was not trying to upstage you, Ned," said Hemings placatingly.

"Well, Lord Strange's Company all stick together, to be sure," said Alleyn with a grimace. "No doubt, they all think that they are much too good to be stuck carrying spears at the back of the stage."

"I have got a place to stick this spear," said Shakespeare wryly, "and 'tis *not* at the back of the stage."

"What was that?" said Alleyn, spinning round.

"'Twas nothing, Ned," said Smythe, giving Shakespeare an elbow in the ribs to stave off his reply.

"I distinctly heard somebody say something," Alleyn said, narrowing his eyes.

"I said—*ooof!*"

Smythe elbowed him again and took hold of him as he doubled over. "Will said he was feeling poorly, Ned," he said. "Look, see how he suffers? It must be something that he ate."

"Well, take him off the bloody stage, then!" Marlowe shouted from the gallery. "We have a play to perform tonight, people! And you, Kemp, you can go with them, until you can learn to stop twitching as if you had St. Vitus's bloody dance!"

"Ohhh, how I *despise* that man," said Kemp through gritted teeth as they went through the doorway at the back of the stage and came into the tiring room, where the players changed their costumes and waited for their entrances.

"Well, I shall grant you that he is not, perhaps, the most amenable of men," said Smythe, still supporting Shakespeare, who was just getting his wind back, "but he is a decent sort at heart, Will."

"*Decent?*" Kemp replied, with disbelief. "*Marlowe?* Are you *mad*? There is naught that is decent about him. The man is a wanton libertine of the first order!"

"Hola, pot! You are black, the kettle sayeth," Shakespeare said, finally getting back his breath.

"And you can bloody well *shut up!*" Kemp said, forgetting his usual cleverly acerbic banter in his frustration. "*Poets!*" he added with contempt, throwing on his cloak with a flourish. "You are *all* mad as March hares, the lot of you! I say a pox upon *all* poets!"

"Hmmpf! He wished a pox upon me, did you hear?" said Shakespeare, watching Kemp depart in a huff. "'Twasn't very nice of him, now, was it? Speaking of which, you might have broken my ribs with that elbow, you great, lumbering ox."

"And Alleyn might have broken your jawbone with his fist had I not stopped you just then," Smythe replied. "To say naught of what Marlowe might have done had he heard you mocking him."

"Ned frightens me about as much as the wind that makes up the greater part of him," said Shakespeare. "And as for Marlowe, well, you must admit, he truly begs for mockery. I mean, come on! Impaled golden virgins and infants swimming in their parents' blood? Lord save us, not even Sophocles would pen such an exaggerated, foolish line."

"You must admit that it conjures up quite the lurid vision," Smythe replied.

"It conjures up what I ate for breakfast," Shakespeare said with a grimace. "'Tis all a lot of knavish nonsense."

"Perhaps, but 'tis what the audiences love about his work," said Smythe. He pointed a finger at Shakespeare's chest. "And 'tis why *you* are trying to emulate him."

"I am *not* trying to emulate him, I am trying to *better* him," said Shakespeare irritably. "There is a difference, you know."

"Fine, I shall grant you that," said Smythe. "Nevertheless, the fact remains that audiences eat up Marlowe's 'knavish nonsense,' as you put it, and you know that as well as anyone. 'Tis why you are so determined to outdo him. His *Jew of Malta* and his *Doctor Faustus* and this new one about the queen of Carthage are all much more exciting than your own *Henry the Sixth*."

"Bah! You compare oranges with apples," Shakespeare said. "They are very different works."

"Mayhap so, but the audiences seem to enjoy Marlowe's oranges much more than your apples."

"Now look, we have staged *Henry the Sixth* but once," Shakespeare said defensively, "and 'twas despite my protests that the play was not yet ready."

"Then why submit it for production?"

"Because . . . well, because Marlowe keeps on writing new ones, and everyone keeps asking when they shall see *mine* and why *I* cannot write so quickly and why all *I* have managed to produce is books of sonnets!"

"Ah, so you allowed yourself to be rushed into submitting it before you were fully satisfied with the result," said Smythe.

"Aye, damn it," Shakespeare said. "I admit it freely, 'twas a stupid thing to do. But even *you* keep chiding me for not yet having finished anything!"

"Aye, 'tis true," admitted Smythe, "but 'twas nothing more than a means to have a bit of fun with you. If it truly troubles you, Will, than I shall refrain from doing it, I promise."

"Nay, it does not trouble me," said Shakespeare. "Well, perhaps a little, but in truth, it does help to spur my efforts. Yet I have learned something from all this, methinks."

"And what is that, pray tell?"

"I have discovered that waiting till I have written something to my final satisfaction is but a means to keep from ever finishing a thing," he said. "For in truth, there *is* no final satisfaction. At least, not for me. A much better way to work, 'twould seem to me, would be to treat a play as if 'twere a gemstone and I a patient and painstaking jeweler who makes my cuts, thus faceting the stone, and then submits the cut gem to the company so that we may all then proceed to polish it together, just as we did when I rewrote some of the Queen's Men's repertoire, do you recall?"

"Aye, but then you did it thus because you had no other choice," said Smythe. "You had to write and then rewrite as flaws were made manifest in the production, because there was no time to do it any other way."

"Quite so," said Shakespeare, "and as a result, 'twas needful to put on the finishing touches in rehearsal, and then revise again after one performance, and once again after the next, and so forth and so forth . . . just as you said to Greene back in the tavern, when you spoke about a play being a crucible in which the intent of the poet and the interpretation of the player comingle with the perception of the audience. 'Twas most excellent, most excellent, indeed! I recall being very taken with that line, even as that vile souse upbraided me, and thinking that I must remember it. 'Twas a memorable turn of phrase, indeed. And much more than that, Tuck, 'twas a rare insight into the alchemy of the crafting of a play!"

"Well, I was but repeating something that you said once," Smythe replied.

"What? *I* said that?" asked Shakespeare, raising his eyebrows with surprise.

"Or else something very like it," Smythe replied.

"The devil you say! When did I say that?"

"I do not remember when just now," said Smythe. "But I do seem to recall that you were rather deeply in your cups when you said it."

"Zounds! I shall have to ask you to start setting down these things I say so that I may remember them," said Shakespeare.

The crashing sound of thunder interrupted them, booming so loudly that it seemed to shake the rafters up above them. The first crash was almost immediately followed by the next, and then a third hot on its heels.

"Oh, dear," said Smythe. "That sounds like a rather nasty storm is brewing."

The next clap of thunder was deafening, and lightning seemed to split the sky as they stepped out of the tiring room. The wind had picked up suddenly, and moments later a torrential rain began pelting down, bringing an immediate end to the rehearsal.

"Well, so much for that," said Shakespeare, watching as the other players scrambled for their hats and cloaks. "We have been rained out nearly every night this week."

"This bodes ill for the companies' already meager purses," Smythe replied, as he buckled on his sword belt. He had of late been trying to cultivate the habit of wearing his rapier everywhere he went, although he still found it rather cumbersome and had an unfortunate tendency to keep catching it on things. His uncle had taught him how to fence, but until he came to London, he had never even owned a sword. He always carried the dagger that his uncle made for him, but wearing a sword had simply seemed like too much trouble, despite the fact that it was much the fashion and, given the steady increase in crime, also seemed very practical.

"Well, this does not appear as if 'twill soon blow over," Shakespeare said, gazing up glumly at the dark sky. "I fear that we shall have no play today."

"Much like the day that we set out in search of Thomas to deliver him his father's message," Smythe replied.

"That troubles you still, I see," said Shakespeare.

"Would that it did not," said Smythe, "but I keep thinking on it."

"'Twas not really your fault, you know, the way that things turned out," said Shakespeare. "You must not blame yourself."

"Do you suppose they have arrested Mayhew?"

Shakespeare snorted. "Not bloody likely, I should say, unless they caught him standing over the poor lad's corpse with a bare bodkin in his hand. Rich men do not often get themselves arrested, you know. 'Tis bad for the economy."

"Well, quite likely, you are right," said Smythe, "else we should have heard something by now."

"Now, if you are asking me if I think that Mayhew was responsible," said Shakespeare, "then I would have to say that on the surface, the odds seem much in favor of it . . . that is, from what we know. Remember, we do not know for a certainty that Thomas was killed because of his relationship with Portia. His murder could have been completely unrelated to that. For all we know, he had some enemy who wished him dead. More than one, perhaps. Or else it could have been a thief who had been trying to rob his room when he walked in, thus setting off a confrontation that ended in his death." He shrugged. "We simply do not know, Tuck. And chances are that we shall never know."

"So what are you saying, then? That because we do not know, we should not care?"

"Nay, I did not say we should not care," said Shakespeare, "for that would make us callous and hard-hearted, and I should not like to think that we were that. But people die in London every day, of many causes and for many reasons. We cannot seek justice for them all, however much we may wish that justice could be served. We did not really know young Thomas Locke. Our paths happened to cross but once, during which time you gave him some advice. Whether 'twas wise advice or not does not make any difference in the end, for 'twas his choice whether or not to take it. In any event, before he could act upon it, he was killed. And there's an end to it."

"He could have been your Jew, you know," said Smythe. "Or else, as it appears that he was raised a Christian, perhaps his mother could have served your purpose and acquainted you with their ways and their beliefs."

"Perhaps," said Shakespeare. "But 'twould be crass of me indeed to ask her now. And I rather doubt we would find welcome at her husband's house."

"Aye, to be sure. Well, 'twould seem the others have all repaired to Cholmley's," he said, referring to the small, one-story, thatch-roofed building attached to the theatre and operated by John Cholmley, Henslowe's partner, as a tavern and victualing house for the patrons of the Rose. "Shall we go and join them?"

Shakespeare sighed. "Cholmley overcharges scandalously, quite aside from which, I have about had my fill of Ned and Kit for one day. But we can go and join the others, if you wish."

"Or else we could make our way back home to the Toad and Badger and see Dick Burbage," Smythe said. "And then you could go upstairs and write, which would give you an excuse to avoid Cholmley's."

"An excellent idea, I must say!" Shakespeare responded, clapping him upon the shoulder. "I would much rather spend some time with Dick, sweet Molly, and that old bear Stackpole at the Toad than overpay at Cholmley's and listen to Ned and Kit attempt to outbark each another like a pair of hounds and lay the blame for every flaw in the production on Lord Strange's Men. Forsooth, I have had enough of that rot. To the Toad, then!"

"To the Toad it is," said Smythe. "What say you, shall we chance it with a wherry in this infernal downpour, or shall we go the long way, by the bridge?"

"In this wind, there should be quite a chop," said Shakespeare, somewhat dubiously. "And many of the boats will have pulled in, though a good wherryman would not be frightened by the weather. Just the same, methinks I would prefer to take the bridge. Either way, we shall get soaked."

"Well, let us walk, then," Smythe replied. "I have always enjoyed a good walk in the rain."

They wrapped their cloaks around themselves, pulled down their hats, and went out into the wind and rain, through the theatre gates. The rain was coming down in sheets as they started walking toward the river, but they were in good spirits. For the moment, at least, the uncertainties and troubles of the world were all forgotten. The Thames was frothed with whitecaps, and the bracing smell of the sea was strong in the air.

As they made their way toward London Bridge, Shakespeare

began to sing a ribald tune, and Smythe laughed, linked arms with him, and joined in. They sang lustily and loudly, looking forward to an evening in front of a warm fire with old friends.

Neither of them noticed that they were being followed.

Elizabeth was growing increasingly concerned about her friend. Already despondent over her father's cancellation of her marriage plans, Portia was plunged into absolute despair when she learned that Thomas had been murdered. When the sheriff's men had come to question them, Portia ran out of the room in tears and fled upstairs to the guest bedroom that she had occupied since leaving home. Now she would not even leave that room. She had taken to her bed and would not get up, not even to eat.

Not knowing what else to do, Elizabeth had sent a servant to Antonia with a message begging her to come at once. But as the day drew on and she did not arrive, Elizabeth grew more and more anxious. It was growing late when Antonia arrived in her carriage at last.

"I wanted to come as soon as I received your message," Antonia explained apologetically, as one of the servants helped her with her cloak, "but my husband was entertaining guests and my presence was required at home. Alas, I could not leave till they had all departed."

"I understand, of course," Elizabeth replied as they made their way together to the drawing room. "And I am much relieved that you have come at last. I am simply driven to distraction. Poor, poor Portia! I just do not know what to do. I cannot think how to help her!"

"You are already helping her, my dear," Antonia replied solicitously. "You have given her safe haven, and a caring heart to see her through this tragic time. And in the end, 'tis said that time itself must heal such wounds."

Elizabeth shook her head. "In this case, Antonia, I am not so certain. Doubtless time could heal grief suffered over an untimely loss, but this was the foul murder of the man she loved, and I do believe she holds her father to account for it, which can only serve to multiply her torment."

"Do you suppose he could have done it?" Antonia asked as the servant poured their wine.

Elizabeth sighed and shook her head once more. "I cannot say. 'Tis not so long ago I would have said that Henry Mayhew certainly did not strike me as a man who would be capable of murder, but I have since discovered that one simply cannot tell such things from appearances and that people one might never think capable of doing such terrible things are, indeed, capable of them and more."

"So then he may have done it," said Antonia. "Or else he may have paid to have it done. Is that what she believes?"

"I am afraid so," said Elizabeth. "What does one tell a girl who thinks her father killed the man she loved?"

"I do not know," Antonia replied. "What has her father said to this?"

"Thus far, he has said nothing," said Elizabeth.

Antonia frowned. "Does he even know that she is here?"

Elizabeth nodded. "He knows. I sent a servant to him with a letter, so that he would know that she was safe with me. It seemed the proper thing to do. Had I a daughter who ran off somewhere, and I did not know where she was, I would be frantic with concern."

Antonia nodded. "You did the right thing. And how did he respond?"

"See for yourself," Elizabeth replied, picking up a letter and passing it to her. "This came but a few hours ago."

With a look of interest, Antonia took the letter, unfolded it, and read:

My dear Elizabeth,

I have received your letter and was gratified to learn that Portia had decided to spend some time upon a visit with you. Doubtless, your pleasant company shall be of benefit to her and help assuage her distress over recent unfortunate events. The sheriff's men had paid me a visit, as they did you, it seems, and I informed them that there was little more that I could add to what they apparently already knew, but that I would remain at their service if they should require anything further of me in their inquiries. They thanked me respectfully and took their leave.

As to my daughter's future, the present uncertainty of which has likely been the cause of her distress, you may inform her that she is ever in my thoughts, and that I have already taken certain steps that will assure her welfare and grant her even greater prospects than she may have earlier expected. With warmest wishes of regard and good will toward your family, I remain, as ever, yours sincerely,

Henry Mayhew

"Well, upon my word," said Antonia, as she finished reading the missive, "he does not seem much concerned. What do you suppose he means when he writes that he has 'taken certain steps that will assure her welfare'?"

"I can only take that to mean that he has already found another suitor for his daughter," Elizabeth replied.

"So soon?"

"Aye, he did not waste any time," Elizabeth said. "I cannot imagine how I shall tell Portia."

"You mean to say she has not seen this letter?" Antonia asked, holding it up.

"I have been afraid to show it to her. There is no telling how she may respond."

"Well, you cannot keep it from her," said Antonia. "She shall find out eventually, from her father if not from you. And the sooner she knows, the better, I should think. 'Tis time that she learned to accept things as they are."

"That was rather an unfeeling sentiment," Elizabeth replied, a bit taken aback. "She is still grieving for the man she loved."

"Then let her don her mourning black, thus giving death its due, and go on about her life," Antonia said.

"Antonia! How can you be so harsh?"

"Oh, truly, Elizabeth, 'tis not my intent to sound hard-hearted," she replied, "but Portia simply must accept that Thomas is dead and there is naught that she can do to bring him back. And if she believes that he died by her father's hand or else by his will, then even so, what can she do about it? Is there proof she may present? And if, by some chance, she has such proof, *would* she present it, accusing her own father? And even if she could, what good would come of it? Who would convict a father for seeking to protect his daughter from disgrace? Who would even fault him for it?" She held up the letter once again. "He writes here in this very letter that the sheriff's men had come to see him. From the sound of it, they spoke to him respectfully and he answered them in kind; thus they were satisfied and took their leave. And there it shall end, Elizabeth. There it shall end. Regardless of what we may suspect, officially the murderer shall remain unknown. Thomas was a young journeyman of much promise but of little means, and a Jew, at that. Henry Mayhew is a prominent and wealthy merchant and a Christian. What more is there to say?"

"There is something more to say for Portia, surely," said Elizabeth.

"Very well, then let us say it," Antonia replied. "She is her father's daughter and must do her duty, as must we all. My father never sought my counsel or consent when he arranged for me to marry. Nor do most fathers do so. And for all of your poetic and romantic notions about love, Elizabeth, the day will come when your father, too, shall decide upon a husband for you, before you become too old for him to marry off and he is settled with a spinster. You and I have talked of this before. Marrying for love is fine for the more common sort of people, but we must be more serious and practical. And the sooner Portia comes to understand that and accept it, the better off she shall be. That is my advice to you, Elizabeth. Do with it what you will, but know this: Neither Portia's father nor yours shall remain patient forever."

"And why, pray tell, should it be a matter of *their* patience?" replied Elizabeth, her temper flaring up. "Why is it a daughter's place to do her duty by her father and not a father's place to do his duty by his daughter? 'Tis a parent who brings a child into the world, and I should think 'tis a parent's duty to ensure that child is nurtured and protected. Why must a daughter grow up to be little better than a slave, destined to marry a man she did not choose, and to spend the remainder of her life at his beck and call, while a man may do whatever he desires?"

"Oh, Elizabeth, there are ways for a woman to do what she desires also, if she does so with careful judgment and discretion," said Antonia. "Look around you at this handsome home. Is this truly what you call living like a slave? You have servants, for God's sake. You have never raised a hand to do anything much more demanding than embroidery! Methinks you see too much of yourself in Portia's plight, if we may truly call it plight. Indeed, how difficult has her life been thus far? Her father is one of London's richest merchants, and from what he writes in his letter, 'twould seem that he has made arrangements for a marriage for her that would improve her prospects even further. She shall marry a rich man of good standing and live a pleasant life of indolence, waited on by servants hand and foot, in return for which, in all likelihood, she shall be required to do nothing more than help entertain his friends and give birth upon occasion. This is a desperate plight? Good Lord! However shall we save her?"

Elizabeth stared at her friend, her mouth set in a tight grimace. "I perceive that I have made a mistake," she said after a moment. "I called upon you because I believed that you would care enough to help, but I see now that you do not care at all. Forgive me, Antonia. I did not mean to waste your time."

Antonia raised her eyebrows. "Well, I see I have offended you, though such was not my intent. Should I take that as a dismissal, then?"

"Take it any way you please," Elizabeth said curtly, turning away from her.

Antonia gazed at her for a moment, her head cocked thoughtfully, then she sniffed, stood, and made her way outside, back to her carriage, without saying another word.

Elizabeth heard the door shut behind her and bit her lower lip. She felt torn. She felt angry with herself for having become angry, and at the same time she felt justified in feeling so. She had known Antonia for a long time. Though she was a few years older, they had grown up together and she had always considered Antonia one of her closest friends. And even though she had not seen Antonia as often since her marriage, she certainly knew her much better than she did Portia. Yet it was to Portia that her heart went out, while Antonia had shown her a side of her character that seemed harsh and insensitive, even a little cruel. And that both surprised and disappointed her.

Yet at the same time, she had to admit that Antonia was not entirely in the wrong. Elizabeth had to acknowledge that she lived a life of privilege, as did Portia. Yet she was still dissatisfied with her lot in life. So did that make her ungrateful? Or was there, in fact, more to life than simply being well taken care of? Had every need truly been supplied?

If a woman were provided with a home, however comfortable that home might be, and if she were well fed and clothed and granted every material comfort that she might desire, then did that mean that she should not wish for anything more—or, if she did desire something further, pursue such desires quietly . . . "with careful judgment and discretion"?

Elizabeth looked inside herself . . . looked hard . . . and found that she could not accept that. It just did not seem right. "Gild a cage howsoever you may choose," she murmured to herself, "and yet still 'twill be a cage. Forge chains from gold or silver, and yet still they will be chains." At the same time, she reminded herself that her own chains, such as they were, were certainly of silver, if not gold, and she wore them fairly lightly. There were many women whose lives were far more difficult than hers. She truly had very little about which to complain.

And yet . . . there was that cage. Let a woman try to step outside, she thought, and the world would gently usher her back in, or else revile her for a shrew and chastise her accordingly. If only I were born a man, she thought . . . and then realized that even if, by some strange and supernatural twist of fate, she could somehow have been given such a choice, it was not what she would have chosen. She would no more wish to be a man than she would wish to be a horse. No, what she wanted was the freedom that went with being a man. She wondered if the day would ever come when women could enjoy such freedom. Most likely, it would not, she thought. Men would never allow it. And women like Antonia would continue having to resort to "careful judgment and discretion." Perhaps, as Antonia had advised, that was what she should do, as well.

Her thoughts were interrupted when one of the servants entered and announced, "Mistress, there is a Master Symington Smythe to see Miss Portia."

She turned. "To see Miss Portia?"

"Aye, mistress, that was what he said."

She frowned. Why would Tuck come to see Portia and not ask to see her first? "Show him in, Albert," she replied.

"Aye, mistress."

A moment later, Albert announced the visitor once more. "Master Symington Smythe," he said.

But instead of Tuck, to her surprise, a man that she had never seen before came in.

"How do you do, madame?" he said, with a slight bow. "Symington Smythe II, Esquire, at your service. Have I the honor and the pleasure of addressing Mistress Portia Mayhew?"

8

✳

THE RAIN HAD ABATED SLIGHTLY by the time Smythe and Shakespeare reached the London Bridge, but the sky was dark and the wind had picked up significantly, producing a sheeting effect that came and went with the irregular gusts. There were still a few wherries out on the Thames, but there was a strong chop out on the water, and most of the boats had pulled in to await a lessening of the storm.

The water moving through the narrow arches between the twenty stone piers supporting the bridge was flowing very rapidly and churning with foam. Originally constructed from a ring of wooden beams driven into the riverbed, forming an enclosure that was then filled with rock and crossbeams, the piers had been rebuilt with stone, along with the rest of the bridge, and then widened a number of times over the years until the openings between them were made narrow enough to cause rapids underneath the archways of the bridge. Even wherrymen were wary of trying to "shoot the arches" at ebb tide, and among those who had tried, not a few had drowned. At flood tide, the arches were impassable.

As Smythe and Shakespeare stepped out onto the bridge, they could hear the loud creaking of the waterwheels powering the cornmills beneath some of the archways. Two arches out from the south bank of the river stood the Great Stone Gate of London

Bridge, originally constructed to help defend the city. Like a medieval castle, it was a gatehouse with large and heavy wooden doors set in a Gothic-arched opening with a portcullis. About a hundred years earlier, this stone gatehouse had collapsed. It had been rebuilt, but ever since, the citizens of London gathering in alehouses sang a traditional song about how London Bridge was "falling down."

It was at the Great Stone Gate that heads of traitors were displayed on iron spikes, where they were left to rot and moulder and be picked at by the rooks until nothing but bone was left and the skull was eventually pitched into the river. Shakespeare paused at one such head as they came up to the gate, gazing at it quizzically.

"I do not seem to remember who this fellow is, do you?" he asked Smythe, as he contemplated the wet and rotting head, all but unrecognizable now after the ravages of the crows, the elements, and decomposition.

"It looks a bit like Kemp, methinks," said Smythe.

"'Strewth, and so it does! Ah, alas, poor Kemp! I knew him, Tuck. A fellow of infinite jest, of most excellent fancy! Where be your gibes now, Kemp? Your gambols? Your songs? Your flashes of merriment that were wont to set the groundlings in a roar, eh? What, nothing to say? Or have you forgot your lines again? Speak up!"

Smythe laughed. "I do not think he can hear you, Will."

"What, drunk and senseless once again? Dead to the world? *Pah!* You are of no use to me, Kemp! Nay, none at all! Stay here and rot, then. Let the crows pick out your eyes." He peered closer at the head. "Oh. I see that they already have. Well, never mind, then."

Smythe laughed once more. "Come on, then, Will, before we get soaked through to the skin. 'Tis a warm fire and a heady brew for me."

"You hear that, Kemp? We are going now to drink with men

who know how to hold their grog. No room for the likes of you, you old reprobate. Go back to the Lord Admiral's Men, for we have had our fill of you."

In good spirits, they passed through the gate together, entering upon the main thoroughfare of the bridge, which was lined with buildings on both sides. These were shops and houses constructed on the bridge itself of timber frames with wattle-and-daub walls. The wooden counters that folded down and out from the shops front windows were now folded up and shut against the weather, of course, which made the bridge appear like a residential block that spanned the Thames, rather than the marketplace it more closely resembled on a sunny day.

There were several galleries that spanned the bridge from one side to the other, connecting the third stories of some of the buildings and allowing residents to cross over. And as in many of the streets throughout the city, the upper floors of many of the houses hung out over the thoroughfare. With the exception of the drawbridge, it looked just like many another street running through the city, save that it was straighter than most.

On this day, with the weather as beastly as it was, there was not as much traffic on the bridge as usual, and there were only a few pedestrians moving along quickly through the rain. Each year, it seemed, the traffic in the city continued to grow worse and worse. Sometimes, the streets became so congested that traffic came to an absolute standstill and fights broke out. On a day like this, however, even Londoners long accustomed to the rain and cold had hurried to find shelter somewhere inside.

"Ah, 'tis a marvelous day, Will, a marvelous day!" said Smythe, spreading out his arms as if to embrace the weather.

"'Tis a very wet day, if you ask me," Shakespeare replied. "'Tis a marvelous day if you are a turtle."

"Well, then I must be part turtle, for I love walking in the rain," said Smythe. "It reminds me of walks I took through the forest in my childhood. On such days as this, Will, do you not find yourself missing your home in Stratford?"

"I seldom find myself missing my home in Stratford," Shakespeare replied. "My wife is at my home in Stratford. And I suspect she seldom finds herself missing me, either."

"Well, marriage is not for everyone, perhaps," said Smythe with a shrug.

"*Happiness* is not for everyone," said Shakespeare. "Marriage, on the other hand, is a most democratic institution."

"One that not all people live to experience," said Smythe.

"I see that you are thinking of Thomas Locke again."

"Aye. Regardless of my disposition, he keeps returning to haunt my thoughts, like some poor, benighted ghost."

Shakespeare shook his head. "'Twill do you no good to dwell upon it, you know," he said.

"Perhaps. But are you not in the least bit curious what will come of it all?" asked Smythe.

"I have found, in general, that such curiosity can be decidedly unhealthy," Shakespeare said. "I have found so in particular since meeting you. In truth, I would have been perfectly satisfied to have remained completely in ignorance of the entire affair."

"And yet 'twas your curiosity, in a manner of speaking, that led to it," said Smythe.

"*My* curiosity? However so?"

"You wanted to learn something of the Jews," said Smythe. "'Twas why we went to visit Ben Dickens in the first place, if you will recall."

"I was merely trying to learn something about them as a people, the better to enable me to *write* about a Jew, so that I would not do quite as laughable a job as Marlowe did."

"The audiences at *The Jew of Malta* were not laughing."

"Well, they should have been," Shakespeare replied. "That they were not merely goes to prove that they do not know any better."

"Be that as it may," said Smythe, "'twas still *your* curiosity that took us to Ben Dickens's shop, where we met Thomas, which was where this whole thing began."

"Aye, when *you* decided to stick your fine, peasant Saxon nose where it most certainly did not belong," countered Shakespeare.

"What, so then you are saying that 'twas all *my* fault?"

"'Twas merely your fault that we became involved," said Shakespeare with a sigh. "'Twas not your fault that Thomas Locke was killed. That, in all likelihood, had nothing at all to do with us and would have happened anyway. However, had you never spoken with him, or sought to counsel him, we could have gone on about our business in blissful ignorance of the poor lad's fate."

"Save that you would probably have spoken to him as soon as you had heard him say he was a Jew," said Smythe.

"Under the circumstances, I doubt very much I would have spoken to him," Shakespeare protested. "The poor lad was much distressed. 'Twould scarcely have been seemly for me to have subjected him to questions at such a time, much as I might have wished to."

"Nonsense. I know you, Will. You would have been unable to resist."

"Oh, I like that!" said Shakespeare, stopping in the middle of the drawbridge and placing his hands upon his hips. "Was I the one, then, who went running off at my mouth about love and elopement and what all?"

Several pedestrians brushed past and went around them quickly, hurrying with their heads down and the hoods of their cloaks up against the rain.

"Will, come on! 'Tis raining cats and dogs out here!"

"But I thought you loved walking in the rain?" said Shakespeare, still standing motionless with his hands upon his hips. "I thought the rain reminded you of your native bogs or some such thing."

"*Forest,*" Smythe said. "'Twas a *forest,* not a bloody bog! And the trees provided a deal more shelter from the rain than do these buildings on this windswept bridge."

"Well, then I am simply going to stand here just like these bloody buildings until you admit that 'twas *you* who could not resist prattling away at Thomas and that therefore 'twas not *my* curiosity but *your* utter inability to keep your busy little mind on your own business that got us involved in all this in the first place!"

"Will. . . ."

"Forget it! Save your breath! I am deaf to your protestations! I am *not* moving until you admit that you are in the wrong and being absolutely bullheaded about it!"

"Will. . . ."

"And do not tell me again how hard it is raining! It may be raining hippogriffs and unicorns for all I care, but I am not going anywhere until you confess that you are—*aiiyeeee!*"

He cried out as Smythe suddenly reached out with his left hand, seized him by his cloak, and yanked him forward roughly, nearly pulling him off his feet as he swung him around behind him. In almost the same motion, Smythe drew his rapier.

Half a dozen men stood only a few feet from where Shakespeare had been standing a moment earlier. All wore dark, hooded cloaks, wet from the rain, and all now produced serious-looking clubs from within the folds of those cloaks.

"Best move along, you men!" Smythe said to them sharply. "You shall find no easy pickings here."

"Master Locke wishes to see you," a gruff voice said from behind them.

Smythe spun around. The men who had passed them moments earlier were now behind them. There were four of them, two of whom were armed with clubs, just like the others. The other two, however, now produced crossbows from beneath their long cloaks. That changed things considerably. Half a dozen men armed with clubs did not make for good odds when there were only two of them, and Will was not armed, not that he would have been much help even if he were. But ten men, two of whom were armed with crossbows, made any resistance absolutely pointless—something the man who had spoken to them underscored with his next comment.

"Mind now, Master Locke did not say in what condition 'e wished to see you," he said, his voice calm and otherwise perfectly conversational. "'E could see you whole . . . or else 'e could see you broke up a bit. It makes not a brass farthing's worth o' difference to us, one way or the other. The choice is yours my friends. And you 'ave the space o' three breaths in which to make it."

"Right," said Smythe, taking a deep breath. "Well . . . when you put it that way. . . ." He slowly sheathed the blade and started to unbuckle his sword belt so that he could hand it over to them.

"Now, that's more like it," said the man who spoke. "No need for 'eroics, eh? We understand each other. I would much prefer to keep this friendly-like."

"By all means, let us keep it friendly-like," said Smythe with a tight grimace, as he handed over his sword belt.

"Oh, hellspite!" Shakespeare said, in a tone of fearful exasperation. "*Why* in God's name do you keep doing this to us?"

"Be quiet, Will."

"It never ends! It simply *never* ends! You positively rain death and devastation upon us!"

"We have not died yet, Will," Smythe replied. "And if we keep our heads about us, we shall not die today. If Master Locke wanted us dead, then we would have been dead already."

"Now, that's what I like," said the leader, his face nearly invisible inside the hood of his cloak. "A man with a practical turn of mind."

He seemed to speak for all the others, who simply stood there motionless, yet watchful and ready. Smythe was all too uncomfortably aware of the two crossbows aimed straight at their chests. He was a good archer, having grown up hunting in the woods around his village, but crossbows made him nervous. He had seen what they could do. And unlike a good, stout English longbow, which required a deliberate pull and release, it did not take much more than a touch to release a bolt from a crossbow. Merely a moment's inattentiveness on the part of either of those two archers and death would come swiftly and decisively.

The clip-clopping of horses' hooves made Smythe look around, though he was careful to avoid any sudden movements. A coach was approaching from the south side of the bridge, the direction from which they had come. It stopped when it drew even with them.

"If you gentlemen would be so good as to turn around," the man said.

They did so, and a couple of the other men stepped forward and tied blindfolds over their eyes.

"Your 'ands behind your backs, please. . . ."

"Tuck, I do not like this," Shakespeare said, trying hard to keep his voice even.

"Nor do I, Will. Steady on. There is naught else we can do but comply with their wishes."

"This is merely to ensure that you do not try anything foolish once we get inside the coach." The man continued speaking to them, though they could no longer see him. "There shall be one of us sitting beside each of you, with a dagger at the ready. So let us all sit quietly and merely enjoy the ride, eh?"

They were assisted into the coach, and then the door was closed behind them. A moment later, they felt the coach lurch forward. They seemed to be continuing across the bridge and toward the city.

"I do not suppose that Master Locke happened to mention why, specifically, he wished to see us?" Smythe heard Shakespeare say.

"I am quite sure that 'e shall tell you when 'e sees you," came the reply. "Now be quiet, like a good lad, eh?"

"Of course," said Shakespeare, and fell silent.

The silence made their ride seem much more tense and ominous. Smythe listened intently, trying to determine where they were by the sounds coming from outside the coach. It was difficult to tell exactly when they reached the other side and entered the city. He could not see anything. The blindfold had been tied well. Alert to every sound, he listened as hard as he could, but could not determine where they where. He thought he could feel it when the coach turned, but even that seemed uncertain. The blindfold made him realize just how much he depended upon his sight. It must be a terrible thing to be blind, he thought. It felt even worse to be unable to see than to have his hands tied behind his back. He had never felt so helpless.

Having his hands tied behind his back also added an element of physical discomfort to the trip, for if he leaned back against the cushioned seat of the coach, then his arms started to go numb and his shoulders ached. On the other hand, if he moved forward toward the edge of the seat, it took the pressure off his arms and shoulders, but made his balance more precarious as the wooden wheels of the coach rattled over the cobblestoned streets, transmitting every bump up through the seats and putting him in danger of pitching forward, which was the last thing he wanted to do, considering that the man sitting next to him had a dagger at his side and might react badly to any sudden movement. All in all, it made trying to keep track of where they were an exercise in futility. Before long, he lost not only all sense of direction but all sense of the passage of time, as well. And that was, doubtless, the general idea, for clearly their abductors did not want them to know where they were going.

Shakespeare had not made a sound since the man had told him to be quiet, but Smythe could easily imagine how he felt. Will was not a courageous individual by nature. He had a quick wit and a keen mind, but physically he was not very strong. Although he was determined, he was also easily intimidated by men who were more physical and larger in stature. Right now, thought Smythe, he must be very frightened, a feeling that was probably exacerbated by his inability to speak. Whenever he was nervous or ill at ease, Shakespeare had a tendency to be particularly chatty. Not being able to speak at such a time probably had him near to bursting with frustration and anxiety. Smythe wished that he could say something to make him feel better, but that would only goad him on to speak. He did not wish to antagonize these men. He had no doubt that they would not be squeamish when it came to violence.

After what seemed like hours, though it could not possibly have been that long, the coach came to a stop. A moment later, the door was opened and the man beside him spoke.

"Right, then. I am going to take your arm and 'elp you down. Do not make any sudden movements. I would not wish to stab you by mistake."

" 'Tis very considerate of you," said Smythe. "Thank you."

"Why, you are very welcome, to be sure. Come on, then. 'Ere we go. . . ."

Feeling himself guided by the grip upon his arm, Smythe felt his way with his foot and then stepped down carefully from the coach. The first thing that he noticed was that the ground beneath his feet was not paved. However, this did not mean that they were out of the city. It merely meant that they were not on a main thoroughfare.

"Tuck?" Will sounded anxious

"I am here, Will. Steady on. Just do as these men say."

"Oh, we are not so worried about 'im," said their unseen companion. " 'E wouldn't be much trouble. You, on the other 'and, look like you might prove an 'andful given 'alf a chance, so we'll be watchin' you right close-like. In other words, mate, be very careful what you do, eh? We understand one another, right?"

"Quite," said Smythe.

"There's a good lad."

Smythe felt himself being patted down.

"'Allo, 'allo . . . what 'ave we 'ere? A bodkin?"

He felt his cloak pulled aside, and then a tug as his uncle's knife came free of its sheath upon his belt.

"You shall not find that of very great value, I assure you," Smythe said. "However, it has some meaning to me, for my uncle made it for me when I was but a lad."

"Your uncle does right good work," the man replied approvingly, from just behind him.

"Make certain that I get it back and I shall make you another just as good," said Smythe.

"Will you, now? Well, that's a right good offer. I shall tell you what I'll do. You promise not to give us any trouble and I shall make certain that you get back your bodkin. And what is more, I shall not only take you up on your kind offer to make me another, but I shall pay you a fair price for it. Agreed?"

"Agreed," said Smythe. "'Tis very generous of you."

"Thank you."

"You are most welcome."

"I cannot believe that I am listening to this," said Shakespeare.

"Be silent, Will."

"Do as your friend 'ere says, Will. 'Twill be best for all concerned, eh? Now move along."

Smythe felt a strong hand upon his arm as he was guided forward. They walked a few paces until the man beside him warned him of a step. He stepped up, going up a couple of stairs and apparently over a threshold. He felt a wood floor covered by rushes beneath his feet. There was a smell of tobacco smoke and ale in the air that told him they were almost certainly inside a tavern or an alehouse. He heard conversation going on around him and could make out some snatches of what was being said, though none of it was particularly helpful. There was some laughter, apparently at their expense, judging by the catcalls that ensued, but he felt himself guided on farther. A door was opened and he was ushered through.

"Goin' up some stairs now," he was told. "Move slowly and 'ave a care."

Smythe felt his shoulder brush a wall and used it to help guide his steps. He could hear footsteps coming up behind him, but had no way of knowing if Shakespeare's were among them. No one seemed to be in front.

He ended up taking one step up too many, having no way of telling where the stairs ended, so that he stumbled as he came up onto the second floor. He heard several people laugh. He could hear the sound of many voices all around him, which seemed to indicate that he was in a large and open room. Once again, he smelled ale and the strong odor of tobacco in the air.

He could not determine how long he had been blindfolded, but noticed how much more he was starting to rely upon his other senses, particularly his hearing and his sense of smell. Things that were not ordinarily so noticeable seemed to take on more significance now that he could not see. Curiously, even in his present highly uncertain circumstances, he found himself thinking that it seemed more and more people were taking up the practice of smoking.

He was starting to encounter it nearly everywhere he went. He recalled being told that the plant came from the colonies in America and that its leaves, when dried and cured, produced smoke that was said to have healthful properties. It was usually smoked in long clay pipes, but on occasion the pipes were carved from cherry wood. The smell was not altogether unpleasant, especially when compared to many of the usual noxious smells of London, but the one time he had tried a pipe, Smythe had found himself gagging and coughing on the smoke. It had made his eyes water, and the taste of it had seemed far worse than the smell. He could not understand why people secmed to like it. For that matter, he could not understand what could be so healthful about inhaling the acrid smoke from burning leaves, or why anyone should wish to do so. Yet those who smoked seemed to encourage others to do so. It was a habit, they often said, that one needed to "cultivate." Smythe could not understand that, either. If it did not feel good the first time, he saw no reason to try it a second. But wherever it was that they had brought him, the smell of tobacco nearly overwhelmed the smell of beer and ale.

"I am going to cut your bonds and remove your blindfold now," said the now familiar voice of his abductor at his ear. "You shall find a stool beside you. Sit, and remain seated until you are told otherwise. Right?"

Smythe merely nodded and swallowed nervously. He could hear an undertone of conversation all around him. He felt his bonds being cut, and a moment later his blindfold was removed.

He blinked several times. Even in the dim light, it seemed too bright at first, but his eyes quickly grew accustomed to it. As he rubbed his wrists, which felt a bit sore from the bonds, he glanced around.

Will was seated next to him, on a wooden stool, about four feet away. He was looking frightened. Their stools had been placed out in the center of the room, and it was a large room, with a wood floor strewn with rushes. All around the perimeter of the room were wooden trestle tables where men sat upon either benches or wooden stools similar to theirs. Smythe saw the one that had been placed beside him and sat down upon it.

The men . . . no, Smythe now noticed that there were women among them . . . were smoking and drinking and talking boisterously, many of them laughing, some pointing toward them and making comments to those around them. Directly in front of them, Smythe saw a table that had been placed upon a small wooden stage, a sort of dais. There were several wooden barrels placed behind this table, as seats. There was no one at this table at present, but as he watched, several men and one woman came out and took their seats upon these kegs. He recognized two of them at once as Charles "Shy" Locke and the notorious Moll Cutpurse.

"Tuck!" said Will. "Do you see?"

He took a deep breath and exhaled heavily. "Aye, Will," he replied. "I do. Lord save us."

One of the men up at the table on the dais picked up a large wooden mallet and brought it down several times upon the table, bringing the conversation all around them to a halt.

"This meeting will come to order!" he announced loudly.

Smythe did not need to be told what meeting it was. The presence of Shy Locke and the infamous Moll Cutpurse meant that it could only be a meeting of the Thieves Guild of London, the largest and most notorious organization of the underworld. And from where they were sitting, it looked as though there was going to be some sort of trial.

9

※

ELIZABETH'S MIND WAS IN A turmoil as her coach drove down the street. She had desperately needed to get away for a while. She needed some air. She needed some time away from Portia, whose despairing grief had made the entire house seem to feel oppressive. She needed time to think. And most of all, she felt she needed some advice.

So that had been Tuck's father, she thought with wonder, as her coach's wheels rattled over the cobblestones. Once she had gotten over her initial shock at seeing him, there had been no question in her mind that he could have been anyone else. The physical resemblance had been telling. Like his son who shared his name, Symington Smythe II was tall and fair haired, and there was a remarkable similarity of features, save that he was slim and not as brawny or as strapping as his son. However, there all resemblance between father and son ended. Much as she had strong affection for the son, she had thoroughly detested the father, and not just because the few things that she had heard about him from Tuck would have disposed her to dislike him anyway.

His manner had been extremely arrogant and condescending. One might have thought that he was a high-ranking nobleman from the airs that he put on. He was dressed in the height of fashion, wearing a soft gray velvet cloak with a matching bonnet and a dark crimson doublet of brocade with the sleeves pinked to reveal the white shirt underneath. Black breeches and black boots had completed his ensemble, along with a handsome sword, which he wore in a cocky sort of way, resting his hand upon the pommel and posing rakishly, like some swaggering bravo half his age.

He had come, astonishingly, to visit Portia, so that he could "gaze upon her" and "embark upon a contemplation to consider whether or not she would be suitable." His remarks had left Elizabeth speechless. She simply could not think how to respond to them. However, an immediate response had not been necessary, as it turned out, for the elder Smythe had continued blithely on, wandering about the parlor as if he owned the place, picking up various objects and examining them, scrutinizing each and every one as if he were a pawnbroker attempting to determine their worth.

Apparently, he had not the faintest inkling that she knew his son, or that Tuck had told her certain things about him, such as the fact that he had bankrupted himself and had been living on his brother's charity, for he had prattled on in a vague yet grandiose manner about his "business" in London and his "country estates," making it sound as if there were more than one, and the necessity of "making a good marriage" because he was a widower and required a woman to run his household properly and so forth. Elizabeth had been quite taken aback by the whole thing.

Had she not known what she knew, doubtless she would have taken him at face value, as apparently Portia's father had, but as it happened, she knew better. And yet, despite that, Tuck's father had seemed so convincing in his manner and his speech that for a moment, although only a moment, she had found herself wondering if it were possible that Tuck might have misled her and not told her the truth about his father. However, a moment's consideration had told her that simply could not be. Tuck would never lie to her. It was not in his character. He had never been anything but honest and straightforward with her and was one of the few men she knew—indeed, the *only* man she knew—who had always been so. And when she had started to look closer, she had begun to notice certain things about the senior Smythe that gave the lie to the tale he was spinning.

They were the sorts of things that many people might have missed, but she had learned from Tuck and Will how to observe and note details that most people might observe but never truly noted. For example, his clothes were very fashionable but of a markedly inferior cut, which suggested to her that he had purchased them cheaply from some cut-rate tailor. And when he had moved a certain way and his cloak swung open slightly, she had noted that his doublet was red brocade only on the front and that the back piece, which was covered by the cloak, was sewn from cheaper cloth. His highly polished boots had rundown heels, and his sword, while it had a hilt that was certainly ornate, had a scabbard that showed signs of wear and age.

When he had finished with his self-aggrandizing speech, she had informed him, in a regretful tone, that it would be quite impossible for him to speak with Portia at present, for she was still grieving over a recent loss, the death of a "close friend," and was consequently feeling much too ill and indisposed to entertain a visitor. She had promised, however, that she would convey his regards to her and carry any message that he wished to leave. The elder Smythe had thanked her, though he had seemed very much put out, and had departed, leaving a flowery message of sympathy and concern and promising to visit again in a few days, when, he hoped, Portia would be feeling better. The entire episode had left Elizabeth feeling stunned, angered, and dismayed.

She had refrained from mentioning anything to the father about her friendship with his son. There was no telling what sort of response that might have brought about. She had been tempted to tell him she knew Tuck, because she had wanted to see if he would be disconcerted and if she could then trap him in his lies, but something had told her that it would be wiser to resist temptation. Now, without his knowing that she knew what she knew, she could communicate the truth to Portia's father at the earliest opportunity. It was the very least that she could do for Portia, who might otherwise find herself married to this impertinent bounder. Poor Tuck, she thought. Small wonder that he had left home and come to London to make his own way in the world. There, fortunately, was one apple that had fallen very far afield from the tree.

She wondered if she should say anything to Tuck about this new and startling development. Clearly, he knew nothing of it, else he would have warned her that his father might suddenly appear. What would he say to this astonishing coincidence? Or would it only bring him embarrassment and shame? Perhaps it would be better to say nothing. She could not decide.

After a while, her coach pulled up in front of a small shop with a green apothecary sign depicting a mortar and a pestle that hung out over the street. She bid her coachman wait and went inside, through the heavy, creaking wooden door. At once, the familiar, earthy, fragrant aroma of dried herbs seemed to wash over her, changing from one moment to the next, depending upon where she stood inside the shop. There was little light inside, and the little that there was came from the small window in the front. Above her, many bunches of drying herbs hung from the beams of the ceiling, filling the air of the small shop with their heady, pungent fragrance.

There were the kitchen herbs, such as sage and savory, bay and basil, chive, rosemary, thyme, and bulb garlic; and medicinal herbs, such as leopard's bane, bilberry, cankerwort, feverfew, and elderberry; and many others that she could not identify, some that were not even native to Europe, but came either from the American colonies or from the Orient, though most of those were stored in earthenware or opaque glass jars on the many wooden shelves that lined the walls. There was a long wooden counter in front of one row of shelves, laden with mixing bowls, funnels, mortars and pestles, scoops, knives and cutting boards, and scales with weights and measures, all tools of the apothecary's trade.

As she came in, a small silver bell above the door rang. A moment later, a painted cloth behind the counter—the poor man's tapestry—was pushed aside and a very tall and gaunt, nearly skeletal man emerged, dressed in a long black robe and a woven black skullcap from beneath which wispy, snow-white hair hung down to the middle of his chest. He had a high forehead and deeply set dark, mournful-looking eyes. The first time Elizabeth had seen him, she had been frightened by his appearance, for he looked the very image of a nefarious necromancer, but soon her fear had been dispelled, for he was kind and gentle and possessed the most prosaic and unsorcerous of names.

"Good morning, Freddy," she said.

"Why, good morning, Mistress Elizabeth," he replied in his deep, sepulchral voice. "'Tis a pleasure to see you once again."

His tone seemed warm and friendly, but for all that, Elizabeth had never seen him smile. She wondered if he could. His expression was perpetually grim and somber.

"Thank you, Freddy, you are most kind. I wonder if I might speak with Granny Meg?"

"Of course," Freddy replied. "She told me just this morning that we could be expecting you."

Elizabeth had heard him say the same sort of thing before and at first had thought that it was just something that he said to make his wife seem more mystical and prescient, but she had since learned that Granny Meg somehow seemed to know things for which there seemed to be no explanation. Unless, of course, that explanation were a supernatural one, which Elizabeth was now more than ready to believe.

Freddy was ostensibly the apothecary of the shop, but although his knowledge of herbs and remedies was undeniable, it was in fact his wife who was the true apothecary. And, rumor had it, she was in truth much more than that. Granny Meg was widely reputed to be a cunning woman, in other words, a witch. People said she was adept at the art of divination with the cards and tea leaves, and dealt in arcane brews and potions, even poisons, some said, although there was never any proof. It was even whispered that the queen's astrologer, Dr. John Dee, consulted with Granny Meg upon occasion.

Elizabeth followed Freddy through the doorway covered by the painted cloth, which depicted stars and moons and suns upon a field of sable sky, and then up the narrow stairway leading to the second floor. The stairs led to the private living quarters above the shop, a small, narrow, one-room apartment longer than it was wide, with whitewashed walls and a clean, planked wooden floor devoid of rushes. It was always kept swept clean, without a speck of dirt or dust. There was only one window, looking out over the street toward the back of the room, and this window was partially obscured from view by a freestanding wooden shelf that held numerous books and also functioned as a room divider and a screen, separating the sleeping area from the rest of the room and cutting off much of the available light.

The furnishings were sparse and simple; there were only a couple of sturdy wooden chairs, several three-legged stools, a trestle table, and a number of large wooden chests covered with carpets. The most unusual feature of the room was the large fireplace, in which hung several black cauldrons of various sizes, suspended from iron hooks. It was rare to see a fireplace on the upper floor of a dwelling, unless it was noble's house, but Granny Meg's residence was unusual in a number of respects.

Although everything was very clean, the overall impression was one of an astonishing amount of clutter. As in the shop downstairs, the walls were lined with shelving holding what seemed like hundreds of glass and earthenware jars, as well as ancient-looking books and scrolls, which seemed to spill out of the shelves and into stacked piles on the floor. Everywhere one looked, there was some-thing to arrest the gaze. On the shelves were tiny figures carved from stone in the shapes of pregnant women or various fantastic birds or animals. Clay pots of every size—some no larger than a baby's fist, others as big as beer kegs—contained all sorts of myste-rious powders and blends. There were pretty beaded necklaces and amulets of gold, silver, and pewter, as well as tiny leather pouches suspended from thongs and meant to be worn around the neck as charms. Displayed prominently upon one shelf were two daggers, one with a curved, single-edged blade and one a straight, double-edged stiletto, as well as a little brass bell, a censer, a plain-looking silver chalice, a silver bowl, a silken cord, two thick candles, and a short length of willow branch.

The fire was lit, for it was a cool and breezy morning, but most of the illumination in the room came from a shaft of sunlight that shone in through the partially obscured window. Yet even though there were no shadows from the flames dancing on the walls, the space still seemed pregnant with an eldritch atmosphere of tension and anticipation. It always felt as if lightning were somehow about to strike within the room.

Elizabeth walked over toward the shelves, staring at the same objects that had captured her interest more than any others each time she had come here: the daggers, the candles, the chalice, and the other items all carefully arranged upon one shelf, along with the willow branch . . . the wand, she thought, as she started to reach toward it.

"Good morning, Elizabeth," Granny Meg said from be-hind her.

She jumped, gasped, and quickly turned around. "Granny Meg! You startled me!" And to herself she wondered, however does she *do* that? One moment she wasn't there, and the very next she was. It was unnerving.

"Forgive me, my dear," said Granny Meg. She smiled. "How very nice to see you. May I offer you some tea?"

"Please," said Elizabeth. As Granny Meg poured her a cup from the teapot, Elizabeth marveled once again at how ageless she appeared. She had to be quite old, for her waist-length hair was pure white, yet it was not limp, as old people's hair often was, but thick and lustrous. Her skin was so pale that it was nearly translucent, yet although it was faintly lined in places it was unwrinkled, with no liver spots or blemishes, and seemed to glow with youthful health. Her features were sharp and elfin, bringing to mind a dryad or a fairy. Her chin came nearly to a point, and her cheekbones were high and pronounced. Her nose, also, had a delicate, birdlike sharpness. She was slim and willowy; even at her age, she possessed a figure most women would have envied, but her eyes were her most striking feature. They were a very pale shade of bluish gray, with a startling, penetrating luminescence, like fire opals. Or the eyes of a changeling, Elizabeth thought.

Freddy had melted away without a sound. They both move like ghosts, Elizabeth thought. What if they were? It was an unsettling idea. She had never seen a ghost, but it was said that spirits could sometimes walk among the living. If they could do that, why could they not work in an apothecary shop? And what if the shop were not really a shop, but instead a gateway to the spirit world?

"What troubles you, Elizabeth?" Granny Meg asked. "Sit down. You look as if you have just seen a ghost."

"Oh, 'tis nothing quite so frightening, Granny Meg," she replied, a bit taken aback. It was as if Granny Meg had known what she was thinking. "I am merely concerned about a friend."

Granny Meg fixed her with a level and unsettlingly direct gaze. "The last time you came to me with such concerns, Elizabeth, I fear that things did not turn out very well."

Elizabeth looked down at the table. "I know," she replied

softly. "But I meant well, Granny Meg, I truly did. I never meant for Catherine to come to any harm!"

"I know that you meant well, Elizabeth," Granny Meg replied. "But then, you would not be the first who, with the best meaning, had incurred the worst."

"But this time is different, Granny Meg."

"Is it?" Granny Meg replied, watching her attentively. "This time you are *not* meddling in someone else's fate?"

Elizabeth looked sheepish. "Well . . . perhaps it may have started out that way," she said. "I mean, in a manner of speaking, I suppose I *did* meddle . . . but 'twas truly her welfare that I was concerned about. And I still am."

"When people seek to interfere with the destiny of others, they usually do so out of a professed concern for them," Granny Meg replied with a smile. "So, what is it that concerns you about your friend, Elizabeth?"

"Granny Meg, do you think 'tis possible that one could go mad with grief?"

"Aye, 'tis possible," Granny Meg replied, nodding. "If the grief is felt over a loved one, it may be powerful, indeed. There are some who may grieve for weeks or months or even years, and there are those who may grieve for as long as they may live. Betimes, the grief may be so powerful that it may even overwhelm the will to live. Do you think your friend may feel such grief?"

Elizabeth nodded. "I fear so, Granny Meg. The young man she loved was killed, foully murdered by an unknown assassin, and ever since, she has been so struck with grief for him that she does not speak, does not go out, merely sits up in her room all day and all night, staring off into the distance. I have tried to speak with her, but she will not respond. And I am afraid for her. I do not know how to help her."

"And so you came to me," said Granny Meg. "Well then, what is it you wish of me, Elizabeth?"

Elizabeth shook her head. "In truth, I . . . I do not know. I came to seek your wise counsel, Granny Meg. I thought, perhaps, that you could tell me what I should do. Mayhap there is some potion or some remedy or charm that would restore my friend to her senses. I would do anything to help her."

"Perhaps the best thing that you can do is to do nothing," Granny Meg replied.

Elizabeth stared at her with dismay. "Nothing? But . . . but surely there is *something* that can be done!"

"Oh, there are many things that can be done," said Granny Meg. "That is not the question. The question is, *should* they be done?"

Elizabeth shook her head. "I . . . I do not understand. If there was something that could be done to help my friend, then why should I refrain from doing it?"

"Because often the best thing is to let people find their own way to help themselves," said Granny Meg. "The grief that your friend feels now is of her own making. She has engendered it within herself, and now she nurtures it, and cherishes it, and will not let it go. And the reason that she will not let it go is that it serves some purpose for her."

"What purpose could that be?" Elizabeth asked.

"'Tis a question that only your friend could answer," Granny Meg replied. "Although 'tis possible that she may not know the answer."

Elizabeth frowned. "You speak in riddles, Granny Meg. I beg of you, speak plainly. Please tell me what you mean."

"Your friend's grief may be her struggle for the answer that she seeks," Granny Meg replied. "Or else it could be her struggle to avoid facing it. Betimes, when faced with a trying situation, one may already know the answer, but be unable to accept it."

"And what would happen then?" Elizabeth asked.

"The answer would not change," Granny Meg replied. "Nor

would the situation, unless one accepted it for what it was and faced the answer."

"So then, you mean that unless she can accept this thing she does not wish to face, then she will be ever thus, trapped within this struggle, within her grief for this young man? Oh, but that is terrible, Granny Meg! What if she can never bring herself to accept it?"

"Sooner or later, Elizabeth, all people must accept their fate, for refusing to accept it shall not change it."

"What, then, is the remedy for my poor friend?"

"Time," said Granny Meg. "Time is often the best remedy of all. Time, and patience, Elizabeth. Your patience. The patience of those who care for her."

Elizabeth shook her head sadly. "I think that I may be the only one who truly cares about her, Granny Meg. Her father has already made another match for her, it seems. And the man with whom this match was made. . . ." She shook her head. "Well, the less said of him, the better."

"If her father truly cares for her, then he must give her time to accept that which she must face," said Granny Meg.

"And if he cares less for her than for himself?" Elizabeth asked.

"Then in the end, he shall fail both his daughter and himself," said Granny Meg.

Elizabeth nodded. "'Twould seem clear, then, what I must do. I must speak with him and make him understand his daughter's plight."

Granny Meg smiled and shook her head. "You cannot *make* him understand, Elizabeth. He must *choose* to understand. In the end, we must all make choices for ourselves. Even when it appears that we have no choice, the truth is that a choice always exists."

"I must present him with that choice, then," Elizabeth replied, "and do all that is within my power to see he chooses wisely. Thank you, Granny Meg, for your good counsel."

"We are not yet done," said Granny Meg, as Elizabeth started to get up. "Sit down, Elizabeth." She pulled out a soft leather pouch and opened the drawstrings.

Elizabeth swallowed nervously, her gaze fixed upon the deck of cards that Granny Meg withdrew from the bag and placed face-down upon the table. "Perhaps now is not the time. . . ." she began.

"Shuffle the cards," said Granny Meg.

Elizabeth moistened her lips and reached slowly for the cards. She half expected to feel some sort of jolt when she picked them up, but she did not. They felt like a perfectly ordinary deck of cards, even though she knew otherwise. Slowly, purposefully, she shuf-fled them.

"Place them down upon the table whenever you feel that you have shuffled them enough," said Granny Meg.

She did so.

"And now cut the cards."

She picked up approximately half the cards and cut the deck, making two neat little stacks.

Granny Meg picked them up and put them together once again, then started to deal out the cards, face up, in a ten-card spread known as the Celtic Cross. The first card she placed face up was the Wheel of Fortune.

"This indicates your present," she said, as she put down the card. "The card of fate and changing fortune."

"We were just speaking of fate," Elizabeth said softly.

Granny Meg smiled. "Indeed." She placed another card down, laying it across the first one. It depicted a woman with her arm around a lion. "The card of Strength. It speaks of courage and con-viction. And this card crosses you."

"What does that mean?"

"It could mean that you are one who has the strength to soothe the grief of others. . . ."

"As with my friend!" Elizabeth exclaimed.

"Or else that there are strong influences aligned against you." Granny Meg continued.

Elizabeth bit her lower lip. "But which one is it?" she asked.

"It could be either one . . . or even both," said Granny Meg. "Let us see what else the cards may have in store."

As she drew the third card, she said, "This shows what may arise from the current situation in which you find yourself . . . or else that which you hope may come to pass." She placed it down upon the table in a position above the first two. "The Chariot," she said. "Interesting. All very strong cards, having to do with destiny and movement."

"What does it mean?"

"The Chariot indicates a moving forward, a sense of purpose, or a triumph over problems or adversity."

"Well . . . this is encouraging, at least," Elizabeth replied. "Is it not?"

"We shall see," Granny Meg replied. She drew the fourth card and placed it below the first two. Elizabeth gasped at the image it depicted, a tall stone tower struck by lightning in a storm, with two people plunging from the heights.

"The Tower," Granny Meg said. "This shows the past, that from which the current situation has arisen. It speaks of sudden change or transformation, of destruction, or of disgrace or loss."

Elizabeth nodded, wide-eyed. "Destruction. Aye, murder is surely the destruction of a life. And when her father discovered that the man she was betrothed to was a Jew, he must have felt disgraced. And loss, which is what she feels now. 'Tis all there, Granny Meg!"

"Let us see what influences the events that are unfolding now," Granny Meg replied as she drew another card and placed it down upon the table to the right of all the others, and even with the first two. "The Five of Pentacles," she said, gazing at the card, which depicted crippled beggars in the snow. "The card of misery. It signifies loss and destitution, loneliness, impoverishment. . . ." She shook her head and drew another card.

She stared at it for a moment, then placed it in the sixth position, to the left of the first two cards, thus completing the cross.

"This signifies what is soon to come," she said. The card showed a dark-cloaked figure in an attitude of woe, standing over five cups, several of which had spilled out upon the ground. "The Five of Cups. The card of sorrow and despair. There will be loss and bitterness, illusions shattered, bonds broken. . . ."

"What sort of bonds?" Elizabeth asked with concern.

Granny Meg shook her head. "I cannot say for certain. It could be the bonds of love or of friendship, perhaps, or else of family or marriage. It could be any of them, or it could even be more than one."

"The sorrow and despair. . . ." Elizabeth said with a nervous swallow. "*Whose* sorrow, Granny Meg? Shall it be mine?"

Granny Meg looked up at her briefly. "Perhaps. Once more, I cannot say for certain. It may mean yours, or not only yours. But sorrow there shall be. Much sorrow."

She drew the next card. This one she placed to the right of all the others, closest to the lower part of the cross formed by the other cards. This card showed the image of a shining woman dressed in bright robes and holding what appeared to be a tall staff.

"The Queen of Wands," said Granny Meg. "This card signifies yourself, a woman with a passionate nature and great vitality, one who has fondness for others, and who possesses a nature that is generous and practical."

She drew the eighth card and placed it directly above the previous one. This one showed a man holding a scale and distributing coins to hands held out in supplication.

"The Six of Pentacles," said Granny Meg. "This card represents the effect of your feelings upon what is unfolding. It signifies gratification, the return of a favor, perhaps, or else the desire to help another."

Elizabeth nodded. "Indeed, I do so wish to help her, if I can," she said. "I am just not certain how."

"The ninth card. . . ." said Granny Meg, drawing it and placing it directly in line above the eighth. Elizabeth saw the image of a juggler or perhaps an acrobat, attempting to balance upon a tightrope. "The Two of Pentacles," said Granny Meg. "This card signifies your hopes and fears. You seek balance; you wish for harmony amidst change and conflict. Perhaps you seek to juggle a number of things all at the same time, thus making your balance more precarious. You hope to find a harmony and balance, but fear that you may not achieve or maintain it."

She drew the final card.

"Justice," she said, as she laid the tenth card down directly above the ninth. The card depicted a robed woman with a laurel wreath, holding a sword in one hand and the scales of justice in the other. "This card represents the final outcome," Granny Meg said.

Elizabeth exhaled, suddenly aware that she had been holding her breath. "Justice," she repeated. "That is encouraging, surely. But justice for whom? For Thomas, the young man who was slain? Or for my friend?"

Granny Meg merely shrugged. "The cards do not say. They speak merely of the resolution. The card of Justice signifies fairness and equality, balance restored, and rightness achieved. What may seem like justice to some may seem unjust to others. But however it may seem, in the end, justice will be served."

"'Tis a hopeful resolution, then," Elizabeth said.

"If one's hope is for justice," Granny Meg replied.

"Well, 'tis clear to me what I must do, then," Elizabeth said, getting up from the table. She took a gold sovereign from her purse and laid it down upon the table. "Thank you, Granny Meg."

"Give my regards to your young man," said Granny Meg, drawing yet another card and turning it face up as she placed it on the table, to one side of the ten-card spread. It was the Seven of Wands, and it depicted a young man armed with a staff, taking a stand against others.

Elizabeth glanced at her with a slight frown. "*My* young man?"

"The one who first brought you to see me," Granny Meg replied. "Tuck is his name, is it not?"

"Oh," Elizabeth replied, looking down. "Oh, I . . . well, that is to say . . . I . . . I am not certain when I shall be seeing Tuck again."

"I have a feeling that you shall be seeing him quite soon," said Granny Meg with a smile.

"Well . . . then I shall be sure to give him your regards," Elizabeth replied, a trifle awkwardly, as she turned to leave.

Granny Meg drew another card and placed it crosswise on top of the Seven of Wands. It depicted a moon with a woman's face rising above a desolate land from which rose two stone towers, with a dog and a wolf howling up at the night sky. She frowned. "Tell him to beware the moon," she added.

10

✳

AS SHE RODE ACROSS TOWN in her coach, Elizabeth kept
thinking about what Granny Meg had said. She was both
fascinated and frightened by the mysterious cards that Granny Meg
used to divine the future. She wished the strange cards could have
been more specific. They spoke of misery and sorrow and destruction, but they also spoke of justice. And then when Granny Meg
had told her that she would be seeing Tuck again soon—"your
young man," she had called him—Elizabeth had felt herself blush-
ing and had looked away. Doubtless, it had been a pointless thing
to do, for it did not seem possible to hide anything from the wise
old cunning woman. Nevertheless, she had felt embarrassed and
had already started for the stairs leading down to the shop when
she had heard Granny Meg add, from behind her, "Tell him to
beware the moon."

That strange and cryptic warning had brought her up short.
Whatever had Granny Meg meant by that? But when Elizabeth
had turned to ask her, the room was empty. Granny Meg was
gone.

For a moment, Elizabeth had just stood there, stunned and
speechless. How was it possible for Granny Meg to have simply
disappeared? Except for the stairs leading down to the shop, there
was no way in or out of the room. It was as if she had never even

been there in the first place. Elizabeth had swallowed hard, thinking once again what she had thought only a short while before: What if the old cunning woman had never really been there at all? What if she truly *was* a ghost? Elizabeth turned and nearly ran downstairs.

The overcast sky had turned dark, and it began to thunder as the coach drove through the London streets, taking her toward Henry Mayhew's house. She did not really know Portia's father very well. They had only met on a few occasions, and then just briefly. For that matter, until recently, she had not known Portia Mayhew much better.

Henry Mayhew had struck her as a man who had a great deal in common with her own father. They shared the same first name, and they were both men who had not been born to money, but had worked hard and achieved success later in life, which made them value what they had achieved all the more. Like her own father, Henry Mayhew had seemed almost entirely preoccupied with business and was probably not the sort of man who had very much time for women. To such a man, as to her own father, a woman was merely a sort of accoutrement, one that served a specific purpose, much like a prized mount or a sporting hound. Elizabeth chuckled to herself at the unintentional and ribald pun implicit in the thought. A "prized mount," indeed.

She tried to imagine if there had ever been a time when her own father had thought of her mother that way. Clearly, there must have been, for she was living proof of that; however, it seemed impossible to imagine. Perhaps they had merely procreated because it was what married couples were supposed to do. She could not believe her father ever could have acted anything even remotely like the characters in the romantic poems she had read. Indeed, he had expressed his scorn for such pursuits on more than one occasion. He believed that poetry was idle nonsense, fit only for players, bards, and gypsies, not "serious" people. To him, the very idea of romance was foolish. And her mother certainly did not seem like the sort of woman to inspire it. Her parents seemed merely to share the same house and the same bed. Each had his or her own duties to perform, and neither seemed to spend very much time even speaking to the other. It seemed like such a pointless way to live. Had they ever even been in love?

She knew that their marriage had been arranged, just as most marriages were these days. Marriage for love, as her mother had often said, was all right for "the common sort of people," but it was hardly appropriate for "the upper classes," who needed to concern themselves with more practical matters. The way her mother spoke, one might think they were aristocrats, rather than members of the rising middle class. Or perhaps that was merely the way her mother placated herself for the lack of romance in her life.

Elizabeth had sworn that she would never do that. She would never marry a man she did not love and simply acquiesce to what he and everyone else seemed to expect of her, regardless of her own desires. And if there was anything that she could do to prevent Portia from having to succumb to such a fate, then she would do it without any hesitation.

Once again, her thoughts turned to Tuck's father. What an appalling, arrogant, selfish, and deceitful man! She tried to imagine whether Tuck could ever become like that when he grew older. She shook her head, as if to dispel the very idea. She felt ashamed of herself for even thinking it. Except for a familial physical resemblance, the father and the son had nothing at all in common—most fortunately, she thought. What could possibly account for the two of them being so very different? But then again, what could account for her being so different from her own mother? Had there *ever* been a time when her mother had thought and felt the same way she did? And if there had, then what could have happened to change her so? Was it merely a matter of advancing age,

Elizabeth wondered, or was it marriage to her father that had beaten her down?

The thunder crashed and lightning lit up the sky outside her coach window. The rain began to pelt down. She felt a little sorry for the coachman, sitting up there exposed to the elements in nothing but his hat and cloak, but then that was his job. And at the same time she thought that no one would ever be telling *him* whom he must marry. He was free to marry anyone he pleased.

She wondered what his life was like. Did he have a wife awaiting him at home? And if so, how long had they been married? Were they like her parents, who merely slept together to keep each other warm? Or did they, despite the little money that they had, still find romance and passion in their lives? Did they make love in bed by candlelight, or perhaps upon the floor, with their sweaty, naked bodies intertwined before the hot and roaring fire in their hearth?

Elizabeth moistened her lips and took a deep breath, exhaling slowly. This was not the sort of thought she should be entertaining as she was preparing to meet Portia's father and convince him of the utter wrongness of his course. She needed to have her wits about her, to be serious and levelheaded. Any sort of emotional appeal would be wasted on him. Her argument would have to be completely logical and practical. It would not do, she thought, to argue that Portia was too distraught with grief and needed time to mend her broken heart. He would dismiss that as a trifling matter, a foolish woman's argument. No she thought, the thing to do would be to focus upon Tuck's father, the man to whom Henry Mayhew was apparently about to betroth his daughter. She would have to convince him of the truth about Symington Smythe II, Esquire, that he was a fraud and a bounder, whose true object was not to find himself a suitable wife, but to get his hands upon her father's money.

Of course, that meant she would have to tell him *how* she

knew. She wondered how Mayhew would respond to that. She was not ashamed of Tuck, and she did not keep her friendship with him secret from either her family or her friends. Her father did not object to it, exactly. He tolerated it, in a rather grudging sort of way, in part because he felt indebted to Tuck and in part, she felt, because he trusted him to behave in an honorable fashion. That seemed somewhat incongruous, perhaps, because Tuck was a player and players were generally considered, more or less, to be on a level with prostitutes and gypsies. A man such as her father—in other words, someone like Henry Mayhew—would not normally think that players *could* behave in an honorable fashion, much less except them to. Nor would her father have thought so, in all likelihood, had not Tuck and Will proven themselves in his eyes. He still did not entirely approve of them, but neither could he bring himself to disapprove. And somewhere in that region of vague tolerance and indecision was bounded her relationship with Tuck.

It was something more than friendship and somewhat less than love. Or at least less than a love that was openly acknowledged or expressed. And if her father should ever suspect that, thought Elizabeth, then what little tolerance he had for their relationship would probably be strained beyond endurance. So long as he believed that it was merely a friendship, or perhaps even a mildly rebellious sort of infatuation on her part, stimulated by its social impropriety, then he could choose to look the other way and sniff disdainfully, shrug his shoulders, roll his eyes, and assume that she would eventually tire of it. However, it was one thing to be vaguely tolerant of her relationship with Tuck because she was discreet about it and never forced the issue or even brought it up in conversation, thereby enabling him to act as if it did not truly exist, yet it was another thing entirely to have someone like Henry Mayhew question him about it. That would throw discretion out the window with all the subtlety of breaking wind at vespers.

"You truly permit your unmarried daughter to associate with *players?*" she could imagine Mayhew saying to her father. "Good Lord, man, what can you *possibly* be thinking? 'Strewth, she has not compromised her virtue so much as dragged it through the mud! Have you taken leave of all your senses?"

She could imagine such a conversation all too easily. And in that event, if he were forced to deal with her relationship with Tuck in a way that would publicly embarrass him, she had no doubt that not only would he put his foot down and forbid it, but he would once again resume his efforts to get her married off . . . except that next time, he might not be so particular about to whom.

She sighed and chewed her lower lip nervously. There was simply no escaping it. Warning Henry Mayhew about Symington Smythe meant telling him about her relationship with his son. And no matter how inconsequential she could try to make it seem, there was no way to make it appear proper and acceptable. Inescapably, trying to help Portia any further meant endangering her relationship with Tuck. But then, revealing the truth to Mayhew went beyond merely trying to help Portia . . . it meant saving her from a disastrous and appalling marriage. And she had already been through enough pain and suffering. To add to it by saying nothing and thus allowing her to fall into Symington Smythe's clutches would be simply unforgivable. And what was more, Elizabeth had no doubt that Tuck would see it that way, too.

It was still raining very hard and the wind had picked up by the time the coach pulled up in front of Henry Mayhew's home. As the coachman came down off the box to open the door for her, Elizabeth pulled up the hood of her cloak and then carefully stepped down onto the slick, wet cobblestones. She quickly climbed the steps up to the house on tiptoe, hoping that it would not take long for someone to answer the door. She did not relish the idea of waiting very long out in this storm. Much more of this, she thought, and her light shoes were going to be ruined. To her surprise, when she went to knock upon the door, she found that it had not been completely closed. Her first knock pushed it open slightly. She frowned as she opened it and went inside, thinking that it was rather careless of the servants not to close the door properly.

"'Allo?" she called out, as she stood just inside the doorway. "'Allo, is anybody home?"

There was no reply forthcoming. It was dark inside. The storm had made the night come early, but there were no candles burning in the hall. That seemed rather peculiar. Even if Mayhew was not at home, surely the servants were. What could they be thinking, leaving the house so dark? It certainly looked as if they were being derelict in their duties.

"'Allo, 'allo?" she called out once again.

There was no answer. A moment later, she heard what sounded like a soft moan.

"'Allo, is someone there?" she called out again, frowning. It was difficult to see well in the dark. She wished she had a candle. She took several steps forward and suddenly tripped over something large lying at her feet and fell to the floor, crying out in alarm.

Someone groaned quite close to her, and a man's voice said, "Oh, my *God!*"

Elizabeth gasped and sat up on the floor. "Merciful Heavens! Who is there?"

She suddenly felt a hand close around her ankle, and instinctively she cried out and jerked her foot away, scuttling backward.

"Ow . . . help me, please. . . ." someone said.

Whoever it was, she realized, was on the floor alongside her. She had tripped over someone, someone who was obviously hurt and in pain.

She took a deep breath. "Steady now," she said, steeling her nerves. Her eyes were growing accustomed to the darkness, and she could now make out someone stretched out on the floor nearby. "I shall try to help you. Here, hold out your hand."

She crawled over to the prostrate figure and saw a hand reaching out, unsteadily. She took hold of it. "Right, I have you. Now you shall have to help me. Can you stand? I cannot lift you up all by myself."

"I . . . shall try. . . ."

They struggled to their feet, Elizabeth trying to hold him steady. Fortunately, he was not a large or heavy man. It took a moment or two, but they managed to stand up together.

"Come on, now, lean on me," she said. "My name is Elizabeth Darcie. I am Portia's friend. Who are you, fellow?"

"I am Hastings, mistress . . . the . . . the steward of this house. . . ."

"What happened, Hastings? Are you ill or injured?"

"Ohh . . . my head. They clubbed me down, the base villains. . . ." He gasped suddenly, though not so much with pain apparently, as with alarm. "Oh, good God! Master Henry and Mistress Winifred! Oh dear, oh dear, I fear what has befallen them! They were at home when those scoundrels broke in!"

"How many of them were there?" asked Elizabeth, alarmed that they might still be in the house.

"I . . . I am not certain. At least three or four, methinks. Perhaps more . . . oh, alas, I fear for Master Henry and poor Mistress Winifred!"

"We shall find them, Hastings," Elizabeth replied. "Calm yourself. Think now, was it already raining when these men attacked you and broke in?"

"Nay, mistress," he answered without hesitation. "'Twas not raining."

"Good. 'Twas a while ago, then, and with luck they may already have fled. You must fetch a candle or a lantern. And a weapon, if you have one. Quickly, if you can."

"At once, mistress . . . perhaps you had best wait here. . . ."

But Elizabeth did not wait. While Hastings went to get a light, she reached inside her cloak and pulled out the small bodkin that she carried with her whenever she went out. It was not a large dagger, but it was very well made, double edged and exceedingly sharp. It had been a present from Tuck, and she prized it because he had made it especially for her. He had given her some lessons in the proper use of it, and although it hardly made her feel invincible, she thought that if she had to use it, she could do so without any hesitation and with a fair degree of competency.

As she moved cautiously through the dark house, she held the bodkin ready in her hand and listened carefully for the slightest sound. She thought that it was likely those men were no longer in the house, but just the same, she moved slowly and tried to keep her footsteps as soft as possible. She felt a tightness in her stomach, and her breaths were quick and shallow. She felt afraid, but she refused to let that stop her. Somewhere in the house, there could be injured people who would need her help.

As she came toward the end of the hall, she heard a thumping sound and froze, the hairs prickling at the back of her neck. She held her breath. Where was it coming from? Could it be the robbers coming back down the stairs?

"Mistress Elizabeth!" she heard Hastings call out from behind her. It nearly made her jump. "Mistress Elizabeth, where are you?"

"Here, Hastings! Hurry!"

A moment later, she saw a light approaching. Hastings came toward her with a lantern and what appeared to be a battle-ax.

"Good Heavens!" she exclaimed. "Where did you get *that?*"

"Master Henry had it hanging upon the wall," said Hastings, who had recovered somewhat, although he still looked a bit unsteady. She could see now that he was not a young man. He was about her height, thin as a rake, bald at the crown, with wispy white hair that stuck out from the sides of his head. "Would that I had this in my hands when those misbegotten wastrels broke in here!" he said, giving the battle-ax a shake. "I would have shown them what for!"

"Be quiet, Hastings! Listen!"

He stopped. The thumping noises continued.

"Do you hear?" she asked. "What is that?"

"The other servants!" he said after a moment. "In the kitchen!"

He led the way and she followed.

They found them tied up in the kitchen. They quickly released the two women, who were frightened, but otherwise unharmed. They lit some candles and together all went in search of Henry Mayhew and Mistress Winifred, whom Elizabeth assumed to be the woman that Portia had told her about not long ago, the one who was going to be her stepmother. They soon found her in an upstairs bedroom, tied up and gagged and stretched out on the bed.

"Oh, my Lord!" cried Hastings when he saw her, and he nearly dropped the lantern. Elizabeth, however, ran immediately to her bedside with the two other women, and they soon had her untied.

"Are you all right?" Elizabeth asked her, helping her sit up. She hesitated. "Did they hurt you?"

Winifred shook her head as she massaged her wrists. "Nay, they did not molest me," she replied with surprising frankness. "'Twas not me that they wanted."

"What do you mean?" Elizabeth asked.

"They took Henry," Winifred replied. She glanced at the servants. "Why are you standing there and dithering? Get some light in here! Look around the house and see if they have taken anything. Go on, now! Be quick about it!"

As the servants quickly moved to follow her directives, she turned to Elizabeth. "I would be much obliged if you would tell me who you are, young woman, so that I may thank you properly."

"My name is Elizabeth Darcie."

"Henry Darcie's daughter," Winifred replied, nodding. "Well, I am most grateful to you, Elizabeth. How did you happen to come here? Is anything amiss with Portia?"

"Nay, Portia is well," Elizabeth replied. "That is, she is still mired in her grief for Thomas, but when I left her, she was otherwise unharmed. You do not suppose those men. . . ." She trailed off, unable to finish articulating the appalling thought that had just occurred to her.

"I do not think so," Winifred replied, getting to her feet. "They demanded to know where she was. They were most insistent, but neither Henry nor I would tell them. Henry stubbornly refused to speak, so, fearing that they might harm him, I told them that she had run away from home and that we did not know where she was. They then took Henry and departed, after tying me up and carrying me upstairs. And save for the soreness in my wrists and ankles where they bound me up, they did not harm me in any way."

"Well, thank goodness for that, at least," Elizabeth replied. "I must say, you have been very brave through all of this."

"Brave?" Winifred snorted. "I was terrified out of my wits. I feel like sitting down and having a good long cry, but there is not time for that. I must try to think how to help Henry." She balled her hands up into fists. "I cannot, I must not, be weak now. I must keep my wits about me. These were no ordinary robbers, to be sure. They kept wanting to know where Portia was. I can only suppose they meant to abduct her and hold her for ransom, and failing to find her, they took Henry, instead, thinking to make me pay for his safe return."

"Perhaps not," said Elizabeth tensely.

Winifred gave her a sharp look. "What do you mean? What *other* reason could there be?"

Elizabeth took a deep breath. "These men sound like rufflers," she replied. "Men who knew what they were about. And unless there were things stolen from your house, 'twould seem to me that they came specifically for Portia and her father. If they truly meant to abduct Portia and hold her for ransom, then when they failed to find her here, why take her father? Why not take you in her place, and thus force him to pay for your safe return instead?"

"Indeed, why not?" Winifred replied. She shook her head. "I do not know. But why else would they have done what they did?"

"Perhaps because someone seeks revenge for the murder of Thomas Locke," Elizabeth told her. "Namely, his father, who I have been told is one of the masters of the Thieves Guild. Thus, 'tis fortunate that you told them you did not know where Portia was. However, they may not have believed you when you said that she ran away, and now that they have taken her father, they may try to force it out of him."

"Then before anything else is done," said Winifred, "we must get Portia out of your house and hide her somewhere."

"I have a coach waiting outside," Elizabeth said.

"Then we must go there straightaway," said Winifred. "Henry is a strong-willed man, but he is no longer young, and if they put him to the question, he may not long hold out against them."

Hastings came back into the room at that moment, looking somewhat perplexed. "Mistress Winifred, 'tis a most curious thing!" he said. "The house is not in any disarray, and it does not appear as if they have taken anything!"

"Then you were right, Elizabeth," said Winifred. "'Twas Portia they were after all along! Let us make all haste! We must get to her before they do!"

Things were looking rather grim, indeed. As Smythe looked up toward the dais where the masters of the Thieves Guild sat, he desperately tried to make eye contact with the one person in the room who could be in a position to help them.

Moll Cutpurse was unique among women in the status she had achieved in her profession. There was not a foist or a pickpocket in all of London who could ply his or her trade without answering to her. It was said—by Robert Greene, among others—that she operated a school for pickpockets and cutpurses, training them in the arts that she had mastered. Many of her pupils were small children, often orphans with no homes, whom she taught to fend for themselves in London's streets and alleyways. Others were people like Smythe himself, who came to London in search of work after the enclosures had driven them from their lands but found, when they reached the city, that work was scarce and difficult to come by. Those who, unlike Smythe and Shakespeare, were not fortunate enough to find work were often left with little choice but to resort to begging or else turn to crime, and these, too, found a friend in the unusual woman who dressed like a man and fought like a man and was known by a variety of names, the most infamous of which was Moll Cutpurse.

Her real name was Mary Flannery, which was a secret few men knew. Smythe just happened to be one of them. And he knew it because he also knew another secret about Moll Cutpurse, one she guarded closely. He knew she had a younger sister by the name of Molly, who worked as a serving wench at the Toad and Badger. Just now, he was hoping very hard that this knowledge would stand him in good stead, for judging by the way things looked, they were going to be in great need of a friend among *this* crowd.

Shakespeare groaned beside him. "Now here is yet *another*—"

"Do *not* say it!" Smythe cautioned him. "Do not even *attempt* to blame all this on me or, so help me God, I shall box your ears right here in front of everyone."

"Having my ears boxed would be the very least of my worries at the moment," Shakespeare replied. "Looking around at this scurvy lot, I shall count myself fortunate if we manage to leave this place alive."

"Well, we are not dead yet."

"Not yet," Shakespeare said wryly. "Do you suppose your friend Moll Cutpurse remembers you and the kindness that you showed her sister?"

"I do most earnestly hope so," Smythe replied. "I have been trying to catch her eye, but she has not yet looked toward us."

"Mayhap she does not wish to see us," Shakespeare said. "Depending upon how the wind is blowing, this may not be a convenient time for her to admit she knows us."

"If that is so, then you may be sure I shall remind her at the very first opportunity," said Smythe.

Shakespeare gave him an uneasy sidelong glance. "Just have a care," he said. "She is the only one we know with any influence among this crowd." He looked around with trepidation. "If, under the present circumstances, we should become inconvenient friends for her, then we are liable to wind up late, lamented friends."

"We shall see," said Smythe, still trying to catch her eye. But she did not look toward them. She seemed to be engaged in an animated conversation with the man upon her left.

"Here we go," said Shakespeare.

Charles Locke picked up the wooden mallet that lay before him and struck the table with it three times. "This meeting shall come to order!" he called out. The noise of the crowd around them gradually died away. He waited until there was complete silence before continuing.

"We shall dispense with our usual order of business on this day," he said. "Many among you already know the reason why. And as for those of you who do not know, I pray, attend me. . . ."

"Oh, this does not look good," said Shakespeare softly.

"Be quiet, Will."

Locke continued. "I had a son," he said. He paused and looked down at the table for a moment, attempting to compose himself. There was not another sound within the chamber. All ears hung upon his every word.

"I had a son," he said once more, clenching his hand into a fist as he looked up. "A son by my wife, Rachel, who had very nearly died in birthing him and was afterwards pronounced unable to bear any more children. No matter, thought I, grateful beyond words that my dear wife should have survived the terrible ordeal of the birth. This one son would be enough. This one son would evermore be my contentment, for upon this one son *my* sun would rise and set. This one son I would cherish and raise up into a man to make a father proud. This one son would be my legacy and my ongoing purpose in this world. And so, throughout his young life, I doted on him, and sought to provide him with every opportunity that I was myself denied. Thus, he grew into a fine young man, well known to many of those among you, a young man who became apprenticed to a tailor, Leffingwell by name, and who, upon completing his term of apprenticeship, became a journeyman in the shop of that same Leffingwell, who had considered him a credit to his business. Thus did a proud father look upon his son, who had grown into a man going out into the world upon his own, and who had become betrothed to a young woman of good family and would soon, no doubt, sire children of his own. I looked upon this one son and was both pleased and proud. Could any man ask for any more?"

"We are dead," said Shakespeare flatly.

"Not yet," said Smythe, for Moll Cutpurse had looked, for the first time, directly at him and had given him a nod.

Locke paused. A murmur went up among the crowd. Then it died away again as he continued. "Of late, it came to my attention that my son, Thomas, was planning to elope. The two men who had brought this news to me are the very men who sit before you now. Their names are Smythe and Shakespeare. They told me that they were players with the company of Lord Strange's Men. I found this rather curious, for I could not think what these two players would have to do with my son Thomas's affairs. And so I inquired of them, how came they by this news? Why, I asked of them, would my son wish to elope when the father of his prospective bride had readily given his consent and blessing to the marriage? And upon being asked this, they then told me that the father of the bride had not only withdrawn his consent to the match, but had forbidden his daughter from ever seeing my son again, and that they had heard this from my own son's lips during a visit to the shop of my son's good friend Ben Dickens, the armorer."

"Nay, this is not looking good at all," murmured Shakespeare.

"Hush, Will," Smythe replied. "All is not yet lost."

Locke continued speaking. "You may imagine my surprise," he said, "when I heard this news from two men who were strangers to me, when my own son had said nothing. And 'twas this very fact which lent credence to their tale, you see, for if my son truly had intended to elope with this young woman, then both he and she would have intended to keep this knowledge secret from their respective parents. There yet remained the question . . . *why?* Why would the father of this girl at first give his consent, only to withdraw it soon thereafter? Why would he at first look upon the match with favor, only to look upon it later with revulsion? What could have brought about so profound a change in his affections? What could bring him to despise my son, whom he had but lately loved as a prospective son-in-law? And so I asked these men that very question . . . *why?* And there came the answer, 'Because his mother is a Jew.'"

The crowd began to murmur once again. Smythe looked around at them, but in the dim light, he could not clearly make out many faces. They all sat in the shadows, like some dreadful court that sat in judgment of their fate. And that was exactly what they were, thought Smythe. A court. A thieves' court, if such a thing could be. And what appeal could be made to such a court, he wondered? How could one sway a court that did not recognize any law except its own? How could he plead that he was not guilty of any crime to a court whose members were guilty of nearly every crime? What would he say to them? And would they even offer him a chance to speak before they reached their judgment?

"Some of you may be surprised to learn that my wife is a Jewess," Locke continued. "And some of you already knew. Those of you who did not know might ask, 'How could he be married to a Jew?' And 'Why would any Christian man make such a marriage?' To those, I say that I did not marry a Jew; I married a woman. And for each Jew that you may show me who is not a Christian, I can also show you a Christian who is not a Christian. If the Lord truly said that thou shalt not steal, then each and every one of us has disobeyed the Lord. And if the Lord truly said that thou shalt not kill, then every soldier who has ever fought and killed an enemy has disobeyed the Lord. And if the Lord truly said that thou shalt not covet thy neighbor's wife, then there is scarcely anyone among us who has not, at one time or another, likewise disobeyed the Lord, for the sin would be in the desire as much as in the act."

There was some general laughter at this last remark, and to his dismay and disbelief, Smythe actually heard Shakespeare mutter, "That was a good line, that one. Would that I had my pen." He quickly shushed him.

"It would not have mattered to me if my wife were Protestant or Catholic," said Locke, "and so it did not matter to me if she came from Jewish stock. Her parents had accepted Christianity, because they had no other choice, as their parents had accepted Christianity, because they had no other choice, for that was what most Jews who remained in England had to do, or else be driven out. Yet even so, they were reviled by many Englishmen, good Christians all, who burned their homes and beat them and abused them.

"My wife, Rachel, lived among us as a Christian," he continued, "but if she was not a true Christian because she did not go to church each Sunday, then neither are many among us true Christians for the selfsame reason. And if she honored the traditions of her ancestors, without doing dishonor to the traditions of anybody else, then where lies the fault in that? Yet I am not here to defend my wife this night; I am here to prosecute the one who killed her son. Our son, who was a Christian, and who attended church each and every Sunday, and who never stole, and never killed, and never coveted anyone save for the girl he truly loved and hoped to marry. He honored the traditions of his mother, although he did not follow them himself, because we had raised him as a Christian. And yet . . . and yet, in the traditions of his mother's people, one is a Jew if one's mother is a Jew. And ironically, this one tradition of the Jews . . . alone among all of their traditions . . . was the one that Henry Mayhew chose to recognize when he refused to let my son marry his daughter."

"Odd's blood!" said Shakespeare softly. "'Tis not us he holds to blame, but Henry Mayhew! And yet if that is so . . . what does he want with us? Why have we been brought here?"

Smythe shook his head. "I do not know, Will. Perhaps, in part, he does believe we are to blame. Or at least *I* am to blame, for 'twas I who had advised Thomas to elope. The fault in that was mine and mine alone. I shall tell them you are not to blame for that."

"'Tis not right to blame you, either," Shakespeare replied. "You were only trying to help. The one who bears the blame for young Locke's death can only be the one who killed him. Surely, they must see that!"

An undertone of conversation suddenly broke out as three men came into the room. Two of them were leading the third between them, one holding each of his arms, while a sack covered his face and head. They led him to a stool that had been placed in the center of the room, roughly twenty feet in front of Smythe and Shakespeare, between them and the dais where Charles Locke and the other masters of the Thieves Guild sat. They sat him down upon the stool, and as they did so Smythe could see that his hands were tied behind him.

"Do you suppose. . . ." Shakespeare began, but then his voice trailed off as one of the men reached out and pulled the sack off their captive's head.

"Your name is Henry Mayhew, is it not?" Locke demanded.

The murmuring grew louder as the man glanced around apprehensively, and Locke picked up the mallet and struck it on the table several times to restore silence.

"You already know my name," Mayhew replied in an affronted tone, "for you have abducted me by force from my own home. And yet I know not yours. Who are you, and what is this place? Why have I been brought here?"

"I shall ask the questions here," said Locke, "and you shall answer them forthrightly, or else face the consequences. But so that you may know why you are here and who I am, I shall tell you that this is a meeting of the Thieves Guild, and that my name is Charles Locke, and that you are here to answer for the murder of my son."

Conversation broke out once again, and this time Locke allowed it to continue for a while, as if to let it all sink in for Mayhew.

"'Strewth!" said Smythe softly. "They are going to hold a trial for him! And we must have been brought here to testify!"

Shakespeare shook his head. "They cannot do this," he murmured. "This is not a trial, but a mockery! There is no justice in this!"

"'Tis *their* justice," Smythe said, "according to *their* law."

"And 'twould seem they have already reached their verdict," Shakespeare said. "The poor sod. He shall have no chance, no chance at all."

Locke hammered upon the table once again to restore order. "What say you to the charge?" he demanded.

"So . . . you are Thomas's father?" replied Mayhew. "How ironic we should meet like this. I must say, you look remarkably well for a man who was supposed to have been dead."

Locke frowned. "*Dead?* What nonsense is this? What do you mean? Who told you I was dead?"

"Your son," Mayhew replied.

Locke leaned forward. "*What?* You expect me to believe that my own *son* told you I was dead?"

"Believe what you like," Mayhew replied derisively. "It makes no difference to me, one way or the other. I have nothing to gain here, and nothing left to lose. 'Tis clear to me that you have already determined my fate. But your son, when I first met him, told me that he was an orphan, that both his parents had died when he was very young. Considering that his father was a criminal and his mother was a Jew, then I suppose that would explain why he chose to lie."

Mayhew's remarks provoked an immediate outburst among the crowd. Locke simply stared at him with cold fury, his hands balled into fists upon the table.

"He is sealing his own fate," said Smythe.

"Nay, his fate is already sealed," said Shakespeare. "He was right about that. But he is acquitting himself bravely."

"There is a difference between arrogance and bravery," said Smythe. "The man is acting like a fool."

"Perhaps," said Shakespeare. "But an innocent fool, methinks."

Smythe frowned and glanced at him. "Innocent?"

"Aye," Shakespeare replied. "He may be an arrogant fool, and he may have refused to let his daughter marry Thomas Locke, but I do not believe he is a murderer. I do not think he did it."

11

✳

HE COACH WHEELS CLATTERED LOUDLY over the wet cobblestones as the driver whipped up the horses to a canter, giving Elizabeth and Winifred a jarring ride over the streets of London. Although the horses were not going at a full gallop, it was nevertheless a risky speed to be driving in the rain, with the slickness of the streets and the poor visibility from the mist and darkness. Fortunately, there was scarcely any traffic, due to the severe weather; otherwise they would almost surely have suffered an accident. Despite the relatively empty streets, however, Winifred was apprehensive.

"Should we not tell the driver to go a little slower?" she asked nervously.

"I am quite sure he would be happy to," Elizabeth replied. "But I would not forgive myself if we arrived too late."

"I suppose you are right," Winifred replied, holding on to the seat grimly.

"Perhaps 'twould have been best had you not come," Elizabeth said to her apologetically.

Winifred shook her head. "Nay, I had to come," she said. "I could not have borne simply sitting there all alone, wondering what would become of Henry, to say naught of worrying about poor Portia."

"How long do you suppose it has been since they took him?"

Winifred shook her head. "'Twould be difficult for me to say for certain. It felt as if I had been lying there tied up for hours and hours, but I do not think it could have truly been that long."

"What would you guess?"

"An hour, perhaps? I cannot say. I do not think it could have been much longer, although 'tis possible, I suppose," Winifred replied.

"An hour," Elizabeth repeated. "Well, if so, then that is somewhat encouraging. They would have needed to take Master Mayhew to wherever they were taking him, and then they would have needed to have time to question him some more. . . ." She stopped when she saw Winifred close her eyes and shudder. "Forgive me. But we must set aside our delicate natures and screw our courage to the sticking point if we are to be of any use to Portia and her father."

Winifred nodded. "Of course, you are quite right, Elizabeth. Please, go on. Continue. I shall bear up as best I can."

"Very well, then. 'Twould have taken them time to make whatever arrangements they were going to make regarding Portia's father, and then. . . ." She took a deep breath. "Well, then 'twould depend upon whether or not he could convince them that he truly did not know where Portia was. If he could do that, well, then I am not sure what they would do. On the other hand, if they did not believe him . . . then I fear 'twould be a matter of how long he could hold out before he told them that she was staying at my house."

Winifred bit her lower lip and clasped her hands together tightly, but said nothing.

"Either way," Elizabeth continued, "we should still have some time to reach Portia, if we hurry." She frowned, recalling something. "I remember that of late I wrote to Master Mayhew concerning Portia staying at my house. Do you suppose he may have left that letter where they could have found it?"

Winifred shook her head. "I do not know. However, I do recall that letter. He had read it to me. But I do not know what he did with it."

"Was he in the habit of saving such things?"

Again, Winifred shook her head. "I cannot say. In truth, it strikes me now that I had never paid very much attention to those things. He has a room in the house where he keeps his business papers, and he often works in there. I had never gone in to disturb him. A man needs to have his privacy. But on the other hand, I have never discussed any of his business matters with him and so know nothing of them, really. If something were to happen to him. . . ." She paused, swallowed hard, and then went on. "Well, I would not know how to sort out any of his business matters. I would not know what to do."

Elizabeth grimaced. "My mother is just the same," she said. "That is to say, her circumstances are the same. Father takes care of everything. The house, the property, the business, all the money matters—Mother has naught to do with any of those things. She would say 'twas not a woman's province to concern herself with such matters, but to keep the house well and see to it that meals are on the table and servants do what they are told and that her husband is free from having to worry about those things. And yet, 'tis clear to me that she would not know what to do if anything were to happen to that husband. She would require some man to come and tell her. And that man could take advantage of her, and what is more, she would never be the wiser."

"Perhaps," said Winifred, nodding in agreement. "Yet, that is the way of things."

"Nay, that is the way things are allowed to be," Elizabeth replied vehemently. "And things are allowed to be that way because we tolerate them. You are fortunate, Winifred, because your late husband left you well taken care of. Before he died, Lord rest his soul, he had made arrangements for you, no doubt with trusted friends, so that you would be provided for and so there would be someone, a man, to take care of his estate and see to it that you were free from such mundane concerns, at least until you had found another husband. And now it seems you have. And if all goes well, Lord help us, and Henry Mayhew is returned to you unharmed, then you shall marry him, and your late husband's estate shall become *his* estate, passed on to him, as it were, along with you. Then he shall take it over, and thus shall you continue to be kept free from those concerns. Well, I do not wish to be 'kept free' from concern. I wish to be concerned with my *own* welfare, to make my *own* choices, and to do what *I* choose to do, and not what some man, be it a husband or a father or a lover, *tells* me I should do!"

"'Twould seem to me that some man has made you very angry, Elizabeth," Winifred replied.

"Oh, *all* men make me angry," she replied with a grimace. "Well, all save one, perhaps, and yet even he has the tendency to irk me now and then. I do not mean to offend you, Winifred, or cause you any more undue distress, but consider your own situation as it stands now. Consider that of my own mother, and that of nearly every woman that I know. What happens to a woman when her whole world, her very firmament, is encompassed by a man? Why, then he becomes her lord, her life, her keeper, her head, her sovereign, one that cares for her and for her maintenance commits his body to painful labor by both sea and land, to watch the night in storms, the day in cold, whilst she lies warm at home, secure and safe, and need offer no other tribute to him but love, fair looks, and true obedience. And so one might well think 'tis too little payment for so great a debt. And yet, what is the payment, truly? 'Tis this: Let a woman make a man her entire world, then take that man away, and she has lost her entire world. What, then, has she got left? Where is her foundation and her firmament? What shall become of her when all that she is has been bounded by a man and she has lost that man? Why, then she has lost herself. Well, I have no wish to lose myself. And if that means living life without a man, why then, I am prepared to do so and accept spinsterhood without complaint. But I would much prefer to live life with a man whom *I* have chosen, and who lets me be myself, who does not compass all my borders, but understands that I need to set my own, who is my mate and works with me the way these horses work together so that they might pull this coach, thus sharing all the burden equally."

"You wish for a great deal," Winifred replied.

"I wish for no more than what many of the simple, common, working people have," Elizabeth replied, "perhaps because they do not have aught else. Is that too much to ask?"

"Perhaps not," said Winifred with a smile. "I hope you get your wish someday, Elizabeth. I truly do, for I should like to live in such a world. And if we do not have that opportunity, then perhaps someday our daughters will."

The coach pulled up in front of the Darcie house.

"Right, we are here," Elizabeth said, as the coachman climbed down and opened the door for them. "There is little time to lose. We must bundle Portia up and be off with her, as quickly as possible."

"But where then shall we take her?" Winifred asked.

"I have already thought of that," Elizabeth replied, as she got down out of the coach. "I know of a place where Portia shall be safe and they shall never think to look for her."

"What do you mean, you do not think he did it?" Smythe asked.

Shakespeare shook his head. "I could be wrong," he said, "but look at him. He is arrogant and angry, and proud, so very proud . . . indeed, just as you said. He is also frightened, surely, and yet he remains defiant. He is outraged that these common criminals should have dared to take such liberties with him. Aye, and he is a fool, too, I shall grant you that, for he truly does not seem to realize the danger he is in. But amidst all the violent emotions that play across his countenance, I still do not see guilt."

"And upon this reasoning you base your judgment?" Smythe asked dubiously.

"Aye, and upon this, as well," said Shakespeare, tapping the side of his nose several times. "'Strewth, I simply do not think he did it, Tuck! It smells all wrong to me. He hath not the aspect of a guilty man."

"If we were to judge all men by their aspects, Will, then many of the guilty would go free and innocents throughout the world would suffer punishment," said Smythe.

"I shall not dispute with you," said Shakespeare. "What you say is sound, indeed. And yet, despite that, I do not think that *this* man would be clever enough to dissemble and conceal his guilt. More like that he would trumpet it, for if he truly did the deed, he would believe 'twas the right deed he had done."

"*Enough!*" shouted Locke from the dais, bringing down the hammer. Once more, the room fell silent. "I shall ask you once again, Henry Mayhew, how do you answer to this charge?"

"I am not obligated to make you any answer," Mayhew replied haughtily. "You are no one to sit in judgment over me. If I am to answer to anyone, then I shall answer to God for all that I have done or not done. And to God I would say that I have had no hand in any murder, either of your son or that of any other man."

"And this is your defense?" Locke replied scornfully. "To perjure yourself before God?"

"I would not expect any defense at all in this outrageous mockery of a court," said Mayhew. He glanced around at the crowd, derision clearly written on his face. "Who, after all, among this scrofulous and motley gathering would rise to defend me?"

"I would," Shakespeare called out suddenly, getting to his feet.

Smythe stared at him, aghast. "*Will!* Have you lost your mind? Sit *down*, for God's sake!"

Shakespeare gave his head a brief shake. "Nay, Tuck," he said, keeping his voice low so that only Smythe could hear, "'tis neither you nor I for whom Shy Locke whets his knife. 'Tis Mayhew. We are but a means to his end. And I intend to thwart it if I can."

"What concern is this of yours?" demanded Locke, staring at him with a frown. "You were brought here as a witness, so that you could tell your story and depart. And yet you would undertake to speak for this man?"

"I would," said Shakespeare, stepping forward.

A buzz of curious conversation swept throughout the room, and Locke hammered several times for it to cease. "What is he to you?" he asked.

"In truth, Master Locke, he is naught to me," Shakespeare replied. "That is to say, not more than any other man nor less."

"So then why speak for him?"

"Because 'twould seem that someone must," said Shakespeare with a shrug. "After all, why bother with the fiction of a trial if no one is to speak for the accused? I am no friend of his, 'tis true, but then, neither is anyone else amongst this company. If what you wish for is revenge for your son's death, and if you are certain beyond any doubt at all that this man killed him, why then, take your revenge and kill him also. What is to stop you? But on the other hand, if what you wish is *justice* for your son, and if that is why you have convened this court of your compatriots, rather than merely to put on a show for them as they do down at the Paris Gardens, then someone must perforce speak for the accused, or else there *is* no justice, nor even any semblance of it. Would you not agree, my friends?" he added, turning to the audience and spreading out his arms to them.

The reaction was immediate. Many of them burst into applause; others still shouted their agreement, calling out such things as "Well said!" or "Aye, let him speak! Let him speak!" or "A trial! A trial! Let us have a proper trial!"

Locke hammered angrily upon the table, while Smythe noticed Moll Cutpurse smiling to herself. She met his gaze and gave him a wink.

It took a few minutes for order to be restored, and then Locke said, "Very well, player. You may speak for the accused. But mark you, this is no stage for you to prance upon. We shall have no jokes or tricks or Morris dances. This is a serious matter, and you shall comport yourself accordingly. Is that understood?"

"In every aspect and particular," said Shakespeare, giving him a small bow. "However, before we proceed, I would like to make but two requests of this fine court, with your permission."

"What sort of requests?" asked Locke with a frown.

"For the first, I should like merely to ask if the bonds of the accused could be removed," said Shakespeare. "Surely, they must chafe and pain him, and it does not seem to me as if he poses any threat to anyone given his present circumstances."

Locke made a casual waving motion with his hand. "Granted. Remove the bonds," he said.

Someone stepped forward and cut the ropes binding Mayhew's wrists.

"Thank you, sir, whoever you may be," said Mayhew, rubbing his sore wrists and staring at him curiously. "I do not know why you are trying to help me, but I am much obliged to you."

"Do not thank me yet," Shakespeare replied to him, in a low voice, "for you may yet find yourself ungrateful."

"And your second request?" asked Locke.

"I should like for my companion to be released," said Shakespeare.

"*Will!* What are you doing?" Smythe asked, shaking his head, but Shakespeare turned and held up a hand to him, admonishing him to be silent.

"In order to conduct a proper defense for the accused," Shakespeare continued, turning back to the dais, " 'twill be necessary for me to call some witnesses on his behalf. And at present, there are none in this chamber I can call. I should like to have permission to summon several to appear before us."

Once again, this brought on an excited murmuring among the audience. Without resorting to his hammer this time, Locke waited for it to die down of its own. His face bore a sour expression, while Moll Cutpurse and the two other masters of the guild clearly looked amused.

"I see," said Locke, after a few moments. "So you expect me to release your friend Smythe so that he can go and gather witnesses for the defense, or so you say, while in fact he may go and gather sheriff's men to come back here with him? Do you take me for an utter fool?"

"Nothing was further from my mind," said Shakespeare. "Why, the very last thing that I would wish to do is incur any enmity among *this* company. I think all here would understand how that could be unwise for a man in my position."

This brought on general laughter. Smythe was not laughing, however. He thought his friend had lost his senses, acting as if this were a play and the people all around him merely groundlings. Damn it, Will, he thought, all the world is *not* a stage!

"What I propose," Shakespeare continued, "is that my friend be released in the company of several members of this court, so that they may accompany him upon his errand. In that way, they would ensure he does it properly and returns, and at the same time they could function to persuade said witnesses to come and testify before this court, for it strikes me that such witnesses just might require some slight persuasion."

Again, this brought on laughter and more shouts of encouragement. Smythe saw Moll Cutpurse lean over toward Locke and say something in his ear. Locke listened for a moment, then nodded and banged his hammer several times to bid the audience be quiet.

"Very well, Master Shakespeare," he said. "The court has decided, in all fairness, to grant you your request. Your friend shall be allowed to leave to summon whatever witnesses you choose. You may confer with him in this regard and instruct him howsoe'er you wish. But mark you, he shall be accompanied, as you propose, by several members of this court, and if he should so much as attempt to give someone a signal or a message, or else attempt to break away from those we send to escort him, then things shall not go well with either him *or* you . . . for we know well who you are and where you may be found and what company you keep, and there shall be no hiding from the Thieves Guild, you may rest assured."

Shakespeare bowed. "I quite understand," he said. "And I do humbly thank this court for fairly granting my request."

"In the meantime," Locke continued, "we shall stand in recess for one hour, and then this court shall go forward with the prosecution. And when your witnesses are brought back to this court, *if* any are brought back to this court, then you may call them and state your case. You shall be given until midnight. If by then your witnesses have not appeared, then we shall conclude without them. You may now instruct your friend as to which witnesses you wish for him to summon to this court. Our esteemed colleague Moll Cutpurse will escort him, together with some members of her company, to make certain that things proceed accordingly."

"I thank the court," said Shakespeare, and hurried back to Smythe.

"You have completely lost your mind," said Smythe. "What in God's name do you think you are doing?"

"Trying to determine the truth," Shakespeare replied. "I had hoped to be done with this entire sad affair, but it seems that the fates have bound us up in it inextricably, and now the only thing to do is see it through. We must act quickly now, and think more quickly still, for time is of the essence. We have only until midnight. . . ."

Elizabeth was becoming exasperated. She had tried her best to explain to Portia about the danger she was in, but despite all of her efforts, Portia still refused to leave. Her eyes looked dark and sunken, she appeared gaunt from eating poorly, if she ate at all, and there was a haunted quality about her gaze that reminded Elizabeth of some frightened little animal. But for all that, she was stubborn and kept sitting in her chair and shaking her head that she did not wish to go.

"*You* try to reason with her," Elizabeth said to Winifred in frustration. "I am reaching the end of my rope. Another shake of that head and so help me, I shall scream!"

"You must calm yourself, Elizabeth, please," Winifred replied. "In her grief, perhaps she does not truly understand "

"Then *make* her understand, for goodness sake!" Elizabeth replied, throwing up her hands. "This is taking us entirely too much time! We do not have all night! You try to talk some sense into her while I go and pack her things!"

"Portia," Winifred said, crouching down before her and taking both her hands, "Portia, dear, please . . . listen to me. Elizabeth only has your best interests at heart, you know. We understand that you came here to be with her because you felt safe here. However, 'tis no longer safe for you here, can you understand that? Some terrible men came and took away your father, took him away I know not where, and I very much fear for his safety."

Portia simply looked away from her without saying a word.

Winifred took a deep breath and tightened her grip on the girl's hands. "Portia, dear, you *must* listen to me, *please*. Those men who came and broke into your house and tied me up and took your father . . . those men were asking about *you*. We believe that they were sent by Charles Locke . . . Thomas's father. Do you understand, Portia? He is an angry man, Portia, grief-stricken in his own way, just like you, and he wishes revenge for his son's death!"

She turned and looked at Winifred.

"You understand now, don't you?" Winifred continued earnestly. "We simply cannot remain here any longer. We have already tarried far too long. 'Tis growing late, and there is a chance that they may find us here, that they may find *you* here. Please, Portia, *please!* We must leave *now!*"

Portia looked down, nodded, then slowly stood.

"Good," said Winifred, feeling enormously relieved. "Come now, I shall help you with your cloak."

A short while later, they came downstairs, with Elizabeth carrying her bag.

"Is the coach still waiting?" Winifred asked nervously.

"He had better still be waiting, or he shall not receive the extra wages that I had promised him," Elizabeth replied, handing Winifred the bag. "Go on, I shall be with you presently. Let me first instruct the servants what to do and what to say should anybody come."

A few moments later, she pulled up the hood of her cloak and ran out into the rain. The coach was waiting, and Winifred and

Portia had already climbed inside. The door was open, and the coachman was already up and waiting in his seat, prepared to leave the moment she got in. Thank Heaven, she thought, we are still in time.

She called out their destination to the coachman, stepped up into the coach, and shut the door behind her. At once, the coachman gave a yell and whipped up the horses, and the coach moved off with a lurch and gathered speed.

With a shock, Elizabeth suddenly realized that both Winifred and Portia were sitting blindfolded in their seats, their hands bound together in their laps. And they were not alone.

"Good evenin'," said a dark-cloaked figure, sitting in the seat across from her, next to Winifred. Elizabeth gasped as she felt her bodkin quickly plucked from her belt inside her cloak. "Ye'll not be needin' that, methinks."

It took a moment for Elizabeth to get over her initial shock. Winifred sat beside the stranger, pale and frozen with fear. Portia sat stiff and immobile.

"Nice little blade, this. Bit small for serious work, else I just might be tempted. Tell ye what . . . be a good lass an' give me no trouble, an' I just might give it back to ye when we are done."

Elizabeth stared at her captor with sudden realization. "Why, you are a woman!" Winifred gasped with disbelief.

"I was last time I looked," Moll Cutpurse replied. "But then he is not," she added, jerking her head toward the coach window. Elizabeth looked and caught her breath as she saw a swarthy face grinning in at her. There was a man hanging on to the outside of the coach, "An' neither is he," Moll added yet again, jerking her head toward the other window, in the coach door where Elizabeth had gotten in. There, too, a man was clinging to the outside of the coach, leering in at them. "An' there are three more up top," said Moll, pointing at the roof. "So be a good lass an' put this on, eh?" She tossed a blindfold onto Elizabeth's lap.

Elizabeth hesitated, then picked it up with resignation and began to tie it on. "I know who you are," she said. "You are the infamous Moll Cutpurse. I have heard about you. And I believe I once saw you, at a wedding I attended."

"I do believe ye did," Moll replied, in her lilting Irish brogue. "'Twas a lovely double wedding, too. You were a friend o' the first couple, as I recall, an' I was a friend o' the second. I do not believe that we were ever introduced on that occasion, but 'tis nice to be remembered, just the same. And now hold out yer hands, if ye would be so kind?"

"We have a mutual friend, as well," Elizabeth continued, moistening her lips nervously as Moll finished tying up her hands. "I . . . I believe you know my friend Tuck Smythe?"

"I do, indeed," Moll replied, leaning back against the seat cushions. "That's him up there, drivin' the coach."

Elizabeth stiffened abruptly. "*What?*"

"Aye, he's drivin' the coach," repeated Moll. "We gave your coachman the rest o' the night off. So just relax an' enjoy the ride."

Elizabeth shook her head. "Nay, he could not be a part of this," she said. "He could *not!* You are lying!"

"If ye had taken a closer look afore ye got in, ye would have seen that I am tellin' ye the truth," said Moll. "But yer kind never do look at the workin' classes very much, do ye? Beneath yer notice, as it were. However, ye can rest assured, Tuck did not have any choice in this. We have his friend Will. We took them both, just as we took you."

"I thought you were a friend of his," Elizabeth said.

"I am," said Moll. "He's a fine lad. Strappin' young man like that, he should have been born Irish."

"Then why are you doing this?" Elizabeth asked.

"Because one o' our own was murdered," Moll replied. "An' we want justice."

"Justice," Elizabeth repeated softly, thinking back to what the cards had said at Granny Meg's. Disillusionment, bonds broken, misery and sorrow . . . it was all coming to pass.

"What will happen to us?" Winifred asked fearfully. "Where are we being taken?"

"To a trial," Moll replied. "An' this coach will come in right handy, thank ye kindly, for we have a few more people to pick up after we deliver you lot. 'Twill be a long night, methinks, but it promises to be an interestin' one."

Shakespeare sat and listened as the witnesses came forward to give their testimony. In one respect, at least, he found that Mayhew had been right. So far as any sort of judicial hearing was concerned, this one was a mockery. He had attended several trials before, back home in Stratford, and he had some notion of what proper procedures were. None were truly being followed here.

Criminals being criminals, they, too, had some notion of proper procedure in a trial, at least in an approximate sense, but as this was *their* trial, they followed their *own* procedure, and it had much more in common with the carnival atmosphere among the groundlings in a theatre yard than with a courtroom. Serving wenches circulated in the galleries and among the benches and the tables, carrying trays laden with breads and drinks and cheeses, all while testimony was being given, and on occasion a wench would be pulled down into a lap and bussed and squeezed until she squealed, which usually resulted in an outburst of raucous laughter from the onlookers, which in turn brought on another bout of hammer pounding from the dais.

Mayhew sat stiffly, shaking his head in disgust as he watched it all, appalled, and for the life of him, Shakespeare could not determine whether Mayhew was more frightened than outraged or more outraged than frightened. He surely had to realize that Shy Locke was out for blood, his blood, and that his chances of escaping this alive were very slim, indeed. And yet, he did not truly act afraid. Apprehension showed clearly on his features, and he seemed tense and strained, but he was not displaying fear. Could it be that he was truly brave? Or was it that he was simply resigned to the inevitable and did not wish to have this rabble see him cowering in fear before them? Perhaps it was that, his loss of dignity, that he feared more than he feared anything else, even death. Shakespeare realized he did not like this man, but at the same time he found him fascinating. This was a man to whom proper comportment and behavior was everything, a man to whom appearances and presentation mattered a great deal. And this was why, of course, he could not have suffered to have his daughter married to a Jew.

For himself, Shakespeare did not feel afraid. He had at first, but now he understood that he and Smythe did not really have anything to fear from this assemblage. They had committed no offense against the Thieves Guild, or even against Shy Locke himself. They had had no hand in the death of Thomas Locke, and his father understood that. Locke wanted his revenge, and they were merely there to be part of the process. But Shakespeare was convinced that in this case the process was misguided.

"Why are you helping me?" Mayhew had asked him, after Smythe had left upon his errand together with Moll Cutpurse and her men and the "trial" had stood in recess for a time. "Truly, why? You do not know me and I do not know you. We are nothing to each other. Why should you take this chance for me?"

"I do not believe that I am taking any great chance in rising to defend you," Shakespeare had replied. "'Tis not me they wish to harm. Shy Locke believes you killed his son, or else 'twas done upon your orders, one way or the other. For that, he hates you with all of his embittered soul and wishes nothing more than to cut out your heart and have his pound of flesh, to drink hot blood to give cold comfort to his desire for vengeance. I have very little import to his plan."

"So where do you fit in?" asked Mayhew, puzzled.

"I understand now that my friend and I were brought here to give testimony as to how he learned you had withdrawn consent for your daughter and his son to marry," Shakespeare answered. "We were the ones who brought him the news, for we had heard it from your son."

"You knew my son?" asked Mayhew. "You were his friends?"

Shakespeare shook his head. "We had but met that very morning," he said, "and we did not speak above half an hour. Perhaps not even that."

Mayhew looked even more perplexed. "I do not understand. Why, then, did you become involved in this?"

Shakespeare rolled his eyes and sighed. "I have asked myself that very question upon more than one occasion since this started," he replied.

"And what answer have you arrived upon?"

Shakespeare grimaced. "When I arrive upon an answer, I shall let you know."

"You play at words and speak in riddles," Mayhew said impatiently.

"I am a poet and a player. What would you have of me?"

"A straight answer, sirrah!"

"Very well, then, I shall trade you like for like. Did you kill Thomas Locke, or order the deed done?"

"Nay, sir, I did not."

Shakespeare stared into Mayhew's unflinching gaze. "'Strewth, it seems I do believe you."

"Why?"

"Because, sir, you have the manner of a lout, but not a murderer."

"You do not care for me."

"Not in the least."

"Yet you defend me."

"To the utmost."

"A straight answer, then, as you had promised. *Why?*"

"Because I do not think you did it."

"And that is why?"

"Aye, that is why."

"That does not seem reason enough to me," said Mayhew.

"Yet 'tis all the reason that I need," said Shakespeare.

"I do not understand," said Mayhew.

"Aye, I know. And more's the pity."

And so the trial began. One after another, the witnesses came forward, men and women not known to Shakespeare but apparently well known to the assemblage. Each of them gave testimony to the character of Thomas Locke, how they had known him as he grew from a child into a boy, and from a boy through his apprenticeship and into a young journeyman, how he had loved and honored both his father and his mother, and how a life of promise and success had seemed spread out before him. There was nothing there with which Shakespeare could take issue, and so he did not try. Through it all, Mayhew sat stonily, listening to all, apparently resigned to whatever fate they had in store for him. And as Shakespeare watched him, he decided that Mayhew was, indeed, afraid, but that to the very end, come what may, no matter what, he would not show it, for that would be the ultimate indignity for him. He was a puzzling man, detestable in many ways, and Shakespeare did not like him. But he did not wish to see him dead.

And then the prosecution called forward its last witness.

"The court calls Rachel Locke!"

Shakespeare sat forward on the edge of his seat. The boy's mother, he thought. And ironically, it struck him suddenly that all of this had started when he had told Smythe that he would like to meet a Jew. And now, finally, he would have his chance.

12

❋

IN HER YOUTH, THOUGHT SHAKESPEARE, Rachel Locke must have been very beautiful. She was beautiful still, though in a different way. The thick, long, braided hair that was once as black and lustrous as a raven's wing was heavily silvered now, though traces of the old hue still remained. The body that once was lithe and supple, with sensual, curvaceous hips, long legs, and ripe young breasts, was heavier and thicker now, yet still feminine and graceful in its carriage. Her dark, Mediterranean skin, once taut and smooth, now bore the lines of age, but they spoke less of time and toil than of experience and character. And the eyes, dark as chestnuts and wide as a fawn's, were still striking and exotic, although they spoke now of weariness and pain. She was dressed plainly, in a simple homespun gown, and did not attempt, as many women did, to compensate for lost youth with accumulated finery. The average man, perhaps, would not look twice at Rachel Locke now, Shakespeare thought, but the observant, thoughtful man would notice her . . . and stare.

The room fell silent as she came in and took her place upon the improvised stand, a small table and stool that had been placed before the dais. There had truly not been any silence in the room at all at any point during the proceedings, Shakespeare thought. It was like trying to conduct a trial in the middle of a tavern, which in effect was exactly what was being done. However, as Rachel Locke took her place, silence reigned supreme. The serving wenches stopped and watched her. No one spoke and no one moved. This was the grieving wife of one of their own, a mother who had lost her son. And the weight of her grief was palpable upon the entire assemblage.

She glanced up at her husband, and he merely nodded gravely. She folded her hands in her lap, and then her shoulders rose and fell as she took a deep breath and began.

"I shall not speak long," she said, the timbre of her voice clear and strong. She paused, considering a moment, then began again. "Many of you know me. And if you do not know me, then you know who I am . . . or at least what I am. I am a woman, and I am a wife. I am a mother, and I am a Jew. And but for that last, I would be thought as good as anyone among you. And yet for that last, I know that there are many who think me something less, even as this man—" she turned to stare straight at Henry Mayhew "—thinks me something less.

"This is not new to me," Rachel Locke continued. "I had grown accustomed to it throughout the years. I am what I am, nor would I be aught else. My people, for the most part, were driven from this country before I was ever born. Some were permitted to remain, however . . . so long as they kept their place and accepted the faith of Christianity. And yet, although their own faith was denied them and they were ordered to accept another, neither were they truly accepted as Christians by other Christians. So then, if they were not accepted by that faith which they were ordered to accept, what were they to accept themselves?

"If, in my heart, I have always remained true to the faith of my people, neither have I ever been false to the faith of others. I have never dishonored Christianity, nor have I ever dishonored any Christian. I have never hated any other faith, nor have I ever hated anyone for having a faith other than my own. And yet there are those who would profess that theirs is a faith of love who yet seem to have no love for those who do not share their faith.

"My son was a Christian." Her voice caught slightly, and Shakespeare saw that she had unclasped her hands and now gripped the folds of her gown tightly. "'Twas his father's faith, and thus he was raised a Christian. But to this man—" she turned once more toward Mayhew with a gaze of anthracite "—to this man he was a despised Jew, because his mother was a despised Jew. Indeed, to a Jew, descent is passed on through the mother. Yet how convenient was it for this one aspect of the Jewish faith to be accepted by this man, who did not accept or honor any other aspect of it? Until he knew that my son had been born of a Jewess, he had considered my son a fit mate for his daughter. He had been pleased to have him at his home, to sup with him at his table, and to introduce him to his friends. He gave his consent for his daughter's marriage to my son, and told Thomas that he would be proud to have him for a son-in-law. And then . . . he discovered that Thomas's mother was a Jew.

"The consent for the marriage was at once withdrawn, and Thomas was forbidden by Henry Mayhew ever to see or speak with his daughter again. And now. . . ." She swallowed hard, having difficulty speaking, but she gathered herself together and continued. "And now my son is dead, because he was in love with Portia Mayhew and dared plan to elope with her. And there before you this man sits . . . the architect of a mother's grief and devastation, and the utter ruin of her life, angrily demanding to know who she is to judge him. After all, who is she but a heathen Jew? And yet, 'tis not only a woman, a wife, a mother, and a Jew who is crying out for justice." She turned to gaze at her husband on the dais. "'Tis also a man, a husband, a father, and a Christian who has likewise lost his son and cries out for revenge. Yet who is *he* to judge him, this man asks? Indeed, who are *any* of us to judge him? Who are any of us, after all, compared to the likes of him? We are poor, and he is rich. We are of the humble working class, and he is of the vaunted gentry. We are those whose duty is to serve, and he is one whose due is to have servants. We are very different in his eyes. And yet have we not eyes to see with for ourselves? Have we not hands, organs, dimensions, senses, affections, passions? Can we not be fed with the same food and hurt with the same weapons? Are we not subject to the same diseases, healed by the same means, warmed and cooled by the same winter and summer as he is? If you prick us, do we not bleed? If you tickle us, do we not laugh? If you poison us, do we not die? And if you wrong us . . . shall we not revenge?"

She stared at Mayhew with a look to freeze the soul, her voice trembling with emotion. "If we are like you in the rest, then we will resemble you in that," she said. She stood and raised her hand, pointing an accusatory finger at him. "The villainy you teach me I will execute," she cried. "Thou stick'st a dagger in me! I shall never see my son again!"

Mayhew's face was white. He sat stiffly, facing her, and yet he did not look away. And Shakespeare wondered, could a guilty man have faced such a gaze unflinchingly?

She closed her eyes and turned away, struggling to keep from breaking down. There was not a sound within the chamber. She won her struggle and managed to compose herself. Then she straightened, took a deep breath, squared her shoulders, and slowly left the room. For a moment that seemed to stretch on and on, no one spoke. Then Shy Locke looked at Shakespeare and said, "And now 'tis your turn to speak for the accused."

Shakespeare stood, thinking it would be impossible to follow on the heels of such a speech. He cleared his throat and faced the dais. "With respect to this court, I would like to request a pause in the proceedings to see if my friend has arrived with all of our witnesses, so that we may plead our cause."

Locke stared at him, clearly not wanting to grant the request, but at the same time not seeing any compelling reason to deny him. He could easily have done so anyway, thought Shakespeare. It was his guild and his court, after all. The fact that he was hesitating was encouraging, indeed. It showed that for all that he might be a thief, he was a fair one.

"Granted," Locke said after a moment's consideration. "Fifteen minutes. And then you must proceed." He slammed the hammer on the table.

Shakespeare glanced around, not certain where to go. After all, he had been brought to this place blindfolded. Fortunately, someone came to his rescue.

"This way," a young man said, coming up beside him. "Moll has just returned with your friend and the last of the people that you sent them for."

"They are *all* here?" Shakespeare asked as he followed the man down a narrow corridor, scarcely able to believe it. "However did you manage it?"

The man simply shrugged. "We persuaded them all to come."

"Indeed," said Shakespeare, partly to himself. "I do hope that you did not persuade too strenuously."

The man shrugged once more. "Well, some required a bit more persuasion than others. But they were all agreeable in the end."

"I am quite sure they were," muttered Shakespeare as they entered a small room. As he came in, he saw Tuck and Moll Cutpurse, together with Elizabeth Darcie, a distraught-looking young woman who had to be Portia Mayhew, and an older woman whom he did not know. He frowned.

"And who is this lady?" he asked.

"Madame Winifred Fitzwalter," Smythe replied. "Henry Mayhew's intended."

"But I did not ask you to bring her," said Shakespeare, turning with a puzzled look from Smythe to Moll Cutpurse.

"They were all together," Moll replied with a shrug. "And after all, if Mayhew is the man that she intends to marry, then why should she not be present at his trial? I shall leave you to make your preparations. I should be getting back out to the hall."

"Trial?" asked Winifred, after Moll left the room. "What do you mean? What trial? What has Henry done?"

"He is being tried for the murder of Thomas Locke," said Shakespeare.

Winifred gasped.

"Tried by whom?" Elizabeth asked. "And by whose authority? Where are we? What is this place?"

"As to where we are," Shakespeare replied, "I cannot say, for we were brought here blindfolded, as I surmise were you. As to what this place is, I would venture to say 'tis an inn, either within the city walls or perhaps across the river, in the Liberties. In either case, we are certainly close by the city, if no longer within its boundaries. As to by whose authority the trial is conducted, 'tis not so much a matter of authority as of main force, though I suppose that one could argue they are much the same. Wherever this place may be, 'tis the meeting hall of the Thieves Guild, and the trial is being held by them, under the direction of Charles Locke, Thomas's father, also known as Shy Locke."

"Dear God," Winifred said, bringing her hands up to her mouth. "They are going to kill him!"

"I would say that there seems to be an excellent chance of that, unless somehow I can do something to dissuade them," Shake-speare replied.

"What is your role in this?" Elizabeth asked.

"Tuck and I were brought here to give testimony, it seems, to lend an air of credence to this trial. We were the ones who had brought Shy Locke the news that his son was planning to elope, and 'tis for that reason, Locke believes, his son was killed."

"And now Will is defending Mayhew," Smythe said, "because he does not believe him to be guilty of the crime."

"But this is madness!" said Elizabeth, glancing from Smythe to Shakespeare. "This is not a real trial or a real court! There is no legal authority here! These people are criminals!"

"Be that as it may," said Shakespeare, "they are very serious in their intent. And 'twould also appear, strange as it may seem, that they are seeking justice and, in so·doing, are actually striving to be fair."

"Fair!" said Elizabeth.

"Aye, believe it or not," Shakespeare replied. "'Tis curious. They are a rough and raucous bunch, and yet, for all that, this is a serious matter to them and, in their own way, they are approaching it as seriously as they know how. And 'twould appear that they are striving to be fair, perhaps because fairness has so often been denied them. And therein lies Henry Mayhew's only hope."

"What do you intend to do?" Elizabeth asked.

"I must do my best to find the truth," said Shakespeare.

Elizabeth frowned. "How?"

Shakespeare sighed. "By seeking to discover lies, perhaps. I do not yet know for certain. But I must do it now, tonight." He turned to Smythe. "I am told the others are all here, as well?"

Smythe nodded. "They are being kept waiting in separate rooms."

"What others?" asked Elizabeth.

"You shall find out in due course," said Shakespeare. He turned to Portia, who had been listening to it all without saying a word. "Mistress Mayhew, you shall shortly be brought out into a hall that is filled with people, people of a rather rough sort that may frighten you, but you must not be frightened. I shall have to put some questions to you, questions that you may not find very pleasant, but you shall have to answer them. I have every confidence that you can do that."

"Oh, for Heaven's sake, Will! She has been out of her wits with grief!" Elizabeth exclaimed.

"You shall not be able to speak for her out there, Elizabeth," said Shakespeare. "So I suggest you do not try to do so here." He turned back to Portia, who simply stared back at him. "All I am asking is that you speak the truth," he said to her. "And if you will not do it for me, or even for your father, do it for Thomas. You shall honor his memory in doing so."

The door was flung open. "Right," said the man who had brought Shakespeare from the hall. "Time to go."

They were led back to the hall.

The masters of the guild were all at their places on the dais. Moll Cutpurse had rejoined them. Mayhew sat where Shakespeare had left him, at the table. He looked a little haggard, but someone had brought him a pitcher of ale and some bread and cheese. He had not touched the bread and cheese, but he had partaken liberally of the ale. His tankard was half full and the pitcher was half empty.

"Do not go getting yourself drunk," Shakespeare told him.

"Why the hell not?" asked Mayhew with a grimace.

Shakespeare opened his mouth, then shut it once again. "'Strewth, you have a point. I cannot think of a single reason."

"Nor could I," said Mayhew. He quaffed the remainder of the ale in his tankard and poured himself another.

Locke struck his hammer on the table several times. "Master Shakespeare, are you prepared to begin?"

"I am," Shakespeare replied, rising to his feet.

"Proceed, then."

"I should like to call for my first witness my good friend Tuck Smythe," he said.

Tuck got up and walked over to the seat placed before the dais. "Do you swear before God, upon pain of your immortal soul, that what you say before this court shall be the truth?" asked Locke.

"I do," said Smythe.

"Be seated."

"Would you please give your full name to this assemblage?" Shakespeare asked him.

"Symington Smythe III," said Tuck.

Winifred caught her breath and stared at him with astonishment.

"And what is your occupation?"

"I am a player with Lord Strange's Men, and a sometime smith and farrier."

"Could you explain to this court how it happened that you met Thomas Locke and what was the nature of your acquaintance?"

"You and I had gone together to the shop of Ben Dickens, the armorer," said Smythe, "who is a friend of ours. Whilst there, we met Thomas Locke, another friend of Ben's, who had arrived in a state of great agitation because the father of his betrothed, Portia Mayhew, had just withdrawn his consent to the marriage and forbidden him from seeing her again."

"Did he say why this consent had been withdrawn?" asked Shakespeare.

"Because his mother was a Jew," said Smythe.

"And how did Thomas respond to this?"

"He was most distressed. He said he loved this girl with all his heart and soul and could not live without her. He could not bear the thought of never seeing her again."

"And what was *your* response to this?" asked Shakespeare.

Smythe hesitated slightly. "I advised him to elope with her."

"Indeed?" said Shakespeare. "And did you know him well?"

Smythe hesitated yet again. "Nay, we had never before met."

"And yet you took it upon yourself to advise him to elope?"

"Aye."

"Were you acquainted at all with his intended, Mistress Mayhew?"

"I was not."

"You had never met her nor even laid eyes upon her, as it happens, is that not so?"

" 'Tis so."

"And yet you still advised Thomas Locke, whom you had only just met, to elope with this girl whom you had never met?"

Smythe spoke under his breath. "Will, what the devil are you doing?"

"Answer the question, please."

"I did so advise him, aye," said Smythe with a grimace.

"Are you ordinarily in the habit of advising strangers to elope?"

"Not ordinarily."

"So then why in this case?"

"Because . . . because I understood how he must have felt, I suppose," said Smythe.

Elizabeth sat up a little straighter in her seat.

"Because something of a somewhat similar nature, so to speak, had occurred in your own life?"

Smythe gave him a hard look. "Aye," he said after a moment.

Elizabeth looked down.

"And what happened then?" asked Shakespeare.

"Thomas said that he would follow my advice and left," Smythe replied. "And then Ben took me to task for not minding my own business. As did you."

"I did, indeed," said Shakespeare. "And what happened then?"

"Upon listening to you and Ben, I decided that perhaps I had spoken rashly, and we—that is, you and I, not Ben—went together to seek out Thomas's parents and inform them of what their son intended."

"The rest you know," said Shakespeare, turning to face Locke upon the dais. "But for the benefit of this assemblage, we came to you and told you what had happened, whereupon you requested us to deliver a message to your son, asking him to come and see you. When we tried to do so, we found, much to our profound regret, that young Thomas had been slain." He turned back to Smythe. "Thank you, Tuck. If it please the court, I am finished with this witness."

"You may step down," said Locke to Smythe.

"I would now like to call forth Mistress Elizabeth Darcie," Shakespeare said.

Elizabeth stepped up to take the stand and was sworn.

"Elizabeth," said Shakespeare, "would you please tell this court your connection with this sad situation?"

"Portia Mayhew is a friend of mine," Elizabeth replied. "Our fathers know one another."

"Would you say that you are very close friends?" Shakespeare asked.

"I would not say that we were very close," Elizabeth replied, "which is to say, I like Portia, but I have not known her very long."

"You knew she was betrothed to Thomas Locke?"

"I did."

"And how did you discover that her father had withdrawn his consent for her to marry?"

"When she came to my home, very upset, and delivered the news to Antonia and myself."

"And who is Antonia?"

"She is a friend of mine, and the wife of Harry Morrison, one of my father's business acquaintances. She was visiting with me at the time."

"And how did you respond to this news?" asked Shakespeare.

"Well, we sought to comfort her, of course," Elizabeth replied.

"And was that all?"

"Not entirely."

"As it happens, 'twas your suggestion to her that she should elope with Thomas, was it not?"

"It was."

This brought a reaction from the assemblage, and Locke hammered for silence, or at least some reasonable semblance of it.

"Curious," said Shakespeare. "'Twould seem that everyone wanted this young couple to elope, save for their parents. And what did you do then?"

"We took a coach and went in search of Thomas," Elizabeth replied.

"And by 'we,' you mean yourself, Antonia, and Portia, is that not so?"

"'Tis so."

"Where did you go?"

"To the shop of Master Leffingwell, where Thomas was employed," Elizabeth replied.

"And what did you discover when you went there?"

"We discovered that Thomas was not there," Elizabeth replied. "Master Leffingwell told us that he had not come in to work that day."

"And was that all he told you?"

Elizabeth frowned. "I believe so."

"Allow me to refresh your memory. Did you not know that Thomas had a room just across the street in the cul-de-sac, above the mercer's shop?"

"Oh. Aye, we did. That is to say, I did not know it, Portia did. But we did not go there, because Master Leffingwell also told us that he had sent one of his apprentices there earlier to see if Thomas was at home, and he was not."

"And so, not seeing any reason to do otherwise, you took him at his word and returned home, thinking to find Thomas later, perhaps the following day. At what point did you discover he was dead?"

"The very next day," Elizabeth replied, "when the sheriff's men came to my house to question us."

"And why did they wish to question you?"

"Because Master Leffingwell had told them we were at his shop, seeking Thomas."

"Portia was with you at the time the sheriff's men arrived?"

"Aye, she was. She had spent the night with me at my home."

"And how did she respond to this tragic news?"

"As you may well imagine, she was horrified and struck with grief. She fled the room, sobbing."

"And the sheriff's men, of course, did not pursue her to press her any further."

"I should say not!"

"After they left, however, I should imagine that you went to her at once, out of concern?"

"I did, indeed."

"And did she say anything to you about Thomas's murder?"

Elizabeth moistened her lips and nodded.

"She told you, did she not, that she believed her father was responsible?"

"She did."

"And did you believe her?"

Elizabeth hesitated.

"Elizabeth . . . did you believe her when she said she thought her father was the one responsible?"

"I did," Elizabeth replied.

"You are doing a bloody marvelous job," said Mayhew, with a disgusted look at Shakespeare. "Keep it up!"

Locke slammed down his hammer. "Silence!"

"Did you have any knowledge, other than what Portia told you, that led you to believe that Henry Mayhew murdered Thomas Locke, or else paid to have it done?" asked Shakespeare.

Elizabeth moistened her lips again. "Nay, I did not."

"But you believed it just the same?"

Elizabeth nodded. "Aye. I did believe it."

"Might I ask why?"

Elizabeth frowned. "Well . . . who else could have done it?"

"The fact is, anyone in London *could* have done it," Shakespeare replied. "What you mean to ask is 'Who *would* have done it?' Is that not so?"

"Aye. What is the difference?"

"Oh, there is a very great difference," Shakespeare said. "A very great difference, indeed. There could have been any number of people who *could* have killed him. The question is, who would have had a *reason* to do so? Aside from Henry Mayhew, that is."

Elizabeth shook her head. "I am sure I do not know."

"Well, that is what we must endeavor to find out," said Shakespeare. "I am finished with this witness. I would next like to call Master Leffingwell, the tailor."

Elizabeth stepped down, and Master Leffingwell was brought out, dressed in his nightclothes. He looked very frightened and disheveled. As soon as he was sworn, Shakespeare tried to reassure him.

"Do not be afraid," he said. "All you need to do is tell the truth, and you should be home in bed within the hour. Now, please tell the court your name and occupation."

"M-M-Master William Leffingwell," he stammered. "I am a t-tailor."

"No need to be afraid," Shakespeare told him once more. "No one shall harm you. All you need do is answer a few questions. What was your relationship with Thomas Locke?"

Leffingwell looked terrified, but he managed to compose himself enough to answer. "He . . . he worked for me. He was my apprentice."

"And you had known him for the entire seven years of his apprenticeship, of course, is that not so?"

Leffingwell nodded. "Aye, I did."

"You were generally satisfied with his work, were you not?"

"I was, indeed, aye."

"So much so that when he completed his apprenticeship, you offered him a position as a journeyman tailor in your shop, is that not so?"

"Indeed, 'twas so, indeed. He was an excellent tailor. I was pleased to have him in my shop."

"And in all the time you knew him, did you know him to have any enemies who may have wished him dead?" asked Shakespeare.

"Nay, not Thomas!" Leffingwell replied emphatically, shaking his head. "He was a fine lad, a fine lad, indeed, well loved by everyone!"

"Would it be fair to say that you never knew him to have any enemies at all?"

"Nay, none at all. None at all. He was an excellent young man. He got on well with everyone."

"So then you were surprised when you learned that he was murdered?"

"Oh, I was astonished! 'Twas a horrible thing, a horrible thing, indeed! I could not imagine who would have done such a thing!"

"You knew he was betrothed?"

"I knew that, aye. He often spoke of it."

"And did you know the young woman to whom he was betrothed?"

Leffingwell shook his head. "Nay, I cannot say I did. He had mentioned her name a number of times, and I . . . I think she may have come to the shop once, but in truth, I cannot say I recall, other than the day she came with those two other women, seeking him. And that must have been the very day he. . . ."

"The day he was killed," said Shakespeare.

Leffingwell looked down and nodded.

"You told the young ladies on that day that Thomas had not come in to work and was not at home," said Shakespeare. "Just as you told us the very same thing. How did you know that he was not at home?"

"I had sent one of my apprentices over to his room to see if perhaps he had fallen ill, and the lad returned and said he was not at home."

"But in fact, he *was* there," Shakespeare said. "The boy you sent merely knocked upon the door, did he not, and when there was no answer, he returned to say that Thomas was not at home. But had he actually tried the door, as we did when we went there ourselves shortly thereafter, he would have found it open, and he would have found that Thomas was already dead. Thank you, Master Leffingwell. I am sorry to have disturbed your rest and troubled you. You may go home now."

As a much relieved Leffingwell was escorted out of the chamber, Shakespeare went over to where Smythe sat and whispered in his ear. Smythe glanced up at him sharply, then nodded and left the room, accompanied by one of Moll's men.

"You have not made much of an argument for the innocence of the accused," said Locke. "Have you any other witnesses to call?"

"I have, if it please the court," said Shakespeare.

"Get on with it, then."

"I call Mistress Antonia Morrison," Shakespeare said.

Elizabeth's eyes grew wide, and she spun around in her seat as Antonia was escorted in. Until that moment, she had not known that Antonia had been brought here, as well. Like Leffingwell, she looked frightened as they brought her in, but unlike him, she was fully dressed. When she saw Elizabeth, she looked a bit relieved, though still apprehensive.

"Please tell this court your name," said Shakespeare.

"My name is Antonia Morrison," she replied.

"Do you know where you are?" asked Shakespeare. "I do not mean exactly where, for I know that you were brought here blindfolded. I mean do you know what this place is?"

She nodded, gravely. "The meeting hall of the Thieves Guild."

"And you have been told why you have been brought here?"

"To testify at the trial of Henry Mayhew for the murder of Thomas Locke," she replied.

"So then you understand the import of all this, and that you must, above all, tell the truth?"

She nodded. "Aye, I do."

Shakespeare looked up and saw that Smythe had returned, together with the man he had left with, as well as several others. He nodded.

"Very well, then. What is your relationship with Portia Mayhew?"

"She is my friend."

"A close friend?"

"Well, she is more Elizabeth Darcie's friend than mine. 'Tis through Elizabeth that we had met."

"Did you know her father?"

"Nay, I did not."

"So then would it be correct to say that you have not known Portia Mayhew for very long?"

"Aye, 'twould be correct."

"And did you know Thomas Locke?"

"Nay, I did not. I knew of him, for Portia had spoken of him often, but we had never met. And now, I fear, we never will."

"Indeed," said Shakespeare, nodding sympathetically. "Where were you when you first learned that Portia's father had withdrawn his consent for her marriage?"

"I was with Elizabeth Darcie at her home."

"And Portia was there with you?"

"She arrived afterwards."

"After you did?"

"Aye, that is so."

"She was upset when she arrived?"

"Very much so," said Antonia. "She was in tears and most distraught."

"Because her father had withdrawn his consent for her to marry Thomas?"

Antonia nodded. "Aye, that is so."

"And did she say why?"

Antonia nodded again. "Because Thomas's mother was a Jewess."

Mayhew shifted uncomfortably in his seat.

"Why did she come to Elizabeth Darcie's house?"

"Because Elizabeth was her friend, and she was distressed and in great need of a friend."

"Whose idea was it in the first place that Portia should elope with Thomas?"

"'Twas Elizabeth who had suggested it," Antonia replied.

"And what did you think of this idea?"

"Well . . . I thought 'twas rather ill advised, to be honest."

"Indeed? You did not find it . . . romantic?"

"I found it rather foolish, if you must know," said Antonia. "Of course, I did not say so at the time."

"Why not?"

"Well, I did not wish to seem lacking in sympathy. Portia was very much upset, and I did not wish to make matters any worse for her."

"I see," said Shakespeare. "'Twas most considerate of you. Why did you believe that the elopement would be ill advised?"

"Because if she and Thomas were to have run away together, they would afterwards have been penniless," Antonia said. "How would they have lived? What would have become of her? Would she have been forced to find work as a laundress or a serving wench? What sort of life would that have been for the daughter of a gentleman?"

"A life with the man she loved, perhaps," said Shakespeare.

"Some may find contentment in such a life. Others may have greater needs. Your husband is a very wealthy man, I understand, is that not so?"

"Harry has been very successful in his life," Antonia replied. "We are very comfortable."

"He is also a good many years older than you, is that not so?"

"Aye. But why do you ask? 'Tis not unusual for men to marry women younger than themselves."

"Nay, 'tis not, indeed," said Shakespeare. He glanced back toward where Smythe stood together with the men who had come back with him. Smythe gave him an emphatic nod. "Especially wealthy gentlemen," he added. "An older man, well settled in his life and in his habits, can certainly provide a secure and comfortable life for a beautiful young woman. But if he is much older, he may not be able to provide *everything* that a beautiful young woman may desire, is that not so?"

Antonia frowned. "I am not sure what you mean."

"I mean that a beautiful young woman like yourself, married to a man many years her senior, may not be able to have all of her desires met. She may have certain needs that he cannot, by virtue of his age, fulfill, is that not so?"

Antonia stiffened. "Your comments are impertinent, sir."

"Ah, well, I would suggest to you that my comments are most pertinent, indeed," said Shakespeare. "Have you ever had a lover, Mistress Morrison?"

"You are a bounder, a lout, and a scoundrel, sir," she replied. "How dare you?"

Elizabeth held her breath.

"What if I were to tell you, Mistress Morrison, that I happen to know that you are an adulteress?"

She rose to her feet, her hands clenched into fists. "Then I would call you an impudent rascal and a villainous liar!"

"So then you deny that you were having an affair with Thomas Locke?"

Elizabeth gasped. Winifred stared, open-mouthed. And Portia sat stiffly, her gaze fixed upon Antonia unwaveringly.

"Of course, I deny it, you worm! I told you that I did not even know him!"

"You had never met him?"

"*Never!*"

"I would ask you to look upon these two men," said Shakespeare, beckoning to Smythe, who came forward with two burly fellows. "Have you ever seen either of these two men before?"

Antonia glanced toward them contemptuously and looked away. "I have never laid eyes upon them."

"Ah, but they have laid eyes upon you," said Shakespeare. "Gentlemen, would you be so kind as to tell this court your names?"

"My name is Evan Drury," said one of the two men, stepping forward.

"And mine is Ian Davies," said the other.

"And what is your occupation?" Shakespeare asked.

"We are paid to act as guards in the street where Master Leffingwell, the tailor, Master Jefferies, the mercer, and Masters Hollowell and Jennings, the silk merchants, have their shops," said Drury.

Antonia turned pale.

"Have you ever seen this woman before?" asked Shakespeare.

"Aye, many times," said Davies.

"Where did you see her?"

"In the street where we are paid to sit and guard the shops," said Drury.

"Specifically, in what circumstances did you see her?"

"She often went to visit the young gentleman who lived above Master Jefferies's shop," said Drury.

"This would be Thomas Locke?" asked Shakespeare.

"Aye, sir. We saw them together upon more than one occasion," Davies said.

"And did they seem as if they knew one another?"

"Oh, I would say they knew one another very well, indeed, sir," Davies replied with a smirk.

"So you would also say that they most likely knew one another often?" Shakespeare asked.

"I would venture to say they did, sir," Davies replied, grinning. "I would venture to say so, indeed."

The reaction of the audience was instantaneous and tumultuous. Locke hammered away upon the table repeatedly, trying to restore order. Antonia stood absolutely motionless, white as a ghost. Elizabeth simply sat there, numbly shaking her head with disbelief. Winifred was speechless.

"*Lies!*" screamed Antonia, her voice rising above the din. "*Lies! Lies! Foul lies! These men have been paid to lie about me!*"

"*Silence!*" Locke shouted, hammering upon the table again and again. "*Silence, I say!*"

"I call Portia Mayhew!" said Shakespeare.

Slowly, Portia stood. For a moment, she and Antonia simply stared at one another. The room became very still. Shakespeare turned his back upon Antonia and came over toward Portia.

"When did you learn that Thomas and Antonia were lovers?" he asked her gently.

She kept her gaze firmly fixed upon Antonia. "The day he told me that she was pregnant with his child," she replied. She winced and brought her hand up to touch her ear.

"And what day was that?" asked Shakespeare.

"The day I killed him," she replied softly. She winced once more and shook her head several times.

There was a collective gasp in the room.

"Oh, my God," Elizabeth murmured.

Mayhew turned to face his daughter with astonished disbelief. "Nay, it cannot be!" he said.

"Tell us what happened, Portia," Shakespeare said. "Please."

"He confessed to me that he and Antonia had been lovers," she replied in a flat tone. "He said that she had seduced him, and that he had not been able to resist. He begged for my forgiveness and said that he was weak."

Once more, she winced, as if with pain, and touched her ears.

"He said that a man had needs . . . and then he told me that Antonia was pregnant with his child, and had threatened to tell my father unless he helped her to be rid of it. So he took her to see a cunning woman, and obtained for her a brew of pennyroyal and mugwort that would banish the child before it quickened. . . ."

She bit her lower lip and shook her head once more, wincing as if with pain.

"And then he told me that it was finished with Antonia and that it did not matter, but that all the trouble he had gone to would be in vain if I did not run away with him at once, because my father had discovered that his mother was a Jew and had forbidden us to marry."

There was not a sound within the room. No one spoke. Nobody moved.

"And what happened then?" asked Shakespeare softly.

"I felt as if my world had crumbled all around me," she said wearily. "I turned away from him . . . my head was spinning . . . and then I saw his dagger where he had laid it down upon the table . . . there was a roaring in my ears, a terrible roaring, like the wind . . . a sound so loud . . . so very, very loud . . . oh, I hear it still . . . I hear it still . . . It will not go away!" She brought her hands up to her ears to block out a sound that only she could hear. "Make it go away! Please, make it go away!"

She sank to her knees upon the floor, rocking back and forth, her hands covering her ears.

"Make it go away!" she whimpered. "Please, make it go away!"

"Oh, Portia!" Mayhew cried, crouching at her side and putting his arms around her. "My poor Portia!"

Charles Locke rose to his feet, staring down at her, holding the hammer clutched tightly in his fist. Then he looked down at it, dropped it on the table, and walked out of the room without a word.

Antonia still stood there, as if rooted to the spot, staring at Portia with horror and dismay. Mayhew sobbed quietly as he held his daughter, who seemed no longer able to hear him. Or anything else.

Smythe came up to Shakespeare and took him by the arm. "However did you guess that she had done it?" he asked.

Shakespeare shook his head. "I had no idea," he said. "'Strewth, I thought Antonia had killed him."

EPILOGUE

✳

"AND SO WE WERE all blindfolded once again, and then taken back to where they found us," Shakespeare said. "Tuck and I were dropped off on London Bridge. Elizabeth and Winifred were taken to their homes, as were all the others, I would assume."

"And what became of Portia Mayhew and her father?" asked John Hemings.

"Well, Portia will likely live out the remainder of her days in Bedlam," Shakespeare said. "And as for Mayhew . . . Shy Locke could not truly blame him for the death of his son. He knew that what happened to Henry Mayhew's daughter shall haunt him evermore. Rachel Locke had lost her son. And now, in a different way, Mayhew has lost his daughter. Mayhap Winifred shall be of some comfort to him."

"'Tis a tragedy worthy of the Greeks," Gus Phillips said, shaking his head.

"Indeed," said Shakespeare. "No one was truly blameless in this sad affair. 'Tis one of those tales where in the end, the stage is littered with victims."

"Truly, not even Marlowe could have penned a more dramatic tale," said Tom Pope.

"I am beginning to grow rather tired of hearing about Marlowe," Shakespeare replied testily.

"Indeed, he does seem to vex you. It does not seem as if the Rose Theatre is big enough for both of you," said Smythe with a smile.

"It does rather make one miss the good old days at our old theatre with the Burbages," said Shakespeare.

"Hark! Did I hear someone mention my name?" a ringing voice called out from behind them.

"*Dick!*" said Smythe.

They all turned as Richard Burbage came up to their table, grinning from ear to ear. "Well met, my friends! Well met!"

"Well met, Dick!" Hemings exclaimed, jumping up and clapping him upon the back. "'Tis good to see you once again, old friend! How goes it at the Theatre?"

"Well, 'tis funny you should ask," said Burbage. "I shall tell you how goes it at the Theatre. The Theatre *goes,* is how it goes!"

"The Theatre goes?" said Pope, raising his eyebrows. "What do you mean it goes?"

"It *goes* is precisely what I mean," said Burbage with a big grin. He winked at them. "It goes straight across the river!"

"What goes across the river?" Smythe asked with a frown.

"The Theatre does!" said Burbage, slapping him on the back with a laugh. "Listen well, my friends. Are you all up for a bit of mischief?"

"Always," Speed replied. "What did you have in mind?"

"Just this: You will recall, no doubt, our old adversary, our money-grubbing landlord? Well, after all of his repeated threats, the rascal has finally decided not to renew our lease. And so, since he owns the land upon which the Theatre sits, he thinks in this way to seize the Theatre for himself, the bounder! But whilst he may own the *land,* my father and I own the *building.* And so, my friends . . . we are going to move it!"

"*What?*" said Shakespeare. "Move the entire theatre, do you mean?"

"Precisely!" Burbage said.

"But . . . how the devil do you plan on doing that?"

"We are going to tear it down completely, and then move the timbers by boat across the river to Southwark, where we shall use them to build a brand-new theatre, even better than the first!"

"You mean the one you told us you had planned?" asked Smythe.

"The very one," Burbage replied. "I had told you that the day would come when we would all play upon the same stage once again, did I not? Well, that day is here! And that very stage is now going to be built! We are going to construct the Globe, my friends!"

"When?" asked Shakespeare.

"It begins tonight!" said Burbage.

"*Tonight?*" they all said at once.

"We must move swiftly, like the wind!" Burbage said. "We must have the building completely torn down by the morning, and the timbers loaded up on boats and floated 'cross the river afore our landlord can seize the property! The carpenters are standing by! What do you say, my friends? Are you with me?"

"We are with you!" Smythe replied at once, getting up from his seat.

"We are your very men!" said Shakespeare, rising to join him.

"Come then, my friends, and let us all away!" said Burbage. "And together we shall confound the landlord come the break of day!"

AFTERWORD

THE MERCHANT OF VENICE, upon which this novel is rather loosely based, is without a doubt the most controversial of Shakespeare's plays. It is difficult, even for those who seem willing to excuse Shakespeare anything, to get around its anti-Semitic content. In the words of Harold Bloom, "One would have to be blind, deaf, and dumb not to recognize that Shakespeare's grand, equivocal comedy *The Merchant of Venice* is nevertheless a profoundly anti-Semitic work." Bloom does go on to say, however, that the question of whether or not Shakespeare was personally anti-Semitic is open to reasonable doubt. This sort of thing is not uncommon among Shakespearean scholars, actually. Most of them do it, this bet-hedging, talking out of both sides of their mouth. It's as if they want to have their cake and eat it, too.

They wouldn't be caught dead trying to assert that the portrayal of Shylock is *not* anti-Semitic (one can only imagine the academic tarring-and-feathering that would follow, the vituperation in the "little magazines," the howling and clothes-rending at teachers' conferences, the sudden denials of tenure, and so forth), but at the same time, they can't quite bring themselves to say that Shakespeare actually hated Jews, because then they would leave themselves open to the charge of having an anti-Semitic writer in their curriculum, and we certainly couldn't have *that*. (Look what hap-

pened to Mark Twain.) Of course, this leaves them in a rather awkward position—somewhere between a rock and a hard place, intel-
lectually speaking. Even Jewish academics seem to suffer from this
problem. They seem to want to say, "Well, all right, the *play* was
anti-Semitic, or at least the character of Shylock was, but just
because Shakespeare may have written an anti-Semitic play or character does not necessarily mean he was *personally* anti-Semitic."
Well, in a word . . . bull.

Not being an academic type, I don't have any problem saying
what I think. And what I think is that Shakespeare was probably no
more and no less anti-Semitic than any other Englishman of his
time. Which is to say, yes, he was. I think that could probably safely
be said of most Elizabethans. And it could also safely be said that
most Elizabethans wouldn't have known any more about a Jew
than they would about a Martian. As Isaac Asimov has pointed out
in his outstanding *Asimov's Guide to Shakespeare* (which should
really be a required text in *any* course on Shakespeare), neither
Shakespeare nor his audience had any firsthand knowledge of Jews,
because the Jews were kicked out of England by Edward I—well
before Shakespeare's time—and they were not allowed to return
until the time of Oliver Cromwell, which was well after Shakespeare's death. So in this case, at least, Shakespeare was not writing
what he knew. He was writing what the people of his time thought
and believed.

To a modern audience, the play certainly has unsettling
aspects. The portrayal of Shylock is a classic example—perhaps *the*
classic example—of cultural stereotyping. To refer to Dr. Asimov
once more:

> Shylock is not a Jewish name; there never was a Jew named Shy-
> lock that anyone has heard of; the name is an invention of Shake-
> speare's which has entered the common language (because of the
> power of the characterization of the man) to represent any

grasping, greedy, hard-hearted creditor. I have heard Jews themselves use the word with exactly this meaning, referring back to Shakespeare's character.

Asimov goes on to speculate as to where Shakespeare actually got the name. He mentions an old Hebrew word, *shalakh,* which appears in the Bible and refers to a bird of prey. It is unclear exactly which bird this is a reference to, but it seems quite possible that Shakespeare used a form of the word as the name for his predatory moneylender, for while he probably knew next to nothing about Jews, Shakespeare would certainly have known his Bible.

So, what could Shakespeare's motive have been in creating the character of Shylock? Since he did not leave behind any diaries (or at least, none that anyone has ever found), we are reduced to guesswork. However, we can make what I think are some fairly logical and educated guesses. And my best guess is the one that I have portrayed here in this book, namely, that he was trying to compete with Marlowe.

In an afterword to an earlier novel in this series, I said that I believed that if Shakespeare were alive today, he would probably be writing for television. I could easily see him sitting around over lattes at Starbucks with the likes of Steven J. Cannell and Harlan Ellison, talking shop. Or perhaps working with Lucas or Spielberg. And the responses to *that* comment were predictable. "*Shakespeare? Writing for television?*" (You have to say that with your upper lip curling in an aristocratic sneer.) Yes, Virginia, writing for television. Because, much as the literati might blanch at the idea, Shakespeare was a *commercial* writer.

He was not writing for the academic, literary writers of his day (in fact, most of them probably hated his guts because he was successful and was *not* a university man, as witness Robert Greene). He was writing for the groundlings, the average working stiffs who paid a penny apiece to stand in the yard and watch a play, which was their era's version of television. And in this regard, a rather hideous modern TV neologism comes to mind that could well be used to describe the work of Christopher Marlowe: "a motion picture event." Apparently, no one makes movies anymore, or even motion pictures. They make "motion picture *events*." (I always thought a motion picture "event" was what happened when the film broke in the projector at the movie theatre.) Well, in Marlowe's case, the silly term actually seems to fit. Marlowe did not simply write dramas. He wrote "drama events." His plays were something completely new to the Elizabethan audiences, spectacles full of lurid violence and bombastic speeches, every bit as over-the-top and overwhelming to the senses as the grisly bear-baitings at the Paris Gardens. And the people ate them up. Shakespeare had to compete with that. He was, of course, to surpass Marlowe and leave behind a far more lasting impact, but at the time he could not possibly have known that. If he was a cocky young Turk, he might easily have believed himself capable of it, but somehow that does not quite seem to fit his personality. Confident, perhaps. Cocky? I suppose it's possible, but I don't think so.

He had to measure himself against Marlowe. How could he not? They were close to the same age, but Marlowe's career was at its zenith when Shakespeare was just arriving on the scene. Marlowe was the big gun. And, while Shakespeare was probably not a cocky sort, Marlowe absolutely was. Marlowe was completely over-the-top in nearly every respect. And if Shakespeare might have been a television writer had he lived today, it would not be much of a stretch to imagine that Marlowe might have been a rock star. Marlowe does not stand up as well as Shakespeare, though. His dramatic work today seems comical, his characters cartoonish. Consider what Shakespeare wrote at nearly the same time, however, and suddenly it becomes clear that it's not simply a matter of Marlowe's work not standing up as well because of the passage of the years. Shakespeare was his contemporary, and Shakespeare was demonstrably better. This is not to say that Marlowe was a hack. Far from it. He was capable of letting rip with some pretty damned good stuff. But he clearly lacked Shakespeare's depth. And Shakespeare, if he did not *know* he could do better, at the very least had to *think* he could. And that meant he had to try.

When considered in the context in which it was written, *The Merchant of Venice* begins to reveal its author's motivation. Marlowe's play *The Jew of Malta* was a big hit, and its lead character, Barabas, is a scenery-chewing, melodramatic villain who gets his in the end. Marlowe's formula was similar to that used by many screenwriters today. With Barabas, he created a character who was so evil and violent and excessive that by the time he gets his comeuppance in the end, the audience is cheering as he gets boiled alive in oil. Marlowe resorted to every trick at his disposal. He made his villain a Jew, a rich merchant, the sort of character who would immediately seem dislikable to his audience, and on top of that, he gave him the biblically evocative name of Barabas. Then, to revenge himself upon the Christians—because the Knights of Malta took away his money—Barabas sets out upon a course of violence that would do justice to the most satanic serial killer, so that by the time he gets what's coming to him, the audience is primed for it. I find myself picturing Shakespeare watching the play and thinking, "Oh, come *on!*"

The Jew of Malta had its debut in 1589. Four years later, Marlowe was dead, murdered in an appropriately Marlovian manner—he was stabbed in the forehead in a room above a bar. (It has been suggested that Marlowe's murder might in fact have been a political assassination, because Marlowe was supposedly a spy who knew too much. Hey, who said literature was boring?) One year after Marlowe's death, there was a sensational trial in London in which Queen Elizabeth's physician, a Portuguese doctor named Roderigo Lopez, was accused of trying to poison her. Lopez was a Jew who had converted to Christianity, but he was still seen as a Jew and a foreigner, which made him doubly damned. He was probably innocent, but given the temper of the times, it would probably have been impossible for a foreigner and a Jew to receive a fair trial. Lopez was convicted and executed. And following the sensational trial and execution of a Jewish villain, Marlowe's *Jew of Malta* was naturally revived, with great success. Once again, to quote Isaac Asimov:

> Shakespeare, who always had his finger on the popular pulse, and who was nothing if not a "commercial" writer, at once realized the value of writing a play of his own about a villainous Jew, and *The Merchant of Venice* was the result.

It had to be almost impossible to pass up. There was Shakespeare, just beginning to make his mark, and here comes Marlowe once more, this time from beyond the grave, to bedevil him again. It was an opportunity for the audiences to make a direct comparison: Marlowe's Jewish villain vs. Shakespeare's Jewish villain. And if there was one thing Shakespeare knew he could do better than Marlowe—he *had* to know it, or at least believe it—it was creating characters who seemed real, who had motivations that went beyond their simply being heroes or villains. It was not enough for Shakespeare to present the audience with a villain and say, "Look, here is the villain! See how he does villainous things?" Shakespeare wanted the audience to *understand* the villain.

Therein lies the problem, of course, because Shakespeare managed to create in Shylock a character who was not only a comic villain, but a tragic villain at the same time. And the fact that Shakespeare's characters can be played with so many different interpretations (Hamlet being perhaps the classic case in point) demonstrates why his work has lived on for so long, while nobody remembers the literary university men of his time (except the literary university men of this time, perhaps). Shakespeare wrote Shylock with all the prejudices and preconceptions of his age. He didn't know any better. It would have been nicer, and more convenient, if he could have, but he didn't. In creating Shylock, he succeeded so well that the unfortunate cultural stereotype lives on, sadly, to this day. That's why the play, and the character, remain controversial. Ironically, it was something he could never have intended. He almost certainly did not have any personal stake in taking down the Jews.

He just wanted to take down another writer.

Simon Hawke
Greensboro, N.C.